Julian Rathbone lives in H *King Fisher Lives* and *Jo* Booker Prize. His thrillers *Killers, The Pandora Optic* *ZDT*, which won the German Crime Writing Prize. His short story 'Some Sunny Day' was awarded the Crime Writers' Association Macallan Short Story Award in 1993. His writing has been translated into fourteen languages.

Also published by Serpent's Tail

Sand Blind
Accidents Will Happen

BRANDENBURG CONCERTO

Julian Rathbone

Library of Congress Catalog Card Number: 97–061911

A catalogue record for this book is available
from the British Library on request

The right of Julian Rathbone to be identified as the author
of this work has been asserted by him in accordance
with the Copyright, Designs and Patents Act 1988

Copyright © 1998 by Julian Rathbone

First published in 1998 by Serpent's Tail,
4 Blackstock Mews, London N4

Phototypeset in 10pt Century Book by Intype, London Ltd
Printed and bound in Great Britain
by Mackays of Chatham

10 9 8 7 6 5 4 3 2 1

AUTHOR'S NOTE

As was the case in *Accidents Will Happen*, the city and region (Land) of Burg occupy the same geographical situation as Bremen. In all other respects Burg is a fiction.

J.R.

Again I owe a debt of gratitude to Pieke Biermann and Thomas Wörtche for doing so much to show me Berlin, and especially to Pieke for lending me two of her characters and giving me her hat.

I was halfway through *Brandenburg Concerto* when I heard, from Thomas, that Ross Thomas had died. Ever since, many years ago, Ross described a villain's eyes as having the cold greyness of year-old ice I have, again and again, surreptitiously acknowledged my debt to him by plagiarising the same metaphor. His thrillers are still, for me, the best.

Ross Thomas
1926–1995

CHAPTER 1

Renata Fechter went into labour on 22 December, which for one reason anyway pleased her. He would be born before Christmas Day.

She had not meant to find out the baby's sex but at the same time, being a curious woman with a lively mind, she had been unable to resist looking at the scans of her womb as the child grew within her. Since it was her first pregnancy and she was in her early forties, by when first pregnancies can be difficult and dangerous for both mother and child, regular scanning and every other test had been made routine.

Back in an April wretched and cold, with an intractable job on which her future career depended, and all the medical advice urging her to consider the dangers of pregnancy at her age, Ersterkriminalhauptkommissar Renata Fechter had opted for abortion. She went through the clerking, allowed her pubes to be shaved. The nurse approached with premedication – and, clad as she was in nothing but a shift that was open all the way down her back bar the ribbon that held it together, she got off the trolley and walked back to her private cubicle.

'I've never run away from anything before,' she told the hastily summoned registrar, 'and I'm not running away from this.'

She patted her lower abdomen.

'Bring me my clothes.'

May had been balmy, warm, perfect. The roses came

out, the trees greened up, and by the end of the month she felt better than she ever had before. She had been at considerable pains to keep herself fit with exercise and a carefully planned and controlled diet for the previous twenty years, but this well-being and physical contentment was something new. She was absolutely sure she had made the right choice.

But by the middle of June she was not so sure. She began to tire more easily and found that for the first time since early adolescence the temptation to eat comfort food was as bad as anything a reformed alcoholic has to put up with. One more chocolate cake won't do us any harm.

Halfway through the sixth month she and the midwife, who was also trained to operate the scanning machine, had been looking through printouts taken from the latest scan. The foetus was in profile and there was a small protuberance just visible below its bottom.

Renata jabbed a finger.

'What's that?' she asked.

'That's his scrotum,' the midwife had replied, with a sort of moist delight, pride as well, that they were looking at a male.

Renata was not pleased. This thing, growing inside her, demanding, shifting, clamouring for chocolate and oranges, had become, in so short a time, so much a part of her that it had simply not occurred to her that they might not share the same sex.

An enchanted castle of dreams collapsed about her with the news. She had had no close ties with anyone since her late teens when her lawyer father suddenly left home with a girl only a year or so older than his daughter. Professional friendships, yes, love affairs, yes. But never live-in friendships or live-in love affairs. Even this . . . *boy's* father, who really had been the best, and whose murder she was obliquely responsible for, had been a weekend distraction, then a real pleasure, even, just before the end, a source of happiness, but never a real intimate.

She did not feel she knew how to live intimately hour by hour with another person, but had felt it was something she could learn, might find very, very rewarding. It would be like growing up again, helping a new friend to grow up over the next fifteen to twenty years. But that was supposing the new friend was a girl. How could she learn growing up all over again – with a boy?

That was the boy's first mistake. The second was to be born by caesarian, on Christmas Day after all, after three days in a labour as horrid as modern technology will allow. And of course, like Aldo Nerone, he had jet black hair, eyes as dark as agates which would clearly lose all their blueness in weeks, and was as large and fat as any bambino painted by Raphael.

Nevertheless, she felt more than a little resentful when, on her return with him to her large and comfortable apartment, he clearly took instantly to María Carmen López Ortega who had raised five boys already and knew what she was about. Her husband, Paco, had crashed his Sierra and killed himself on his way back to the Ford factory in Köln after attending his mother's funeral in a village near Granada. Carmen had no desire to return to Spain, but was very happy to be a mother again, even a surrogate mother. Renata resentful? But deeply grateful too.

After submitting to a close inspection by the Regional Department of Social Services of her circumstances, including Carmen, her apartment and her financial status, Ersterkriminalhauptkommissar Renata Fechter of the Regional Department for Environmental Crime went back to work on the first day allowed by the Region of Burg, 15 January. And reported immediately to her boss – who gave her a nasty shock.

On the outskirts of Burg, on the top floor of the Regional Ministry of the Interior, Secretary Drenkmann endeavoured to assure EKHK Renata Fechter of the Regional Department for Environmental Crime, that the winding down of her department and her shift sideways to a new job was no bad thing. Drenkmann, however, never told the whole truth about anything, was always duplicitous, always had a hidden agenda. This, Renata believed, was why his head was always shrouded, Jove-like, in clouds – not those of Olympus but the smoke produced by the English Whisky Flake he stuffed in his pipe. Problem, Renata reflected: everyone within fifty metres has to smoke it too. Mind you, the room they were in was almost that big. Nevertheless it got to her. It always did, but never more so than now.

She fixed her eyes on *Cohesion 3*, a huge, sprawling, blotchy mess of a painting on the wall behind him. It was meant to express institutionalised structural harmony. At the same time, she strove to take in what he was saying without actually puking up on the hectare of expensive carpet that lay between them.

Drenkmann, very fat, with a pendulous lower lip, pendulous jowls and big tobacco-stained hands, laid out his stall.

'The Green Party is insisting that environmental crime is serious . . .' He took time out to rekindle the pipe. Lightning flashed through the smoke, sparks flew, he brushed singeing tobacco shreds off his waistcoat. 'And since it is serious it should be dealt with by Serious Crime. You can see what the implications are.'

Renata, tall, already tolerably fit and almost thin as a result of compulsive adherence to the post-natal exercises and routines that had been prescribed by a handful of therapists and counsellors, chestnut hair bobbed now, considered the implications. The new head of Serious Crime (she herself had been instrumental in ensuring that his predecessor took early retirement) was nominally ranked level with her. If her department was subsumed into his, she would have to do the unthinkable and accept a drop in rank or do the equally unthinkable, and resign. She assumed Drenkmann had something else in mind. She waited.

She might, she realised, have to wait some time. If Drenkmann was going to come to the point he would have to be direct, unequivocal. And, decades ago, he had ruthlessly suppressed whatever tendency he had ever had towards those qualities. He would not have reached the very highest grade in a major regional ministry if he had not.

'I can,' he rasped at last, 'offer you the directorship of a cross-regional task force.'

He shuffled some papers, wheezed at his pipe.

Renata was puzzled. Cross-regional task forces were unusual. The Bundeskriminalamt existed for such projects.

Drenkmann was rambling on.

Renata re-crossed shapely legs below the knee and re-angled her body in the leather sling mounted on chrome tubes that passed for an armchair. Drenkmann blinked and the droop of his lower lip became more obvious. It was odd the way pregnancy and now achieved parturition impelled her to adopt more feminine modes of dress and posture. She was aware of it, but confused as to the why of it. She was even wearing fuck-me court shoes that showed the cleavage between her big toe and the next one, shoes that had been in the bottom of her wardrobe for a decade.

Drenkmann edged a little nearer the nub. 'You will recall reports in the press that stated that forty-two trainloads of assorted ammunition, stored at the Russian arsenal in the Region of Brandenburg, went missing last year. What was not reported, or only in small paragraphs, was the, to the media, rather boring fact that thirty-eight were found. The Russian railway authorities had made a clerical error. However, they still insisted that only thirty-eight arrived, whereas the records in Brandenburg clearly showed the departure of forty-two.'

Secretary Drenkmann pushed on, laboriously fighting his instinct against ever saying anything that could be attributed to him in the future. But the gist became clear. He wanted her to find the missing trains.

'As I see it, the work will be mainly paperwork. At least in the initial stages. Indeed, it is possible that the loss of these trains is simply a paper loss. A loss on paper. What used to be a clerical error, more probably now a computing error.' He puffed away, leant forward, offered a husky grunt which Renata supposed might be taken for a laugh. A chuckle anyway. 'In fact I don't suppose there's anything on paper at all. It'll all be on disks and inside computers.'

Renata felt that the time had come to get a grip on all this. She shifted her whole body into a new diagonal, bringing legs to the left, shoulders to the right, perching her right elbow on the chrome arm-rest and her right index finger against her cheek. Her caesarian scar tweaked a little, even though the stitches had come out a week or so earlier.

'Surely,' she said, 'even supposing there were forty-two trains and not thirty-eight, the contents will have been sold, distributed? We are talking about, what, eight months ago?'

'We think not. First of all you must consider the scale.

Four train-loads of assorted ammunition are enough to keep a small army, say two divisions of infantry, operating offensively against a well-armed adversary for at least a month. So I have been told. The Federal Office for the Defence of the Constitution, liaising with similar agencies in other countries, are sure that there has been no substantial upsurge in illicit marketing of ammunition since these trains went astray. We believe the trains are still intact, but hidden.'

'Is that possible?'

'Do you know how many thousands of kilometres of rail-track there are between the Rhine and the Volga? And while almost all of it is useable, only about ten per cent is in regular use.'

'The Volga? Will my enquiries be authorised by all the governments between the Oder and the Volga? The Poles, the Ukrainians...' She began to tap them off on her fingers.

'The Poles have agreed to co-operate fully. If or when you need to go further east, we'll look into it.'

It did not occur to her then that this was the merest whisper of a hint that Poland alone might be involved.

'Secretary,' she said, injecting enough firmness into her voice to prevent him from overriding her intervention, 'the moment I start asking for records of freight-train movements anyone who was involved in the disappearance of freight trains is going to do everything they can to obstruct me.'

The clouds parted, and through them she could see a smile form on god's face.

'Absolutely, my dear. Which is why I and my colleagues in the other relevant regions all agree that you are ideally situated for the job. And indeed better placed than the Bundeskriminalamt. You, your department, already have an ongoing investigation into freight trains carrying industrial toxic waste into Poland for onward shipment into the Eastern republics. While much of your department's other activities will be transferred to the new sub-department in Serious Crime, you will continue to manage a small team looking into this, ah, unfinished business. That will be your cover.'

'A small team?'

'A small team but with virtually unlimited access to available resources.'

He put his pipe in a big ashtray, sat back in his big chair, laced podgy fingers across his global waistcoat. Renata, without changing her posture, chewed for a moment on the corner of her right middle finger. Then she straightened a little, but leant back too. To Drenkmann the body language was explicit – she'd decided to take it. But she'd want to press a little, show she had clout of her own.

'These train-loads were reported missing some time ago. Why the interest now?'

'When they went missing they were on German soil. Not East German soil. German soil. If they turn up, shall we say, for example, in the Balkans – it scarcely matters on which side – the world and his wife will assume that the German government colluded in getting them there. That must not happen. Bonn has said that that must not happen. You see, if the Moslems get them the Jews and Americans will be upset, if the Serbs get them the Croatians and Moslems will be upset, and if they end up in Croatia then the whole world will say we are helping the Catholic Fascist Croats just as Hitler did. More particularly, a lot of German voters will believe that.'

A general election was looming and the Christian Democrat-led coalition was behind in the polls.

He lifted his hands, spread his hands, shrugged. The

smile was now almost wistful, pleading, a little boy asking mummy for sweets.

Renata was caught. How could she not be? To save central government, Bonn, Herr Cabbage himself, from very considerable embarrassment did not seem to her to be necessarily a tremendously good thing – but it would be one hell of a career move.

When the early evening settled in she drove her small red BMW back to her apartment, first through fields powdered with snow, then the misty, drizzly, cold suburbs of Burg. She was happy again, happy to be back in harness, happy therefore to be welcomed by Carmen, and by . . . Brat. Her name for him, short for Bratwurst. Grilled sausage. His real name was Karl-Rosa, after Lieb-knecht and Luxemburg, but that was her secret. In 1968 she had been sixteen. She had watched, on the TV, all the disturbances that occurred over the next few years from the safety of her bedroom; had longed to get up and go, join in, but her father left home and she withdrew into work studying law and criminality and, besides, with the coming of the RAF it all turned sour. But a streak of rebellion, of idealism remained. A closet revolutionary, she fought her way to the top of a man's profession, maintained her independence and now named her son after the martyrs of 1919.

Carmen called him Carlo', dropping the 's' as Andalus-ians always do.

CHAPTER 2

On or around the day this conversation between Renata Fechter and Secretary Drenkmann took place, Kim Kind was also ready for a career move, which was why he was saying goodbye to his old mates Jace and Ash on Hamburg's Altona station, before boarding the Inter-City for Berlin.

'Well, darlings,' he cried, 'the little man's going to blow his whistle and wave his pretty green signal thingy any moment now, so I'd better get my ugly old self on board.'

He touched the corners of his eyes very carefully with the corner of a tissue, determined not to let the mascara run.

'Take care now, and thank you, thank you, darlings, for everything you've done for me in the last four years . . . Oh, you know I mean it.'

The three men, all well over six feet, looked at each other and for a moment the eyes of Jace and Ash went a touch cold. Kim read them.

'Don't be a pair of sillies. I'm not going to kiss you, though I know I'd like to.'

Jace and Ash relaxed, grinned a little, let Kim reach over and pat their cheeks before boarding the train. Then the doors closed and Kim was on the other side of the sealed, tinted window, waving as the train began to inch away.

Jace and Ash, Jason and Ashley, identical twins, early forties but still as lean and tough as they had always been, turned away. Kim watched them go, their dark close-shaven heads above black bomber jackets, tight jeans, tight arses, speed-lace designer boots.

'What a pair of pets,' he murmured. Then he unzipped his soft black leather bag, took out a glossy semi-porn, semi-gay magazine, stood, put the magazine on his seat and his bag on the luggage rack. He caught sight of his reflection in a mirror, deep large eyes, good cheekbones, generous mouth, used his right pinkie to even out a thickness in his peach-coloured lipstick, smoothed his left eyebrow, then adjusted the tilt backwards of the floppy grey beret. He sat in the window corner and opened the magazine.

The young black man opposite him, wearing a knitted grey jumper and baggy trousers tucked into socks above Wrangler boots, offered him a shy grin before turning away to watch the parks and boulevards of Hamburg slip by on the right-hand side. A flurry of snow drifted across them. Presently the train crossed the bridge between the two ornamental lakes, one with a Geneva-scale fountain making a white scar against the grey of a leaden sky.

'Oh, yes?' thought Kim. 'That could help while away the hours very nicely,' and he gave his bum a wriggle so the seams in the crotch of his tailored jeans settled a little more comfortably to the right.

He let the magazine fall open where it wanted to, which was naturally at the interview with yours truly about how, after working for four years on the Reeperbahn, mostly at Ass'nJass, Kim Kind now felt it was time for a change. Outside the tourist season he was old hat as far as the regulars were concerned and it was time to twitch his mantle blue, pass on to pastures new.

All a bit lost on the Hamburg journo, who had not known Kim was quoting Milton's elegy for a handsome young man drowned in the Irish Sea three and half centuries ago. 'Lycidas', along with 'In Memoriam', was one

of Kim's favourite poems. A young lad he had been in
love with had died as prematurely as the lads commemor-
ated in the poems. Very prematurely. Along with six
others in an APC he had been rocketed in a friendly way
by a passing US AH-64 Apache gunship in the last stages
of Desert Storm. Kim, at that time the lad's company
commander, had been three vehicles ahead of him.

The twins returned to the short-stay carpark, Ash elec-
tronically unlocked the doors of the black BMW 318i
convertible and got into the driving seat. Jace chucked
the German-made Senior Service he had fired up as soon
as the train pulled out, knowing Ash would object if he
smoked it in the car, and got into the black leather bucket
seat beside him. Ash covered the short distance back to
the Reeperbahn and parked in the service area behind
Ass'nJass, now, thanks to several factors, one of the smar-
test and largest joints on the strip.

It had all started ten years earlier when they trashed
the original premises after a pair of hookers had tried to
roll them. Not wanting publicity, the divisional commander had offered them honourable discharge instead
of a court martial – but no handshake or pension. Since
neither had any close relatives or ties in the UK and they
liked Hamburg, they decided to stay there. At that time
Uncle Harry Sheen was doing very well in entertainment
and property deals – this was during the Lawson boom
– and he had loadsa money looking for a home. He lent
them half a million, they bought the joint they'd wrecked,
borrowed from the Deutsche Bank to refurbish, and had
never looked back.

Ash pocketed the keys, Jace paused to fire up another
Senior Service with his gold Zippo and they trotted up
the fire-escape above the dark green wheelie-bins to the
first floor. Ash used a Yale mortice key on an iron door

and Jace let it slam behind them. Once beyond a velour
curtain, they were in what looked like a largeish café-
theatre, chairs and tables circling a small stage, only
most of the chairs and tables had been pushed back to
make room for a minimal film-crew, 16mm camera on a
dolly, lights, sound, a couple of grips, a couple of gofers.
On the stage a large, very fat white blonde was kneeling
in a heap of cushions with her spread buttocks in the air
and a deep yawn on her face. Nearby a much sexier
oriental sex therapist in a white overall and probably not
much else was doing her best to stimulate a cock back
into serious erection.

It belonged to a tall black man whose carefully built
muscles shone with oil. The cock was long, very long, but
still pointed south.

'Shit, man,' he was saying, 'all I need is a half-hour
with a T-steak and a couple of beers . . .'

The sex therapist scowled, spoke angrily: 'And thlee
hours zizz to forrow.' Letting go of him for a moment, she
looked at her watch. 'And our lental on the set luns out
in an hour and a half.'

'Less,' said the man who was clearly the director – he
was old, wrinkled like an emaciated elephant, wore
glasses beneath a green eye-shade. A light-meter was
slung on a black cord over his check-shirt and cardigan,
together with one of those gadgets that help you frame a
shot.

'Don't call me "man",' the sex therapist added.

Jace and Ash squeezed their way through the periphery
of all this, where the furniture had been pushed, with
barely a glance at any of it, though Jace registered that
he reckoned the crew should be out on the hour if they
didn't want the rent to go on to double time.

A tall man who filled an electric-blue suit to overflowing
and was built like a Turkish wrestler, which is what he

was – they come in not much below the weight of Sumo wrestlers, but less flabby – was leaning against the wall by another velour curtain, arms folded, but showing some interest in the filming. That was because the big fat white woman was his wife – a marriage of convenience five years ago to get him the equivalent of a Green Card, but now they were really fond of each other. He himself was one of a team of ten minders–bouncers Jace and Ash employed, five of whom were always on the premises, armed and in touch with each other by RT. No-one was ever going to trash Ass'nJass the way Jace and Ash had done.

'Your uncle came,' he said to the twins as they came up to him. He spoke accented German. So did they, but different accent.

'On his own?' asked Jace, with a hint of excitement in his voice, enough to make Ash look at him expression-lessly.

'Two blokes with him. And a girl. I put them in the suite.'

They took the lift up to the eighth floor, past the quite classy restaurant, the casino, the private rooms where the really heavy stuff went on, including until very recently Kim Kind's activities, and the two floors occupied by their speciality mail-order firm together with the offices from which their little empire was run. The ground floor, which the fire-escape had by-passed, was a conven-tional topless bar with booths facing a stage where every hour on the hour a ten-minute sex show of staggering banality was performed by women built like gladiators. Between shows, a combo of middle-aged to elderly men played be-bop with better than average competence – the Jass of Ass'nJass.

The suite was where the twins lived when they felt their presence was needed or when they had nowhere else more exciting to go. Since it was furnished and decorated entirely in the style of the most anonymous international hotels, it was in fact one of the least exciting places in the world.

The lift opened on to a foyer decorated with prints of Hamburg when Telemann was writing the music, and beyond it, seen through glass, spider plants and Swiss cheese plants, a reception room with chrome and black leather furniture, and glass-topped tables. The pictures this time, framed in matt steel, were prints of Impressionist paintings with 'The Museum of Modern Art, NY' printed boldly across the bottom margins. The view was the best thing about the room – across the Elbe, with the passenger boats and ferries on this side and the serious container port on the other. The tinted glass made the river a ribbon of mercury and exaggerated the contrasts of light and shade in the clouds, which were beginning to spill real snow.

Sheen Associates had draped themselves around the central and largest low round table.

Harry Sheen, late sixties, with the skull-like face, brown eye-sockets and nicotine-stained knuckles of someone who has chain-smoked strong cigarettes for more than fifty years, looked up with a glimmer of a grin, even before the automatic glass door swung back in front of the twins. Eloise Harman, daughter of Sergeant-Major Harman, who had been Sheen's mucker back in the fifties on the Rhine and who had married a German bint so El was bilingual, straightened her back with a touch more excitement than Sheen had shown.

The last time Jason had seen her, ten months before, her hair had been a pleasant unobtrusive brown and fluffily long. Her usual clothes had been a conventional suit, shoulders lightly padded, pencil skirt to her knee, slit at the back, white frothy blouse, black tights, court shoes, minimal conventional make-up.

Since then she had transformed herself, and it was a shock. Hair, almost white now and streaked with red, chopped to look like a toothbrush the day before you throw it away, rouge on her cheeks, a mouth painted up in a Lana Turner bow. She was wearing a black velvet jacket, cut low so you could see the tops of her boobs, with a tight waist which then flared out again above floppily flared trousers in the same material. Jace was stirred but bemused, chucked the cigarette he was no more than halfway through into a chrome and matt black free-standing airport-type ashtray but lit another, all before he was over the threshold.

Herbert Doe, next to Sheen, being a gent by nature if not by birth, pulled himself to his feet. Doe was about the same age as Sheen, much fitter since the hip replacement he'd earned from the Burg regional police after getting the original arthritic one shot away by a drug-crazed policeman. He was a big man, ex-professional wrestler, ex-con for GBH, ex-army where he'd met Sheen on the Rhine thirty years ago. Now employed as Sheen's minder – and chauffeur when they could afford a car.

The fourth member of the group looked up from the laptop he'd been working on. Fat, with small eyes set in a weaselly face, his name was Sam Pratchard. Being nearest the window, he had to crane round El to offer the twins a welcome – a sick, shy smile in his case.

There was an awkwardness about all four of them. Ten months ago, as much as that? Sheen had called the twins to Burg, forty miles down the motorway, to sort out a spot of bother for them, taking out a couple of corrupt ex-policemen with whom he'd been involved in some shenanigans that Jace never got to the bottom of – though he did know they'd roughed up Sheen, Doe and above all El in a not-nice way some days previous. El had handled it all with a gutsiness he had more than admired.

'Sorry we're late, Harry.' Ash took over. 'Had to see a friend off at the station. Drinks?'

He moved to a bar in the corner to the left of the entrance. Sheen had scotch and water, no ice, Doe a Beck, Sam a diet Pepsi, El a Campari soda. Jace had a Beck as well, and Ash took the top off a small Perrier for himself. Jace handed round nuts and garlicky olives he'd prepared himself. Bit of a gourmet cook, was Jace.

'Jace, you smokin' again?' Sheen asked.

Ash replied. 'He's in love. He always smokes when he's in love. Till he's laid her, anyway.'

'Who's the lucky girl?'

'He won't say. Never does. In case I get the hots for her too.'

Oh God, thought El, let it be me, let it be me.

'So, Harry,' said Ash, when they were all settled, 'What's it all about, then?'

Harry Sheen put aside his scotch and cleared his throat. Wet concrete slipping off a shovel.

'You know how we was shipping toxic waste through Lübeck and Rostock up the Baltic to Riga, Tallinn and Novgorod using these Ossi freighters we got cheap? Well it were doin' all right till some Brussels piss-artist blew the whistle on the seaworthiness of our boats. They've all been grounded, pending compliance with EU regs. Stupid fing is, ad we ad the sense to register them in Panama or wherever we'd av bin laughin'. An Sam don't you tell me "I told you so" for the umpteenth time. It would've meant delay, interest building up on the capital we'd borrowed, plus a few backhanders we couldn't afford.'

Christ, thought Ash, he's in the shit and he's going to ask us for a fucking loan. And since he set us up here, a refusal might cause offence. Jace thought: who'd have thought in, what, ten months she could change herself so much? Is she the same woman she was? Does the personality change too? He reached for his Senior Service, but found he still had one going in his hand.

'So,' Harry Sheen concluded, stubbing his Piccadilly out in the onyx ashtray, 'we're in the shit, paddle-free. Except Sam has this wheeze he thinks might run. Tell 'em, Sam.'

Over to Sam Pratchard. Disbarred from the Royal College of Accountants' Charter some years earlier, taking the rap for a media tycoon who topped himself a year or so later when he found he couldn't handle things without him, Sam was a whizz with figures. But, as he was wont to say, you can't make bread without flour and most of his life he'd been doing just that – for other people. He had a squeaky voice. When he got excited it was as bad as chalk on a blackboard.

'Just after that other business had been concluded,' he began, 'and Herbert Doe here was still in hospital on account of his hip, Jace here told us how ammunition train-loads the Russkies were shipping out of Germany, Brandenburg actually, which is the Region round Berlin—'

'We know where Brandenburg is,' Ash growled.

'Of course you do . . . these train-loads, as many as forty-two, some said, had gone missing. Now I felt that here was a middleman situation. Stuff like that is very tricky to handle. No one wants to be revealed as seller or buyer. It's the sort of situation where a broker, an agent is virtually a necessity.

'Anyway,' Pratchard squeaked on, more raspingly than ever, 'it's the sort of situation we at Sheen Associates feel specially able to handle and we want to get an in on it. We've tried. El here knows her German, speaks it like a native' – Eloise felt her colour rise, not with embarrassment but with anger, and re-crossed her trousered legs – 'and even after all these years Harry has his connections, but times have moved on and we didn't get anywhere. Wasted a few weeks on it, then gave up and went back to Blighty. But jus' recently we had a whisper or two about it all again, enough to make us come back. Like we wondered whether you knew an in into this situation or someone who might have an in. Lodovmoney in it. Way I see it, everyone from Dubrovnik to Vladivostok has guns, rocket-launchers, mortars, but they must all be fucking low in ammunition.'

He sort of sighed, then leant forward, looked around as if he suspected eavesdroppers might be present, and lowered his voice. Which was a relief.

'There is another aspect,' he went on. 'We have had experience in this area in a small way in the past and we really do know the role we actually play. You see, it's like this. People who have arms to sell, like, take a for instance, certain British firms aided and abetted by civil servants and ministers, do often need to conceal from everyone else concerned that they are the actual sellers. Which is why a trustworthy middleman is a necessity. Say a load of ammunition turns up in the hands of, for example, the Iranian government, then the position everyone wants to be in is to be able to say this ammunition did not come direct from Vickers or wherever, but from a bona fide, internationally based dealer, just doing his business in the international market-place. He happened to be warehousing, in, say, Cyprus, just what the ayatollahs needed at just the moment the ayotollahs called on him, so the deal he made with them was legit and had nothing to do with HMG or the manufacturers. That's the sort of situation we want to get into, be part of, take ten percent from both sides in exchange for holding the stuff for a month or so, on paper, I don't mean really holding it. Just paper. I can juggle the paper about, trust me.'

Silence fell for a moment, apart from Sheen's wheezy chest. Then Ash spoke.

'First,' he said, 'thirty-eight of those trains have been accounted for. There's only four still missing,' then, seeing despondency settle over Sheen's and Pratchard's faces, 'but that's still, money-wise, a lot. Forty-two trains could keep forty-two infantry divisions moving forward with all the firepower they could use for three weeks, two anyway. Fighting a real war. Four trains ... what shall we say? Enough to make the Chetniks a serious nuisance for a year? Give firepower to any of the Balkan factions for six months? Enough to be seriously decisive.'

'Money-wise?' Pratchard, of course.

'Shit, how do I know? Partly it depends how the trains were made up. If all the AK rounds were in one, all the RPGs in another, the mortar shells in the third, that wouldn't be so good. But if each separately represented the needs of a whole infantry division, and that is quite possible since the Russians kept around forty divisions on standby in the DDR and east Poland through most of the Cold War, then that would be a hell of a bonanza for whoever picked them up. You're talking serious money. Off the top of my head, and I could be wrong by a factor of two if not ten, I'd say three million sterling.'

Sheen and Pratchard relaxed, and Sheen beamed. Lit himself another Piccadilly and finished his scotch. Ash freshened it for him.

Jace coughed politely and leant forward.

'But, Harry, it's not our scene. I mean like really not our scene. Berlin. Berlin's where the action will be.'

He killed his Senior Service.

'Of course,' he said, 'we do now have a man in Berlin.'

He looked at his watch.

'Nearly,' he added.

Kim Kind zipped up the black boy's baggy trousers.

'Did you like that,' he asked.

The black boy grinned moistly and nodded.

He murmured, 'Yes.'

Kim looked out of the window. Scruffy-looking town with a lake beyond it. He'd done the guard detail there in the prison ten years earlier on his first tour as first lieutenant. Jason, ten years older than him, had been his corporal. Just the one prisoner – Rudolph Hess. When he committed suicide a couple of years later, they pulled down the prison and built a NAAFI supermarket.

The train crossed the Havel, passed through Spandau station without stopping. Ten minutes to Zoo.

'Nearly there,' he said, and patted the black boy's cheek.

CHAPTER 3

Kim had been planning his move for some weeks. But
only in the last ten days had he found a room so cheap
he'd have been a fool to refuse it. One of the agents he
had approached, a Silesian with an atrocious accent, who
until then had only shown him luxury studios at five
hundred marks a week, suddenly rang him in Hamburg
to say he had a room near the centre for a hundred.
Unusual, yes, but it might do. Kim made a special trip
to see it, liked it, as much for its oddness as for its
cheapness, and took it. No one, offered a room for half
the rent they can afford, questions just why it might have
been made available to him. One puts it down to luck.

It was at the top of a large brick-built, five-storey stuc-
coed nineteenth-century apartment block built round a
courtyard, on Brandenburgische Straße. The not unim-
posing entry was just a hundred metres or so above the
Fehrbelliner Platz U-Bahn station, just ten minutes by
tube from the Europa Center.

Since the nineteenth century the building had been
gutted, rebuilt, gutted again, and not just by war. Some
of the original internal structures remained unchanged,
pariculary the broad and handsome, if rather worn,
wooden staircase. Most of the building was occupied by
offices, some of which had put new, steel-lined doors in
instead of the old wooden ones and many of which had
knocked down walls between apartments, adding extras
like air-conditioning and modern central heating.

Kim climbed to the fifth floor – the lift worked only

intermittently and today was one of its off days – and let himself through a small but old door with a key that was already his. The part of the block he was now in had been set aside for the servants of the haute bourgeoisie who had lived above the classy shops and cafés at street level. For the most part these top two storeys remained a warren or hive of tiny rooms linked by narrow corridors and narrow staircases; however, one section, facing the street and originally made up of many small rooms, had been knocked down to create a sound-stage for low-budget films. Such ventures fail and it was now a big empty barn, gathering dust, but brightly lit by two storeys' worth of windows. There were a few film-cans stacked in a corner and some loose cable which ran from some of the many power points and ended in sockets like the antennae of space creatures. Nothing else.

A narrow wooden staircase had been left exposed, clinging to the inner wall. It climbed to a door on what had been the top floor. Next to this door there was a pane of rectangular modern glass – Kim guessed that it had been put there to convert the room behind it into a sound-proofed control room overlooking the sound-stage. The room he had rented was behind it.

He climbed the narrow stair with its rickety banister, used a second key to open the door, and went in.

It was a narrow but long room, running the entire width of one side of the block, a good eight metres, though it was only four metres wide. As well as the internal pane, which had a lowered Venetian blind, there was a small dormer window piercing the slope of the roof, overlooking similar windows and chimneys on the other side of Brandenburgische Straße. The wall facing the window on to the studio was broken by the plastered-over chimney-stack which still vented the central-heating boilers below and gave the room a slight but welcome background heat. It also created two deep alcoves. No lavatory, but there was one in working order at the foot of the stairs. There was, however, a basin with a cold-water tap.

The cardboard boxes he had had sent on ahead from Hamburg had been dumped on the almost bare boards near the door. Almost bare? There was a new circular Indian rug, fluffy, embroidered in wool with stylised flowers; a small framed oil sketch of a female nude, pos-sibly, Kim thought, the work of one of the group of early-twentieth-century painters known as Die Brücke and if so worth a bob or two. And there was a fresh but part-used small cake of Nina Ricci soap by the washbasin tap. Only one piece of furniture: a large but broken-down old sofa upholstered in chocolate-brown cord with four extra cushions and a thin eiderdown, the sort of covering Euro-peans had had on their beds in summer before duvets became universal. It stood alongside the wall by the door. Here too the roof sloped above a dado of red-painted panels.

It added up, he realised, to an occasional squatter, someone who came and went but did not stay. He wondered if it were a he or a she and how long it would be before they became acquainted.

He opened the dormer window, let in a gust of icy air. Berlin was a lot colder than Hamburg. A shadow slipped over the lead and slates and he looked up to see what had caused it. For a moment his heart stood still with delight. A falcon with white underbelly and wings stip-pled with charcoal grey was losing height in wide circles above the street, heading towards the roof behind him, above his head. As it came in on shallow, quick wing-beats he could clearly see the broken-necked pigeon clutched in its talons. One last sweep took it close over the arched window and he fancied he could hear it land, the rustle of sheathed feathers as it folded its pinions.

Not easy to tell falcons apart, but one or two pointers, not least that of distribution, indicated a peregrine.

'Don't worry about me,' Kim murmured. 'We'll be mates, you and I, up in our eyrie.'

He closed the window – it was too cold to leave it open – turned away and began to unpack.

An hour later he had a couple of hundred books piled against the walls – he'd build book-cases out of bricks and planks; clothes including a Versace suit, a couple of cashmere sweaters, and eight pairs of stylish boots and shoes – he thought he'd buy a self-assembly wardrobe; a mini sound system with a hundred CDs already stacked in black plastic, so that was no problem; a portable TV with video player and about fifty videos also already stacked; a selection of postcards and small prints which shortly he'd Blu-Tack to the walls; and, almost new, the full range of Calvin Klein toiletries. He wasn't yet sure he liked them, but the advertising campaign had been irresistible. There was also his gun.

It was a Smith & Wesson .38 British Service revolver that had been issued to his Granddad in 1940. Apart from target practice, it had been used only once in earnest. Granddad, in a fit of deep depression as a result of being in the detail which opened Belsen in 1945, had blown the back of his head out with it on VE day. Kim had thirty-six boxed rounds for it. He hoped he would never have to find out whether or not they still worked.

'Nice weapon. May I?'

Shit, he thought, and froze. He was almost but not quite sure it was a woman's voice – husky, quite deep, but soft. Whatever, she or he was a neat mover and had a key. The fly-by-night squatter? He or she had asked to look at the gun he was holding – did that mean she or he had a gun on him? He reversed the Smith & Wesson so he was holding it by its six-inch barrel, grip outwards. And, still hunkered over the canvas wrap-around he had taken it from slowly turned to face . . .

Five seven in height, one thirty pounds, give or take. A bistre velvet fedora with a broad black gros-grain headband, bright woollen scarf, mostly red, Royal Stuart tartan, a long pearl-white woollen duster coat, which could have been worn by a man but wasn't because it partly covered a knitted silk and cotton mixture bustier, also in a subtle shade of brown (the breasts beneath it probably bra-less, not big but low-slung and flat), creamy white chinos, pleated to be baggy below the waist, full enough at the cuffs to lie over black medium-heeled ankle boots, the heels fashionably indented.

'I don't like the shoes either,' she said as she put down the shiny KaDeWe carrier bag with string handles she was carrying. She took the gun. 'But they were the only ones, um, available at the time.'

Thin wrists and long fingers but not apparently bothered by the weight. She pushed the sliding catch that released the drum, spun it, listened to the lubricated hum it made, held it to the light, squinted down the chambers, reversed it so she could get light down the barrel, sniffed it, snapped the drum back into place, pulled the trigger slowly till the hammer reached its critical point and snapped back like a trap. All the time she did this Kim wondered how she could have got hold of footwear worth at least a hundred and fifty marks without being able to choose something she liked. Then he peered up at her face.

She was blonde, somewhere between mouse and straw, cut, as far as the hat allowed him to see, to a four-millimetre pelt. Pale skin, not quite pasty but certainly not blooming, cheeks raw with cold. Indeed, he noticed now that she was almost shivering. Wide-spaced pale blue eyes, shapely small nose, thin lips painted terra-cotta, good chin, neck that more than anything else he had seen so far betrayed her age. At least forty-five. A guess borne out by what she said next.

'This gun must be all of ten years older than me.'

She handed it back.

'If you're ever going to use it for real, I'd tighten the main-spring first,' she went on. 'Otherwise you might find the hammer blow too weak. Especially if you're using British-made rounds. There's a screw above the grip on the right-hand side that does it.'

He knew all that, but was surprised she did. Her English was as good as it appears written down, but accented Berlin style, a softer approach to the language than the stereotyped 'Achtung, English swine' of escape movies. And why did she speak to him in English? Because in the fleeting moment before she spoke she had taken in that most of his books were in English.

She moved to the panel that looked down on the big hall below, separated the slats of the blind a quarter-inch or so, just enough for her to see beyond it. And she waited like that for a full minute.

Why?

Because she was afraid she might have been followed.

At last she turned, looked over the room.

'I guessed right,' she said.

'Guessed what?'

'That you wouldn't have what's needed to make this place a reasonable place to live in.'

She hunkered again over the big KaDeWe bag and pulled out three items, unboxed and unwrapped: a Braun electric kettle, a small Brother microwave and an AEG room-heater with blower.

'Demonstration, display models.'

He began to understand why she thought she might have been followed.

'Compliments ... what do you say? Of the management?'

'If someone was after you,' he said, 'you'd be trapped here, cornered, like a rat.'

This was the one thing that worried him about the pad he had rented.

'Oh no, I don't think so,' said with a cryptic smile. But she couldn't help giving a fleeting glance at the brownish red gloss-painted hardboard behind the sofa, below the slanting part of the ceiling.

'Hi,' she said. 'At the moment I answer to Piotra. Piotra Grabowski. Do you like the name?'

'It's all right.'

'I made it up. What's your name?'

'Kim. Kim Kind. I made it up too.'

CHAPTER 4

EKHK Renata Fechter called her team together for a work-in-progress conference.

Her team? Of the original five she had had when they were the Eco-squad, one had proved to be a crook and had killed himself, one an alcoholic who had to be dismissed after he crashed a police car at a crucial moment. A third had been a drug addict. In order to stop him from shooting Harry Sheen and Herbert Doe in the Schiller Park in Burg, she had killed him. The weapon, literally in her hand at the time, had been a slate-grey 1958 soft-top Pininfarina-styled 250 GTS California Ferrari which had belonged to her already murdered lover, father of Karl-Rosa.

That left Firat Arslan, who had made a good but slow recovery from the head wound he'd received the same night as all the other incidents, and Sharon King, the half-black daughter of a US Army sergeant. The three older men had been replaced, but she had released two of the replacements to form the nucleus of the Eco-department in Serious Crime. She kept the third because he was a computer nerd, and this job, she guessed, was going to need a computer nerd. His name was Norbert Eintner, so they all called him Albert – for Einstein.

She kept on Firat and Sharon because they were familiar and loyal and she knew she could rely on them.

They sat round her desk in the Regional Interior Ministry with pads on their knees. The Ministry was on the outskirts of Burg, virtually in the countryside, and was surrounded by lawns, flower-beds, walks and a screen of poplars. There had been a fairly heavy fall of snow in the night and the fourth-floor room was filled with a cool reflected light which spoke of cold and made her shiver, even though the central heating was more than adequate.

'Firat?'

Firat Arslan had originally come to Germany on an exchange, the sort of exchange that happens when your father, now retired, had once been a very senior police officer indeed, first in Ankara, then in Istanbul. Firat had done well, stayed on, taken German nationality: the German police needed officers who could cope with Turks – whether guest-workers, illegals, or naturalised. And from Serious Crime in Burg he had been moved to the Eco-cops because the hardened detectives he worked with in Serious Crime had not much liked having a Turk for a colleague.

'Not a lot to say, Renata. As you know I've been coping with the cover. The idea is that what we're doing is completing an enquiry into tracking down freight trains carrying toxic or worse waste across borders to Poland and beyond. Actually, this really means just carrying on as we were before. There's a firm out at Burghaven makes those tiny batteries you get in cameras, watches, infrared signallers and so on, seems to be getting rid of mercury-based compounds to Poland. The thing is, this indicates they're using processes banned by EU Directive K stroke six eleven . . .'

'OK.' Renata turned to Sharon.

Sharon, capuccino-coloured, still in her mid-twenties, attractive but overweight as ever, perhaps even more so, was squeezed into jeans that really would not do beneath a hugely chunky woollen top with a halter neck.

'Oh, nothing much. I'm just the hey-you, the gofer, the messenger person. Put stamps on envelopes, occasionally get to drive a car. I'm doing a fair bit of in-training too. Rape counselling, that sort of thing.'

Renata felt a sudden wave of impatience. She was already pissed off with this assignment, this so-called cross-regional Einsatzgruppe, and it didn't help to know her subordinates were as pissed off as she was. Was this post-natal depression? Bit early, surely, if it was.

'Alber—Norbert.'

Eintner, bald, spectacles, cleared his throat and actually opened his notebook.

'The trains were loaded from arsenals and magazines in the Region of Brandenburg. These were sited on spurs from the main railway lines and close to autobahns nine, two, twenty-four and of course ten, which is the motorway box that links the others and circles Berlin. Supposing the trains have hardly moved at all, they'll be somewhere west of Potsdam, east of Brandenburg itself, hidden among lakes, forest and arable land. But is it really conceivable they could remain hidden?'

Is it? Renata asked herself ironically. We'll soon know, because you are going to tell us.

And sure enough he did.

'The whole area is up for grabs. Landowners are returning from the West claiming properties that were requisitioned or compulsorily purchased by GDR-controlled authorities. Businessmen are looking all through the area for cheap sites and cheap labour. The infrastructure is there, rail and road especially. It is not likely – no, it is not possible – that every siding and spur has not been explored.'

He squirmed in his seat, shifted his pad from one knee to the other, used his ball-point to flick over a page.

'So, the trains have gone. But how far? And in which direction? East, for sure. And the more I think about it the more I think of Poland. I remember Rzepin. I've studied the maps. I have decided that the one area between Germany and Russia where these trains might be, has to be close to Rzepin. And no further than Rzepin – that is, assuming their contents have not been sold. At Rzepin they are centrally placed to go south, east or back into the West.'

Renata sighed, stood, walked to the window. Tracks in the snow that had not been there before. And then one of the poplars shed a load of it. Must be thawing already. She chewed on a hang-nail. She could not remember ever having had a hang-nail before. How was Brat? Getting his second bottle of the morning by now. He'd cried a lot of the night and she'd left him to Carmen to comfort and still felt guilty that she had.

Could she put up with Carmen much longer? The apartment was beginning to smell. Of nappies (Carmen used terry-towelling cotton ones which she steeped in disinfectant before putting them through the washer), of olive oil, of eggs, of garlic, of furniture polish.

'Firat . . . No, Sharon. We'll go to Rzepin. Wherever that is. And speak to whoever is in charge. Set it up, will you?'

Sharon, plump but darkly attractive, a bit of a bimbo until you got to know just how clever she could be, drove. Firat, suppressing, just, all the worst attitudes to women a Turkish upbringing and a police career can bring, sat beside her. He knew that he would normally have been asked to drive, even with a woman as the boss, but the hair had not yet grown over the grafted skin that concealed the small steel plate above his right ear, and he was still prone to violent headaches and occasional black-outs.

Eintner sat in the back with Renata. They went by car, a comfortable Opel, because the air and train connections at Berlin were impossible. The route was Burg via Hannover and Potsdam, by-passing Berlin, to Frankfurt an der Oder. The Oder had frozen, thawed partially and frozen again so that there were huge chunks of broken ice like slabs of concrete from a destroyed town heaped at all angles beneath the new motorway bridge. On the far side a group of men had made holes in it and were fishing while a black dog scampered around them. They drove through into Poland and so on down the last few kilometres to Rzepin.

It was a depressing drive, over five hundred kilometres in five hours, arriving, as arranged, at two o'clock with one toilet and fast-food stop on the way. Mostly it was on autobahns or near-autobahn-standard trunk roads, and mostly through forest or prairie-farmed arable.

Half a decade since unification and almost nothing had changed. There was a poverty, a meanness, everywhere, even in the very soil itself, over-used in forty years of collectivised farming: the root crops looked etiolated and scraggy compared with what poked through the thin snow-fall in the smaller fields of the still largely peasant-farmed West. The villages were drab, with flaking stucco and rusting rubbish through which thrust the brown spikes of last summer's sorrel and brambles. And the further east they got, the more the road-surfaces needed attention.

Poland was worse.

Rzepin was a small town of yellow-stuccoed houses serving what had been one of the largest marshalling-yards in Europe. Here, deep in the Polish forest, the armour of the Wehrmacht had assembled on endless lines of waggons which trundled across Poland to the eastern front from Leningrad to Volgograd; five years later the Red Army moved in but facing the other way and stayed there for forty years. There were hectares, many hundreds of hectares, of sidings racked across the forest in a giant fine-meshed grid, interspersed with sheds, turntables, gantries of signals, points marked with counter-weighted handles so they could be shifted manually, signal boxes, control towers and at the peripheries smaller watch-towers. It wasn't just the armour that came through but trains capable of shifting ten thousand men in an afternoon, and then all the logistical back-up too, the ammunition, spare parts and replacements, food, cattle, cattle-trucks too.

Many of the sidings were still occupied with rolling stock of all sorts, empty, abandoned, useless, not worth scrapping, war's litter. There were even locomotives which you might have thought were worth breaking up – giant steel monsters, black where they weren't rusting, steam engines. In the old days anoraks from the world over, but mainly it has to be said from Britain, used to get visas to visit Warsaw down the line just so they could be trundled through Rzepin, twice, there and back, and see the steam engines still working. Risking at best a beating and their cameras smashed, they'd take photographs from behind one another's back-packs, not of Soviet matériel, including nuclear warheaded missiles, but of steam engines, steam engines working.

With most of the restrictions lifted, a few still came back, but not many – no longer a working place for steam, it was now a graveyard.

And of course Rzepin itself suffered. The traffic through the marshalling-yards was a mere five per cent of what it had been and what was left was about to be automated. There were no jobs. With no legitimate use (if you can call war, hot or cold, a legitimate use) it was probable that some at least of an unemployed but skilled workforce who knew how the yards worked would make themselves available to a new breed of racketeers. Arms- and drug-dealers, yes, but there were black markets less evil too, the people who, for instance, could steal a thousand tons of cement from a still state-owned Russian cement works and who needed to get it, no questions asked, with all the right paperwork, to the contractors who were re-building the new, glitzy Berlin, making it a worthy capital from which Herr Cabbage could rule new Europe.

Or so Renata suspected.

Two o'clock, and there was no-one to meet them. They hung around the main entrance to the marshalling-yard for twenty minutes. Firat and Norbert stood outside the Opel and smoked. Sharon, who was trying to give up, stayed inside.

There were concrete posts with red and white striped barriers which were locked down and there was no one there to lift them. Not that they would have known where to go if they had got in. Outside the three-metre fences the forest of fir and larch collected the snow, particularly on the north-east sides of the trees, where it froze. Inside ice formed on the stunted gorse and broom that had grown up between the tracks, and the pools of stagnant water, oily though they were, shone with a sick sheen. The new car's dash registered an outside temperature of minus seven Celsius. Sharon left the diesel engine running and the heater on. After ten minutes she asked if she could play a tape. Renata said yes. Garage. Three minutes and Renata told her to take it off. Amicably they settled on Miles Davis, digitally re-processed *Kind of Blue*.

The fidgety, almost train-like scurry of the opening riffs of 'All Blues', with the melancholy, slow, haunting melody coming over the top on Davis's muted trumpet, suddenly filled Renata with deep anxiety, angst. Why? She realised she was worried about Karl-Rosa. Was he all right? Chewing a knuckle, she cursed herself. It was the first time being away from home had bothered her – but it was also the first time she'd been any distance away from him.

Presently a small Fiat Panda-type car, with the ubiquitous body-work which factories from Valencia to Belgrade have been turning out under different names for a decade chugged to a halt beside them. Two people in it, not counting the driver.

One was a young woman with fair hair and a large nose, wearing an old business suit into which someone had inexpertly introduced power shoulder-pads.

'My name is Wisa, and I will interpret for you. May I introduce Walery Kalinka, Acting Deputy Controller?'

Sixty or more, frail, steel-framed specs, a heavy nicotine-stained moustache, a bad cough which sounded terminal. He wore a grease-stained trilby and shabby, threadbare overcoat whose astrakhan collar, however, looked new and warm.

They explained and apologised. Wisa had written the fax giving instructions as to where they should meet. She had supposed Kalinka meant the entrance they were now at, but he had meant the entrance to the small part of the yard where they actually worked. They got back in their cars and Sharon followed the ersatz Fiat.

Kalinka took them to a three-storey concrete shoe-box close to yards where some activity was apparent though not much. He took them up concrete stairs painted with gloss paint the colour of blood. It felt slightly sticky on the soles of their shoes and indeed there were slight indentations in it. Renata supposed that when the summer heat returned it would be a problem.

They were shown into an open-plan office filling most of the first floor. Tables, desks, filing-cabinets with doors rather than drawers, a few monitors and keyboards. Three clerks, smoking and drinking coffee with the remains of pastries in their saucers. She knew the signs – three people doing the work of one. The heating was by paraffin stoves that filled the air with damp, oily fumes. Renata felt slightly sick now and exhausted rather than tired – a dragging weightiness impeded every effort to move. Her forehead prickled in anticipation of a headache. It was still January, less than six weeks since Karl-Rosa had been born. Her breasts hurt, felt swollen. She had not fed Karl-Rosa herself, but had been expressing milk. The midwife had said she should.

Through Wisa they repeated what they had already said by fax: they were looking for four train-loads of unspecified freight which they believed had crossed the border en route to Russia during the second week of January 1994. There had in fact been forty-two of them, but only thirty-eight had arrived in Russia. The Russians had serial numbers, times, and documentation showing the missing four never reached their destination. They had documention that showed the trains had been in and out of the freight yards across the Oder in Frankfurt an der Oder. Rzepin was the next place they should have been put – in sidings, perhaps, to wait for clear track between scheduled traffic. There should be a record here if that was what had happened.

'Nineteen ninety-four? January?' Kalinka pursed his lips, shook his head, grunted orders, requests to the three clerks. Very reluctantly they left their cigarettes and coffees. They sort of milled around for a bit, argued, thought about it.

Wisa explained. Although they had been computerised at the time they were still, then, using five-and-a-quarter-inch floppies for records and now they'd gone IBM on three-and-a-half and although they still had the old disks they didn't have the old machines to load them on.

'Hard copies?'

y.'

.pboard filing-cabinets were opened up, the doors
.g. Hanging files of brown card were emptied across
the ables. Reams of continuous printout, de-concerti-
naed, tumbled folios to the floor. The print was dot matrix,
not a lot of dots, and mostly faded. And all, of course, in
Polish. Firat sneezed and felt that he had almost blown
out the steel plate above his ear. He and Sharon went out
on to the staircase and Sharon had her first cigarette for
six months. Renata sat down, looked out of the window,
wished that it was open. Einstein poked about amongst
the sea of paper but gave up – the Polish was beyond
him. After an hour Kalinka was fervently positive. Wisa
translated: 'There were no trains came through with
those serial numbers. They never reached Rzepin.'

'Nevertheless, we should like to take the printouts and
the five-and-a-half-inch disks back with us for further
analysis. If that's possible.'

This was a tricky moment. Renata had been as polite
as she could be; by her standards she had positively
crawled. Why? She knew well that not only the Poles
but the Danes, even the British, reacted badly to any
suggestion that she was imbued with the mastery of the
Herrenvolk – that, because she was not just German
but West German, people less fortunate would do as she
asked.

But to no avail. Or perhaps Kalinka spoke the truth.

'Obviously,' he said, through Wisa, 'I cannot let you
have the masters. I shall have to make a formal request
to Warsaw for permission to make copies . . . But I repeat.
No trains came through with those serial numbers. They
never reached Rzepin.'

For no better reason than to make a change they took
the road through Słubice and Frankfurt an der Oder,

rather than the autobahn. While they waited at the bridge to cross the Oder and the border back into Germany, Einstein unfolded a map of the area.

'The thing is,' he said, 'Frankfurt an der Oder is a major junction. But also a terminus. Trains come in here but cannot go through. They come in from each point of the compass. From the north from Szczecin, from the west from Berlin, from the south from Dresden and Prague, and from the east from Warsaw and Russia. They come in from all these places and they go out again. To any of them. Those four trains need not have gone to Rzepin. From here they could have gone anywhere.'

Renata forbore to comment that it was his hunch that had brought them to Rzepin but yawned with boredom and fatigue, looked out across the parapet at the cathedral with its twin spires and another big church in the German town. They were being restored after more than half a century of neglect, not to mention being shelled from across the Oder in 1945. It looked better than Poland, but not a lot. It would be midnight before she was back in her own flat. With her son. And Carmen.

From the front passenger seat Firat complained, 'I left my fucking lighter there. My Zippo. The one my dad gave me.'

Back in Rzepin Kalinka held the lighter up, grinned somewhat wanly at the three clerks and Wisa. He scraped his thumb inexpertly on the milled wheel, then got a flare. He touched it to the reams of dry continuous stationery close to the floor and watched the orange flame snake up. All five of them left quite quickly but without panic. The red paint already had a touch more give in it as they went down the stairs.

CHAPTER 5

Sheen Associates went back to UKania, virtually disbanded. Jace and Ash had told them that it would take their man in Berlin some time, weeks anyway, to search through the city's underworld for a whisper about the missing trains. There were now so many 'mafias', interlocking circles of organised crime, that someone would know something about it all, but clearly it was a matter where a deft, careful approach was necessary. There was so much treachery, ah! treachery, double-crossing, grassing, undercover cops – he was walking through a minefield. He'd take his time.

Privately, Jace and Ash had not the slightest hope that Kim would do anything about it at all – it simply was not his scene. Moreover, it wasn't their scene either. They had no intention of getting involved, however peripherally, in illicit arms-dealing, but at the same time they recognised that they did have an obligation to Harry Sheen. Even though they had paid back the half mil that set them up years ago. So, without considering the possible consequences, they contacted Kim and asked him to keep his ear to the ground with regard to missing freight trains filled with ammunition and let them know if he heard anything.

So Harry went back to his mock-tudor in Godstone, Surrey, which he hated. It was pure Arthur Daley. There was even a 'her indoors'. The real money and the serious crooks were down the M4 in Cotswold pads not a hundred miles from HRH himself. Herbert Doe cracked his knuckles in East London gyms and offered good but unheeded advice to West Indian youngsters who all knew they were the next Bruno or Eubank. Squeaky Sam went to the dogs, literally, and made an almost honest living working various gambling systems he'd devised. Eloise went back to what she had hoped would be a temporary job as sales rep for a small but adventurous publishing outfit operating out of Finsbury Park. In the nine months she had been there she had doubled the sales in her area.

Slowly the powerful presence of Jace in her mind and her longing for him faded. And, for his part, Jace smoked less and less until, after four weeks or so, he realised he'd given up. Again.

Back in Brandenburgische Straße Kim too was having problems. The gay S&M scene in Berlin was very different from Hamburg's. Berlin has a reputation for being the omphalos of the gay world. Isherwood, dodgy cabarets and all that, remain in the great collective consciousness. Indeed once it was so. In the area round Nollendorfplatz in the heart of Schöneberg, to the south and west of Zoo and north of Brandenburgische Straße, back in the twenties gay life was open, institutionalised, with its own papers, community associations and art. That is until Hitler rounded them all up, made them wear pink triangles on their sleeves, and finally sent them to the ovens.

The result, Kim found, was that although there were many gay bars in the area the whole ambience lacked frivolity. He found himself saying again and again, 'They all take themselves so fucking seriously.' There were bars that seemed to be used exclusively by PWAs and HIVs. There was even a red granite triangular plaque at the U-Bahn station erected in memory of the thousands murdered by Hitler.

All of which he approved – up to a point. But, as far as

Kim was concerned there was not a lot of point in being gay if it didn't mean fun. And fun which people were ready, one way or another, to pay for. Basically, sexuality aside, which was real enough, Kim saw himself as an entertainer. In Berlin, compared with Hamburg, he was an entertainer with a disappointingly meagre market. In short, he was not making the money he had hoped for.

With his height, his sculptured good looks, a body he kept in good nick without going for the full iron-pumped pectorals, he got some film work quite quickly. He had to take the U-Bahn across the city to Prenzlauer Berg. There the gay scene was not so obvious as it was round Nollendorfplatz, but, once you'd found it, was harder, tougher, more exciting in the run-down, tired, still unre-constructed (in every sense of the word) east of Berlin.

However, there were limits, even for Kim, and he pulled out when he discovered the crucifixion he had been cast for was to be simulated only in part. OK, he said to the outfit who had hired him, piercing, OK. Crown of thorns, fine, especially if they threw in a decent purple robe. Flogging, of course. The English vice. Not in moderation, but neither in too exaggerated excess, yes, he could go along with flogging. Coming from where he came from, his first sexual experience, so formative don't you think, had been having his bleeding buttocks licked by the beefy adolescent who had just beaten them with a sawn-off hockey stick. Who then went on to suck him off, before buggering him. But nails? Through my palms? Leave it out, man.

He did a couple of floor-shows at weekends and hustled a little. Trouble was that servicing extremely fat Russian 'businessmen' was almost as crucifying as crucifixion.

Piotra came by every now and then. Sometimes breath-less and anxious, spending a few minutes at the Venetian blind before relaxing and then unloading a couple of bags of stuff she'd hoisted along Ku'damm. In exchange for the refuge he provided she gave him presents – but always on the condition that 'cross-my-heart' he wouldn't try to flog them.

'You don't know how. You don't know where to go.'

The odd thing was that most of what she lifted was male-orientated. Shoes. Silk ties and shirts. Leather waistcoats. Sweaters. Suits. Cashmere coats, even. Posh spirits – malt whisky, class cognac. Smelly foreign cheese. Watches, good ones. Caviare.

'Why?'

'Most shoplifters are women. The security's good where women shop. Some of the department stores even use shoplifters on probation for their security. Bastards. Where men shop it's different. Men are lousy at it, so the security isn't so good. They're looking at the men anyway – the girlfriend or wife has come along only to make sure the stupid male isn't buying something hopelessly stupid.'

'Is it because the clothes you lift are always menswear that you dress like a man?'

'Fuck off.'

One afternoon, towards the middle of February, she came by without anything at all, just threw herself on to the sofa and asked for tea.

'I'm broke,' she said. 'The shops are so fucking empty they watch you every second, hoping you'll buy. The summer stuff is in, but no-one's buying yet. Who thinks of summer when it's this fucking cold? I could have lifted a couple of kilos of sun-tan lotion but what the fuck use is that?'

She accepted a cup of the Jackson's of Piccadilly Lapsang she'd brought him a month before.

'How's the family?'

She meant the peregrine.

'Surviving. I give her a bit of warmed-over raw liver every now and then. She likes that.'

'No sign of a mister yet?'

'No. Wait till the fourteenth. St Valentine's Day. That's when birds pair off.'

'Of course. Listen, Kim. This won't do. We need a real bust. A proper con. We need to move up. You hustling your ass, me scampering down Ku'damm with a loada security guards on my tail, we're getting too old for this sort of lark. We have to move up. Up the social scale. Upward mobility. OK?'

Her English was always almost perfect – but she would attempt to be idiomatic and it always came across a touch out of kilter.

'Sure.'

'Any ideas?'

And then he remembered. Remembered the rather vague invitation he had had from the twins to see if he could find out anything about four missing freight trains loaded with Russian ammunition. If he could, English friends of theirs would be be able to handle the business angle.

'Well,' she said, 'that is a good idea.'

And she sat bolt upright, knees spread. She was wearing yellow silk velvet corduroys beneath a very warm-looking cashmere coat, whose price tag must have been all of two thousand marks. Not the clothes you associated with someone who was broke, until you remembered she was probably on her way to sell them for a tenth or at most a fifth of their retail price. She looked up at him.

'That is a good idea,' she said again.

'Yes?'

'Yes. I'll put it around that we know where these trains are.'

'Oh yes?'

'And what will happen is this. First of all, a lot of buyers will come on the scene wanting to know how they can buy the stuff. Second, if these trains really do exist, then whoever has them is going to be pissed off we're claiming ownership and they'll come on the scene too.'

'This could be dangerous, you know. I mean, if any of this happens how will you play it?'

'How will *I* play it? We . . . *We'll* play it by ear. How else?'

Dangerous? Three nights later he came back from cruising Schöneberg's avenues and squares, heard heavy movements on the other side of the door to the ex-sound-stage, let himself through the door as quietly as he could and found three crew-cut, leather-jacketed men in jeans attempting to do nasty things to Piotra – except that one of them wasn't in jeans because he was raping Piotra while the other two held her down.

CHAPTER 6

The first thing Kim had to decide was whether or not to kill them. In less than a second he decided not to. How far short of killing them he'd go would depend on how well they behaved.

The huge, high, empty room was unlit apart from street-light and moonlight. They were all in a huddle in the corner nearest the windows and the door. There was a lot of dust, much of it swirling in the spaces round them, as well as empty film-cans.

One of them saw him coming, released Piotra, stood, pulled back his fist, then, for a second, paused. He'd taken in that Kim was just on two metres tall and probably a healthy eighty kilos. The hesitation cost him. Kim delivered a roundhouse left-footed kick to his diaphragm with all of that height and weight behind it, and then spun on his right foot. As the man's head came down, Kim's fists, now linked, came up under his chin. His head snapped back and the dust billowed out from under him as he hit the floor.

If I've killed him, Kim thought, well . . . I didn't mean to. He ducked the clumsy windmill of a blow the second guy threw at him and thought, I'll be a touch more careful with this one. Kim caught the arm as it swung and gave it the sort of shake or flap you give a heavy rug when you want to get it clean and you don't have a vacuum cleaner; dislocating it at the shoulder.

That left the rapist. But Piotra already had her teeth in his neck and his balls in her hand. And she showed no sign of letting go of either. The man screamed, really screamed, screamed like they do in hell – Michelangelo's version, anyway. When he went limp she let go, and as he tried to get up Kim kicked him in the head.

She stood up. Looked around for a moment and then picked up the plum-coloured leggings she'd been wearing, her fedora and her long woollen coat.

'I need a wash,' she said, and headed for the narrow, exposed stairs that climbed the inside wall. At the top she fumbled her key out of the linen jacket she still had on and let herself in.

Kim stood at the bottom of the stairs with his back to her, watching the three men. He was pleased to find that his breathing and pulse were already almost back to normal. It was the adrenalin rush that had raised them rather than the physical effort. Kim walked towards them. The dust was settling, but there was still enough to give shape to a moonbeam. His foot kicked a film-can, sent it skittering a metre or so across the floor. He could smell fresh urine, fresh shit, fresh blood and maybe semen too. I'd make the fuckers clean up, he thought, if there was any chance of them making a reasonable job of it.

The one he'd kicked and then chinned was still out cold. Kim felt his neck for a pulse, found one. Fast, fluttering a bit, but he wasn't about to pop his clogs. He got hold of his ankles and hauled him out on to the landing. The one with a dislocated shoulder was sitting up, leaning against the wall, holding his shoulder with his good hand while the other arm hung twisted and skewed. He was whimpering. It crossed Kim's mind that he could rig him up a sling, even reset the joint for him, but he decided not. If it had been a straight fight, even three men on one woman, he might have done. But rape? No.

He hooked his hands in the man's armpits, which considering the nature of his injury was not kind, and hauled him too out on to the landing.

That left the rapist. Oh dear. Even in a bad light which left deep shadows in the areas it could not reach, he was clearly in a very bad way, gonad-wise. Would be some time before he'd be sexually functional again, perhaps never. Piotra had made a fair shot at castrating him, possibly, technically at any rate, had succeeded. Kim put him out on the landing with the others, closed the door, locked it.

And then the reaction came. Nausea and self-disgust. He blundered into the lavatory at the foot of the stairs and heaved up the beef stroganoff and rice he'd just had at a fairly authentic Russian restaurant a hundred metres from his front door. He cleaned himself up but found he was still shaking – as much at the horror of self-discovery as anything else: the techniques and above all mental attitude that had been instilled in him during the ten years he had been a trained, professional killer in the British Army had come back unreconstructed and as instinctive as they had been five years ago, when he had turned his back on it all. He looked at himself in the mirror, smiled ruefully. Plans he had had for a sex change might, he thought, be a touch premature.

He climbed the stairs, knocked.

'You can come in.'

She had no clothes on at all now, was hunkered over the electric kettle she'd hoisted for him. The room-heater was blowing hot air at full blast. She'd turned on the spotlight he'd rigged up but left it so it lit the end of the sofa furthest from the door, which was where he liked it when he was reading himself to sleep. It cast a warm, soft light over the rest of the room. The kettle came to the boil just as he closed and locked the door behind him. She lifted the cordless jug from its low pedestal and poured about half into the washbasin, which was already half filled with cold water. The Nina Ricci soap had gone but in its place was the black Spanish soap he liked called Magna, a fairly fresh ovoid cake of it.

'Hang on,' he said, and chucked her a clean white T-shirt. 'Use that.'

She washed herself slowly and carefully, twice, all over, with fresh water the second time, using the T-shirt on her body, and her fingers on her short hair, but skillfully, neither spilling nor dropping more water than she absolutely had to.

Her body was older than he had expected.

Her shoulders were broad and a touch mannish, her breasts small with small nipples. She had a hint of a spare tyre above her pelvic girdle and her buttocks were dimpled. However, her thighs and shins were lean and muscled, and he wondered why, but remembered that on the two occasions he had seen her outside, by accident, she had been cycling. Perhaps she cycled a lot. All in all, her body was not very specifically feminine – indeed much of it was hazed with blond fur. Feminine, no. Female, yes. But somehow, only just.

There were several nasty red blotches on her skin, some, round her neck and upper thighs, actually lacerated. In an hour or so they would be bruises.

She put her feet, first one, then the other, on the arm of a cane chair he'd bought for himself, and dried between toes that were slightly misshapen: her big toes half lay over the ones next to them. The feet themselves were long, yellowish, and on the left one there was an incipient bunion.

He felt no desire for her, but tenderness, yes. Sensing she was nearly through, he found tobacco, pellets of hash, cigarette papers, and rolled a couple of joints. She wrapped herself in a big towel, a seaside towel with an awful picture of Marilyn Monroe on it. She'd picked it up for herself off a stall outside the Europa Center, and left it in the room, telling him he could use it if he wanted to, but it was really there for her. Now, she tucked it high up under her armpits. She sat on the end of the sofa opposite him, swung her legs up, pulled the towel down over her shins, took the joint he had lit for her, inhaled, held it, let it hit. He adjusted the spotlight so it was not in her eyes.

'There. That's better.'

'Are you all right?'

'Never felt better.' More a grimace than a grin. Time passed, marked by the sudden revving of a performance car as it roared away from the lights at the junction of Brandenburgische Straße and Hohenzollerndamm. 'Ah. Are you speaking . . . technically?'

He shrugged. She tossed her head.

'Do you mean, did he penetrate?' she asked. 'Not far. Did he come? I think not. Not inside me, anyway.'

He recalled that she had examined the T-shirt after washing her genitals.

'So what was all that about?'

'That, dear Kim, was about your fucking trains.'

He waited. She took another toke.

'They wanted to know where the trains are.'

He took a toke, held it, and felt a lot better. The shaking had stopped. He was sitting in more or less the same posture as she was and, in the middle of the sofa, her feet lay over his sneakers. His knees were slightly spread and the joint, hanging from his right hand glowed like a nebula between his face and hers.

He tried to remember what the three men had been like.

There had been some words among their grunts and moans, and not German. They were quite well-built, two

of them small but stocky. He hadn't really made much of
their faces but had an impression of small noses and
thickish lips. Two had close-cropped hair, but the rapist's
was quite long and full, probably dark.

'Well, darling,' he said, a hint of a laugh in his voice as
well as apology, 'it was your idea. Who were they?'

'Serbs,' she said, 'fucking Serbs. Buyers, anyway.'

She explained. Or at any rate gave him an explanation.

She had spent two nights on the eastern side of Berlin
cruising the cafés and clubs in Scheunenviertal where
she knew petty criminals and two-dime gangsters hung
out, hardly any of them of German origin.

A fat barman in Oranienburger Straße, not far from
the restored art nouveau synagogue, turned out to be a
Pole. Since Piotra spoke Polish well, he had been ready
to gossip. And treat her to a vodka he kept under the
counter. He assured her it was pure grain spirit made by
his uncle, who had a farm, and a still, near Poznań. It
tasted much the way she thought paint-thinners would
taste.

'He'd heard about the trains. He'd heard they were in
a big marshalling-yard near Rzepin – that's where you'll
find them.'

But she had been looking for buyers as well as sellers,
and having drawn a blank in east Berlin she had moved
back west to Kreuzberg, close to the Schlesisches Tor U-
Bahn station, where most of the illegal immigrants and
poorer guest-workers hung out, especially those from ex-
Yugoslavia.

There, on the third night she had been tracked down
by three louts who insisted she knew where the trains
were and was about to tell them. They followed her into
the U-Bahn system, shouting abuse and jostling her. She
needed help. She headed not back to her own room in
Schöneberg, not far from where Isherwood remembered,

as if he were a camera, an English girl who sang in the gay clubs, but further west to Fehrbelliner Platz. She ran down Brandenburgische Straße, thought she was far enough ahead to get through the locked front door, but just as she was closing it on them a young woman who had been visiting her mother on the fifth floor had appeared in front of her and insisted on being let out.

This gave the leader the chance he needed to get his foot in the door.

She slept on the sofa, he on the floor. When he woke, she'd gone. She left the linen jacket. There was blood all down the left lapel – not hers, but from the neck of the man she'd bitten.

CHAPTER 7

Kim sat in his cane chair in an early beam of sunlight
that penetrated the dormer window, drank instant coffee
and tried to think it all through.

The bastards of the night before were spearmen merely,
heavies sent to intimidate and extract information,
though possibly one of them, the rapist perhaps, had been
in charge, was under orders to get from Piotra what their
bosses thought she had.

They'll be back. They'll be back mob-handed.

He stood up, looked down into the hall below. Move
out? Unthinkable. Improve our defences? Some sense in
that.

He let himself out, paused at the top of the stairs. The
door was panelled, with signs of woodworm at the bottom
but substantial in itself. It was the lock and then the
hinges too that needed replacing – either or both would
burst if a reasonably strong and heavy man took a run
up the steps at them. And a child could manage it, given
a jemmy or a crowbar.

He went down the open stairs and over to the corner
where the battle had taken place. There were scuff marks
in the dust and some small patches of blood and other
bodily fluids, but not as bad as he had expected. He'd
borrow a mop and bucket from one of the offices he shared
the landing with, or maybe just buy a floor-cloth.

The door on to the landing was more substantial than
the one at the top of the stairs. He reckoned a more
serious lock would do the trick. He'd need tools. A

powered screwdriver, chisels, a hammer, maybe a drill as
well, and of course the locks and hinges. The post-army
Kim sighed with the boredom of it all, the expense. The
man who had had his captaincy and command of a
company by the time the Gulf War came along, knew
better. But it was post-army Kim who went back upstairs
to put on his war-paint before going out – the brick-
coloured lipstick, the mascara, and, because he was
feeling a little wan after all he'd been through, a hint of
blusher.

He found a good hardware store and bought what he
reckoned he would need. The cost was outrageous – everything like that was so bloody expensive in Germany, and
of course of superb quality. Which he could have done
without. When again would he use a set of cold-forged
steel chisels with rubberised handles? It was only when
he got them back and looked at the writing engraved on
the blades that he realised that they weren't German at
all but from Taiwan.

He worked all morning and rather enjoyed it. The big
room filled with sunlight. The frost melted from both
outside and inside the windows. His fingers were almost
too cold to work but he trimmed a pair of leather gloves,
making mittens out of them, and managed. The street
noise was a problem but he unplugged his music system
and took it down to where he was working. Techno, then
Mozart.

By one o'clock he reckoned he was through. He put his
shoulders to both locked doors in turn and exerted all the
pressure he could. Not even a creak. He felt good about
it, about the way he'd spent a sunny morning occupied
meaningfully with strenuous physical work. Better than
a work-out in a sweaty gym or lane-swimming in chlori-
nated water. Should do it more often.

He cleared up, stacking the tools close to the film-cans

– no point in cluttering his room with them – and using his dustpan and brush swept the sawdust and chippings into a supermarket plastic bag.

Feeling pleased with himself, he went down to the nearest Turkish fast-food stall and got himself a doner kebab with chilli and a litre of Évian. He ate and drank sitting on a window-sill in the big room, from where he could see down into the street. And bit by bit a sense of unease built up inside his head – it was not enough, what he had done, not enough. All right, he had added at least twenty minutes to the time it would take determined people to get in, but it would not stop them. Even foxes' earths and badgers' setts usually have a way out as well as a way in. He pushed the *imbiß* wrapper into the bag on top of the wood-shavings, tightened the top on what was left of his Évian.

Problem! He couldn't use the new locks until he had given Piotra the new keys – but he had left the old ones in place too, so he engaged them but not the new ones.

He climbed the stairs and stood facing the sofa and the red-painted panel of hardboard behind it. It was only just over a metre high, reaching to the point where the roof began to slope inwards. It was secured with six cross-head screws. He had often heard noises coming from behind it, scuffling, shuffling noises, sibilant and squeaky. He had assumed rats, maybe, if there were gaps in the leading, birds, starlings, pigeons, though this was unlikely with the peregrine around. And once, just once, he'd heard, for a moment he was sure it was so, a human cough.

Three o'clock in the morning, a bit drunk, bleeding slightly from the bum (a Japanese businessman who really didn't seem to know what he was doing – or perhaps he did), he had nevertheless had a go at the screws with a knife-blade, but the cross-heads had defeated him. He had gone to sleep and thought no more about it when he woke.

The screwdriver he had just bought had interchangeable heads, one of which was for cross-heads. He pulled the sofa into the middle of the room, and went to work, carefully placing the screws, which were long, at least two and a half centimetres, in the soap-holder in the washbasin. They came out really rather easily and he recalled the glance Piotra had given the wall on the day she called when he was unpacking. Perhaps he could have tried harder with a knife-blade. Perhaps she always carried a cross-head screwdriver with her.

Quite soon he was able to lift the hardboard clear. It was heavier than he had expected, being mounted on a frame of dressed and finished pine a bit smaller than English two by four, but not much. The gap was similarly framed with an upright in the middle and with the six screw-holes he had withdrawn the screws from. A wall of icy air toppled slowly into the already cold room. He put his head into almost complete darkness and sniffed without thinking – just as he had been trained to do.

The smells were mixed. Mustiness, the ammonia of animal urine, but there were other smells too: a definite suggestion of garbage, vegetable and fruit garbage. That gave him pause for thought.

He pulled back into his room, hoicked the Smith & Wesson out from its hiding-place between the back of the sofa and the cushions, unwrapped it from its canvas pouch, loaded it but left empty the chamber that would come under the hammer when he pulled the trigger or cocked it – a safety device more reliable than the catch: no chance now of shooting himself in the foot. He pushed it into the broad tooled and studded belt that held up his jeans. Then he unhooked the reading spot and holding it

well in front of where he was going to put his head, and
to the side too, pointed it into the darkness.

To his left a solid brick wall, hung with dusty cobwebs.
It was, he realised, the end wall of his block. But to his
right he was looking down a narrow tunnel shaped like
a right-angled triangle. The inner side was the continu-
ation of the wall the hardboard had replaced. The outer
longer side, the hypotenuse, was the roof, supported by
heavy dressed but unfinished timber beams set at metre
intervals. There were slats and smaller beams set hori-
zontally and filling the spaces between the big beams.
Above them, what? Probably tarred material of some sort
beneath lead or slate.

He paused again and thought. The whole block was a
vast rectangle built round a courtyard. The longer sides,
on one of which he was, faced the streets, the shorter
ones backed on to the neighbouring blocks. Remembering
the buildings on the other side of Brandenburgische
Straße, the roof would be at two pitches, a shallow one
coming from the roof-tree that ran along the middle of
each side, then a steeper one that ended in guttering
behind a low parapet. On the street side, the steeper side
was pierced with dormer windows, but not apparently on
the side overlooking the inner courtyard. The tunnel he
was looking down was therefore formed by the steeper
pitch and an inner load-bearing wall.

He looked back in again, took in the floor this time.
It was narrow, only about a metre wide and broken by
horizontal beams that ran laterally out to support the
floor of his room. The height of the tunnel, even right up
against the wall where it was highest, was also about a
metre.

With his original purpose well in the front of his mind
– to see if there wasn't a second way out – he realised
he'd have to go further in. It would, in fact, be sensible

to explore the whole roof area. But the flex on the lamp
was already almost at its full stretch and he had no torch.
Should he go and buy one? No. He was now quite excited
about the whole business and anyway knew that if there
were any danger ahead he'd face it better with his own
adapted vision than with the deceptive and limited light
a torch would give.

He climbed through the hole, contrived to pull the hardboard on its frame almost back into place, and hunkered
down with his back to it. He kept his eyes away from the
few small slits of narrow light that ran mostly along
the level of the floor, glanced at the illuminated hands of
his watch and waited for twenty minutes, during which
the cold crept into him like a disease. But his night vision
returned. All the time he listened. Distant traffic noises.
A scrabbling from above somewhere and a faint kittenish
mewling. Cats? Rats? He realised his removal of the
screws and entry would have made enough noise to
frighten into hiding whatever life there was up there.
Perhaps, as time passed, courage was returning. His was,
particularly as he could now see quite well. Stooped
almost double, he moved off down the passage, his hands
above his head, palms in turn flat against each beam as
he passed beneath them, eyes fixed on the floor a metre
or so in front of him, occasionally peering into the
dimness ahead.

Soon he came, as he knew he would, to the top of the
lift-shaft. It was enclosed, at least on the side he was on,
in sheet steel painted dark green. There was a narrow
gap round it, which he could just squeeze through. At
least here he could stand upright. Another gap brought
him to a passage identical to the one he had come down,
continuing in the same direction. He felt a dull moment
of tedium. It seemed he could follow this new passage
down its length and then along the other three sides

and so back to where he had come from, without finding anything significant, certainly not an escape route.

From below, but amplified by the lift-shaft, a concertinaed gate rattled, followed by the more definite slam of the lift's newer inner door. The machinery whirred, quite uncomfortably loud, and the casing that held it vibrated heavily when he put his palm against it. He visualised what was happening. There was a stairwell. The stairs climbed three sides of the well, landing by landing. At the back of the well was the lift-shaft. Sometimes lift-shafts were put in in the middle of the well, sometimes at the back. This one was at the back.

The well itself, seen from below, had a high ceiling with a stucco circular ornament in its centre. Probably, in the block's glory days, it had been the fixture from which a chandelier, or at any rate a candelabra, had hung. Lowered by the concierge each evening, it would have been lit and hoisted back up to illuminate the whole well. The rose that remained had been painted over so many times that the actual nature of the ornamentation could no longer be discerned. But what it meant was that there was quite a substantial area above it.

He continued to think it through. Lifts break down, need servicing. There had to be access to the top of the lift-shaft. But that would probably be from outside, from the roof, up discreet little ladders set in the brickwork leading on from the fire-escapes that dropped down to the inner courtyard. Certainly a way out. If you could get there. Again he remembered Piotra's glance at the false wall in his room. He had, without properly thinking it through, assumed a trapdoor, access to the landings on corridors below. But these would lead back to the staircases and the lift, and could therefore be very easily covered. But access to the fire-escapes that ran down the inside walls of the courtyard, which at every level had access to rooms and apartments ... There had to be a link, a way of getting from where he was on to the roofs and down the fire-escapes.

He went back to the first side of the casing that enclosed the lift machinery and ran his hand down the inner wall close up to it. It gave. It yielded. It was a canvas curtain, less than a metre across.

His vision was now very good, and anyway on the far side there was more light. He saw what he saw quite clearly. A Wehrmacht uniform hung from the roof, shredded by age but still recognisable, the uniform of a private, a cadet even. The forage cap with its simple badge of a black circle within a white one was perched absurdly on top of a crumbling skull.

The breeches pathetically concertinaed on the low floor. The roof was not quite high enough.

Beyond it a man wheezed, coughed and spat.

Behind Kim a torch came on.

Not, he thought, the moment to go for the Smith & Wesson.

'On the other side of Martin Bormann, you'll find Fritz.' The voice behind him was Piotra's. Once again, in spite of all his training, she'd got close without him hearing her. 'I'd like you to meet him. He's going to help us screw the Serbs. And make a pfennig or two for us all.'

Kim edged round 'Martin Bormann'. A small skylight let into the roof, possibly to give access to the top of the lift-shaft, shed a grey light.

Fritz looked up at him. Long, filthy grey hair tumbled from beneath an old leather hat, the sort pilots used to wear, and bikers wore before they had to have helmets; a face almost as grey as his hair, huge bushy eyebrows, eyes that glittered from the back of deep brown sockets, a big bony nose, its size exaggerated by his skeletal thin-ness, the brown stumps of old untreated teeth. And for the rest, a huge pile of old blankets, old eiderdowns, and pigeon feathers.

'Hi, Fritz,' Kim said in German. 'Can you really do that?'

'Yes, he can. About this time every year Fritz makes a trip. Don't you, Fritz? Over the border to Rzepin and the forest beyond. He can show us just the sort of place where these trains might be.'

Kim looked down at the old man, who looked back from cold, expressionless eyes, surprisingly clear.

'But not the trains themselves?'

'No. But then you never know, do you? Anyway, I think we should go along with Fritz and have a look.' She looked at her gold watch. 'No time to do it today. Fritz, if we're going to do this tomorrow, you need to clean up. You can do it in Kim's room. You know, what was my room. Down the end of the passage.'

At last Fritz spoke. A guttural, harsh voice.

'Is it warm there?' he asked.

'Warm enough.'

'All right.'

The mountain of blankets and eiderdowns stirred, heaved, broke open. There were smells, but not noxious – warm, damp odours. The old man was wearing a long black overcoat of heavy wool. He reached out a claw of a hand. Kim took it. It was not cold, but the nails were very long, cracked and yellow. Kim helped him to his feet. Piotra, who had obviously been there before, delved into the heap and came up with a large carpet-bag. She followed the men back to Kim's room, the room that had been hers.

CHAPTER 8

They spent the evening cleaning Fritz up. First, while the room warmed up with the fan-heater on full blast, Kim, who knew how to do such things, gave him a short haircut, and trimmed the beard down to an Edwardian moustache and goatee. Naturally Kim's travelling accessories included barber's scissors and an electric trimmer. Then they stripped the old man down and washed him in hot water, with plenty of Magna soap. He was not particularly dirty, not even about his genitals and anus, but his skin seemed stale and old. It revived a lot as they worked on him, sometimes standing him up, sometimes sitting him on the sofa.

He was very thin, hardly any fat on him at all, just bones, tendons, sinews; arms and legs not quite stick-like and useless, but with some muscle, the joints standing out like the knobs on frequently pollarded branches.

'He gets out about twice a week, always at night,' Piotra said. 'Scavenges the garbage heaps in the markets after they've shut down, gets stale bread from the back of restaurants, that sort of thing.'

'So there is another way out?'

'Was that what you were looking for when you found him?'

'Yes.'

'Several. I'll show you some other time. Here. I'm not strong enough to do his nails. You'll have to do them.'

Kim took the claw, saw the star-shaped scar on the back of the hand, turned it over, saw the same in the palm.

'Who ... What is he?' He remembered the movie he had dropped out from when things seemed to be getting a bit heavy.

'Well, he's not Jesus Christ, that's for sure. Back in the early sixties there was a craze for porn-snuff movies featuring crucifixions. Some of them were made down there' – she gestured towards the internal panel of glass – 'which is probably why Fritz ended up here.'

Sure enough there were similar wounds in his long yellow feet, which were purpled with split capillaries round the ankles, more life-menacing than the old scars. There was even a crescent cicatrice under his left ribs, pure white like a very new moon, which Kim had missed but now looked for and found.

The full five wounds. Kim thought: perhaps he shouldn't have chickened out. Had it hurt? he wanted to ask. Did they pay well? Using a pair of ordinary nail scissors, he attacked the nails. They had grown to a forwards droop a centimetre clear of the ends of his fingers, and, though ridged, were remarkably undamaged. They were very tough and not all that brittle, not at all easy to trim.

At times Kim wanted to weep. He felt he was looking at himself in forty years' time, but also at a sort of father or elder brother who had gone the same way ahead of him. Not at all like his real father, of course, a retired police chief inspector who lived in a bungalow in Feltham, Middlesex. Mum, as often happens with wives of dedicated policemen, had done a runner when Kim was ten. With a Tesco store manager. She had not wanted to take Kim with her. Kim's dad's unmarried sister had moved in to take her place. Kim had had, still had, an intense admiration for his dad, which was why he had done his utmost to please him by joining the army. He'd been kicked out shortly after getting his captaincy for being caught in bed with the company sergeant-major's bummer boy, and hadn't seen or spoken to his father since.

The carpet-bag ('I nicked it for him,' Piotra claimed) held clothes: thermal underwear, a shirt, a good Scottish tweed suit, good shoes ('I nicked those too'). But they saved them for the morning. They gave the old man a packet of Knorr soup, chicken and noodles, in a mug and some bread. Then they wrapped him in the bed-coverings and put him on the sofa. Fritz slept.

All through the whole business he hardly said a word, not even offered a grunt, but submitted to it all in the way a patient who knows he is terminally ill submits to the ministrations of generous nurses.

'I don't get this,' Kim said at last, once Fritz was on the sofa and asleep. Until then he had followed Piotra's instructions and suggestions without question.

'Nor do I. But I can tell you what I know.'

Crouched by the heater, now on half power and hardly noisy at all, she did just that.

'I found him here five years ago when I first used this room. I heard him behind the wall. It was a wall then. Like you I needed an escape route, knew I would feel more comfortable if I had one. I took the wall down—'

'How?'

'With a sledgehammer. How else? I put in the panelling, explored the roof-spaces and found him where you found him. Funny thing. It was the same week the other Wall came down. We didn't bother each other at all for several months, but every now and then I looked in on him to see how he was. And he told me about the three ways out of this place.'

'You said "several".'

'Three is several. Then three years ago he checked out with me that the Polish frontier was now open. He'd picked up the idea from a scrap of newspaper he'd bothered to look at. I told him it was. He asked me to go with him into Poland, not far into Poland, just to Rzepin. It seemed important to him so I organised it. Got him the clothes. He had an old ID, I got him a new one. None of it was difficult.'

'So you went to Poland with him. To Rzepin.'

'Yes.'

'And?'

'Nothing, really. We'll do the routine tomorrow and you'll see.'

'Routine?'

'This will be the fourth time.'

'But why "we"?'

'I told you. Those trains are there, in Rzepin. I'm sure of it. And if they are, they'll be close to the bit he goes to.'

Kim thought she was telling the truth – some of the time. But her eyes flinched off his face every now and then, and sometimes he felt she was composing.

In the morning, at a quarter to nine they took the U7 line from Fehrbelliner Platz to Wilmersdorfer Straße and then walked through the pedestrian precinct with, Kim was amused to note, its C & A store – of course, there were C & As in Hamburg too, but it always made him feel a touch less foreign when he saw the familiar logo – and on past the inevitable stalls selling New Age trinkets, thong 'jewellery' and so on. A long, wide, dull street beside and below the railway and S-Bahn took them to Charlottenburg station. There they caught the S-Bahn to Hauptbahnhof. It was bitterly cold, with a grey sky and occasional flurries of powdery snow.

Up to then Kim had always taken the U-Bahn: the overhead railway gave him a view of the city he had not seen before. From the misnamed Bellevue to Friedrichstraße and beyond it was a landscape out of hell: especially close to the line the Wall had taken. Small factories, disused warehouses, demolition sites, decrepit housing, and a few blackened leafless trees in small snow-swept parks. But what made it extraordinary was the graffitti: every available surface had been sprayed in the lurid colours of the art, mostly slogans, nihilistic and anarchic. Clearly, every possible site had been seen as a challenge by artists who must also have been skilled alpine climbers or steeplejacks.

Beyond it all the huge cranes clustered like the birds they are named after over Potsdamer Platz and Friedrichstraße, building the glitzy Berlin of 2001.

Fritz sat in a corner by the window but did not appear to be looking at anything. His pale blue eyes, beneath the brim of the tweed hat, did not shift. His cheeks, above the white goatee Kim had left, were pink from the brief walk. Occasionally he rubbed the knuckles of his brown-leather-gloved hands as if attempting to soothe the nagging pain of arthritic joints. He did not speak, but then neither did Piotra or Kim.

At Hauptbahnhof they had fifteen minutes to spare. Piotra went down to ground level, bought some chocolate from one of the many kiosks and got their tickets for Frankfurt an der Oder. Back on the platform, she explained that there was only one through-train a day across the border and that didn't leave until the afternoon. So the routine was that they took the train as far as Frankfurt, walked across the bridge, then took a taxi for the last twenty-five kilometres.

'Why not a train?'

'We tried that the first time. But the first railway station isn't the border town of Słubice but is eight kilometres down the road at Kunowice. And the buses are not frequent. You end up waiting on platforms in weather like this, waiting for hours for the next train.'

'It's always been this time of year?'

'Always.'

It was bitterly cold. And the station, a big hangar done in black and grey, was desperately bleak. In fact, the architecture and design was stylish, as indeed was the ground-level concourse, a showcase for the old GDR, but on a February morning with the public temperature displays registering minus ten and a chill factor doubling that figure, it was bleak.

The train arrived, on time, at 10.07.

A moment or two of anxiety as Piotra ran up and down the platform searching out a carriage where smoking was allowed. Most of the travellers waiting with them were doing the same. Kim eventually used his height and size, combined with pleas for the old man with them, to get them the situation they wanted. Kim sat opposite Fritz in window seats. Piotra sat next to the old man. A young Polish boy sat next to Kim, across the gangway from the rest of his family. The carriage was grubby but not really dirty, the seats tolerably comfortable, upholstered in grey leatherette. Piotra lit a cigarillo. Occasionally Fritz held out a hand and and she put the cigarillo in it. He took a drag and handed it back.

Kim looked out of the window. Drab complexes of three-storey workers' flats gave way to small factories, a huge coal-fired power station with massive belts carrying the coal from barges on a canal up into giant silo-like hoppers. Was it the weather, the time of year, that made it so depressing, or was this still Ossi-land waiting to share the miracle of the West?

Piotra leant across to him.

'There's a lot of smuggling goes on on these trains.' A lift of her shoulder indicated the Polish family across the way. 'Cigarettes and vodka out of Poland, luxury goods back in. Drugs probably both ways – pot out, heroin and charlie in, courtesy the Russian and Estonian mafiosi.'

She leant back again, lit up another cigarillo.

Small run-down industrial estates drifted into forest, some of it young oak, birch, beech with fir and larch. Kim recalled that a few years earlier he had been in Vienna and seen a very early Klimt in the Belvedere, a radiant painting of a wood with bluebells. Its title was *Buchenwald*. At the time he had thought it was the name of a place. Only much later did he realise that it simply meant 'Beechwood'.

The ground was powdered with snow, and the east-facing sides of exposed trees were crusted with frozen fog. The occasional villages were made up of post-war chalet-style small dwellings – Kim remembered that the fiercest battles of the war had been fought over this land-scape as the Third Reich defended every inch of the way to Berlin and beyond. Thousands, millions, had died on this terrain, Soviets and Germans. This was where the war was finally won and lost, not that you'd ever know it if you relied only on US or UK versions of history. Hardly a house had been left standing and he had read of how still in these forests and lakes, where Berliners came camping, hunting and fishing in the summer, one came across helmets, skulls, belt-buckles and even occasionally the burnt-out, rusting, twisted, holed shell of a tank. Most of the landmines, however, had been exploded or lifted.

Occasionally, and then more frequently as the fifty-five-minute journey neared its end, the forest was broken by prairie-like expanses of open ground, much of it winter-fallow beneath a thin covering of coarse grass, or some green low crop that he thought might be grown for fodder or green manure to be ploughed in when the frost broke.

It all looked bleaker, more overused and then thrown away than most landscapes do, even in February.

They didn't talk much. A chain of questions clanked though Kim's mind, questions and doubts. But he wasn't bothered. Today was different, a sort of outing. He was content to let it unfold. The questions he would ask at the end of it would be different from those he might ask now, so why bother?

The train jiggerty-jugged through a station called Briesen. No apparent reason for there being a station there at all, just a handful of those chalet-style, cheap-looking houses. An inspector came, looked at their tickets, thin strips of card, computer-printed. She wanted two marks from each of them. Why? For some reason Kim could not understand, the clerk at Hauptbahnhof had undercharged them. All the staff on the Deutsche Bahn appeared to be women – the inspectors, the guard, perhaps the driver. Women in their forties and fifties, no doubt paid poorly but perhaps vital supports of their families now the children were leaving school and failing to get jobs. At any rate they were competent, and if not exactly happy certainly pleased to be where they were. Men who work on railways in such positions are either – and this applies to anywhere I have ever been, Kim thought – little Hitlers or servile, usually depending on how they read the clothes you are wearing. These women were simply, quietly, efficient.

This, he suspected, was the sort of thing the GDR had been good at.

Jakobsdorf. Again a station with no reason. He leant across to Piotra and asked why. It was, after all, a question of no real importance.

'The stations are often as much as a kilometre away from the villages they serve.' She looked out of the window, half caught his eye in the reflection and without turning from it asked, 'Have you been tested?'

Of course he knew what she meant. Of course. If you don't tell, eventually they ask.

'Yes.'

'OK?'

'Yes.'

'Good.'

He felt a sudden surge of anger.

'Why do you ask?'

She looked back at him directly, put her hand on his knee.

'Sorry. It was silly of me to bring it up.'

CHAPTER 9

Pillgram, Rosengarten. Funny how the German word for rose-garden suggests to your ordinary Brit something Jewish. Almost as much as Jakobsdorf. Rosengarten, Rosenkranz – a garland of roses. But here comes Frankfurt an der Oder. Frank's ford. A suburb, marshalling yards, a big station. Why is it bigger than any of the Berlin stations? Kim asked himself as he helped Fritz down on to the platform. Because trains come in here from every point of the compass, whereas in Berlin they tend to be east–west with the north–south filtered in, or ending in stations in the suburbs.

Piotra knew the way. She and Fritz had been here before, twice, or was it three times?

She led or directed them through a vaulted concourse with shops and stalls selling, of course, cheap silver jewellery, gewgaws and knick-knacks, out on to a small, mean plaza where taxis waited listlessly and buses and trams chugged through.

'You don't mind walking a couple of kilometres?'

'No. But what about him?'

'It is what he prefers.'

They set off down a hill. The road curved on to a boulevard of sorts, past a church converted into a gallery for children's art. Kim rather wished they could stop and go inside, see the paintings.

Some of the buildings were pre-war. Pre several wars. But as they got nearer the Oder they were either restored or replaced. They walked through a small modern mall.

There was a very good bookshop, much like the one he had found on Ku'damm in Berlin, a McDonald's – of course. At the other end of the mall they faced a classical façade which proclaimed it was the Universitas Viadrina.

Kim wondered why Piotra had asked if he were HIV-positive. Was she planning a seduction? He'd met several women who looked on his sexual orientation as a challenge to which, a couple of times, he had, as it were, risen. Or was she simply expressing concern for someone she was learning not just to like but to look on as a friend. Mentally he shrugged and pushed on down the icy pavements.

Their route took them past two more churches, one of which had more or less survived the war, while the other was now being rebuilt. They were both big, high-roofed barns of places. Then a right-angle took them along a long terrace of two-storey apartments put together from prefabricated concrete slabs, and there, at the end, was the Oder. The ice, white, grey and pale greyish green, was piled up high like rubble – even higher than when Renata and her team had crossed it a fortnight or so before. They walked along the riverside walk above it towards the bridge between Germany and Poland, seven or eight spans of ironwork mounted on massive stone piers at a point where the river narrowed. Upstream, where they had first reached its western bank, the Oder was at least a quarter of a mile wide and even more further up. Though Kim supposed it might have flooded low-lying fields before it froze.

They walked three abreast with Fritz in the middle. The old man's eyes were watering with the cold. His big, bony nose, jutting out like a prow beneath the brim of his hat, was pink too. He walked a little stiffly, head and shoulders thrust forward. It was an attitude that was somehow questing, yet determined too – it was as if he knew danger or pain lay ahead but he was pressing on nevertheless.

Steep stairs took them up on to the approach to the bridge and into a fenced in queue for the border control. There were two identical kiosks next to each other and it appeared to Kim that only one was being used, so he stepped out of the queue to go to the one that had no-one in front of it. Consternation. German spoken more quickly than he could cope with and Polish too. The first kiosk was the German control for exit, the second was the Polish for entry. He had assumed that the Polish control would be at the other end of the bridge. It seemed wrong that it should be on German soil.

Out on the bridge, and more completely exposed now to the icy thrust of a strong north-easterly breeze, strong enough to make both Piotra and Fritz hold on to their hats, Piotra grunted from behind her up-turned collar, 'That was a pretty stupid way to behave.'

Kim grinned down at her.

'Farting about like that at this frontier post would have got you shot five years ago,' she went on.

Out on the ice below, several men were messing around a hole in the ice. A dog, a bit like a Welsh collie, scampered around them. Were they fishing, perhaps? Perhaps.

Bare black trees, a roundabout, metal-linked panels round a building site, a sign – Słubice – then a street of town-houses with some balconies and moulded stucco above small shops took them past exchange booths in one of which Piotra exchanged seventy marks for a hundred and nineteen new złotys. The shops sold spirits, ciga-rettes, jewellery, clearly cheaper here than in Germany. Many of the people who had been crossing on the other side of the bridge back into Germany had been carrying cartons of Marlboro and clanking carriers. Presumably there was a limit that was legal, but worth making the crossing for.

The street dropped, rounded a bend into a wide, bleak square. More high, blank fencing round more building sites, low single- or two-storey shops, no longer for tourists but empty and tired-looking. A taxi rank with three taxis, two old Mercs and an even older Opel – better than the Zarzawa or Lada Kim had been expecting. It turned out that Piotra had actually booked the Opel by phone; the driver had taken them on this trip the year before. He was middle-aged, with a beer-gut and a Lech Wałęwsa moustache. He wore a brown leather fur-lined hat with ear-flaps buttoned to the sides, a jacket to match, and jeans. She addressed him as Joe.

He and Piotra exchanged a few words. She put Fritz in the front seat next to him, she sat behind Fritz, and Kim behind the driver. As soon as they were settled the driver lit a Winston and reached behind to fire up Piotra's Lucky Luciano for her. The petrol fumes from his overloaded Zippo momentarily filled the interior until the harsh smell of the tobacco, always worse in cold air, took over.

He set the engine going and used the gear stalk mounted on the steering wheel column to get into first. The Opel was that old. Presently they left the town on the Poznań road but almost immediately took a left on to a more minor road signposted Kunowice. The countryside was no different from what they had seen from the train. Prairie farming with forest, the forest becoming thicker, the fields less frequent. Kunowice was nothing – again the chalets in their little allotment-like gardens, some mustard-yellow stucco in the centre, a railway station. After a time they took a right, the forest closed round them, and presently they crossed under the railway. For a time they were always quite close to it, glimpsing its embankments through the regimented larch, pine and fir. A huge pipeline ran alongside it, carrying natural gas from Russia to Berlin. The signposts briefly indicated they were on the road to Rzepin, but before they got there they took an even more minor road and the forest closed even more closely around them.

There had been little traffic so far, now there was none. The surface was no longer tarmac but cracked and pot-holed concrete. High wire, the top strands barbed, fenced them from the forest – or the forest from them. They passed a deep layby where stacks of sawn timber, poles twenty metres long, awaited collection. The falling snow, intermittent and powdery, began to thicken a little but the flakes were still small enough to dance on the breeze and swirl in the car's slipstream. The railway was no longer a presence.

Fritz leant forward, peering ahead. He was about to speak, indicate, but before he could the driver pulled in to the side by a gate in the fence.

'You see,' said Piotra, 'he remembers.'

They all got out except the driver, who remained where he was. A few words in Polish established, presumably, that they would not be long and that he would wait for them. The gate was fastened with a chain and padlock – except it wasn't. The chain was twisted round a lateral strut of the gate and locked; so no-one could steal it. But the gate was not secured. A vague, unexpressed feeling Kim had had for some time crystallised into words which, however, he kept to himself. We're expected.

The gate clanged behind them and the three of them set off down a wide ride or fire-break. Their feet crunched in snow, ice, and the dried debris of the previous summer. With the snow now falling more thickly and the breeze dropping, it was not so cold as it had been in Frankfurt an der Oder. There were deer hoofprints in the snow and others too: birds and possibly a fox.

'Could even be a wolf,' Piotra said, as if reading Kim's thoughts.

No humans had been this way before them, not since the most recent snow-fall.

After a kilometre or so Fritz took them left down a much narrower track, between plantations of younger trees, narrow enough for their shoulders to brush the lowest branches of larch and shift the powdering of snow so that it swirled briefly round them. It was all very quiet, the silence a wall round the small noises they made, their breathing, their footsteps.

The clearing was visible at a hundred metres or more, a lightening among the trees, a whiteness where the snow reflected the white lead of the sky above. And then they could see the trucks, the waggons.

The clearing was about three hundred metres by one hundred, a rectangular hole in the forest, open to a sky filling with snow. Four sidings split off from track which came out of the forest and ran along one side. Four lines of trucks filled each siding, all carrying standard-sized containers twenty feet by eight feet square. Each siding held thirty waggons.

'See,' said Piotra, 'I told you so.'

Questions bubbled up in Kim's mind, but he repressed them. Later perhaps. He walked up to the nearest truck on the end of the the first train. The doors were secure, with padlocks fastening down hasps attached to bolts. There were also what appeared to be electronic locks. A more immediate question framed itself in his head. How can we be sure they hold what we think they hold? But just as the words came to his lips they heard, close to, from the other side of the waggon, a long-drawn-out rasping cough, followed by a rough hawking and a spit. Footsteps clunked through snow and loose ballast.

A man and a woman came round the end of the truck. The man looked frail, elderly, wore an overcoat with an astrakhan collar and a grey sheepskin hat. The woman was much younger, wore a black coat whose hem came down to her shins and cracked black boots. Her hat was also sheepskin but black. She had a large nose.

'My name,' she said, in German, 'is Wisa. This is Mr Kalinka, Walery Kalinka. I can interpret for you if you do not speak Polish.'

'I speak Polish,' Piotra said, and went on to do so.

Kim looked round for Fritz, suddenly aware that he was no longer with them.

The old man was already almost a hundred metres away walking alongside the track, past the trains. The track appeared to go on into the forest and Fritz followed it, took a turn and was suddenly out of sight.

When he could get a word in edgeways, Kim asked, 'Where's Fritz going?'

'Fritz has his own agenda. Nothing to do with us. He'll be back,' Piotra replied. 'Listen, these people are selling. Will these English people you know of buy?'

'I suppose so. Yes. That was the idea as I understand it.'

She talked some more with the Poles, for about ten minutes.

When she was finished, they shook hands and walked away down the track that led into the clearing. As they went Kim asked, 'How did you know these trains would be here? How did those people know we were coming?'

'I didn't know. I guessed. I knew these sidings were here, from coming here with Fritz. I knew that they have been forgotten, are not used. As you see, the rails are rusting. It seemed not impossible that the trains would be here.'

'And these two people? Here to meet us?'

'My contact in Scheunenviertal told me the trains were still in the rail network around Rzepin. If that was the case, Walery Kalinka would know of it. He controls the freight side. And if he knew, then he'd have some control over how they are to be sold. They can't move from here without his say-so. I got in touch with him, told him we were coming. Look, here comes Fritz. We can go now. He's done what he came to do.'

And what was that? Clearly she didn't want to tell him. Kim sensed it was not the only thing that was being kept from him.

CHAPTER 10

Piotra Grabowska poured boiling water from a cheap tin kettle into a cracked basin, added cold water from the one tap and then, using a set of Nina Ricci toiletries she had hoisted from the perfumery counter at KaDeWe, gave herself yet another all-over wash. She knew perfectly well that she was, still, a week later, reacting to what had been, technically, attempted rather than actual rape, but it had been a near thing. It wasn't exactly that she 'felt dirty', it was more a case of soothing herself, making herself feel that her body was something to be respected, cosseted.

As she worked herself over she half hummed half sang along to the Benny Goodman Trio, 'Oh Lady Be Good'. At last, feeling better from the warm water, the soft delicately perfumed white soap and the touch of real sponge, she towelled herself dry in front of a free-standing clouded full-length mirror framed in chipped gilded stucco, pouting as she usually did at the signs of age revealed by an otherwise fit body.

It was her feet she disliked most – too long, yellowish, and on the left one that incipient bunion. With distaste she remembered, as she usually did, that her mother had had just such feet, just such a bunion.

Piotra had not been fond of her mother.

Around her the room watched, the many mirrors its eyes. In effect the room and she were the same organism, more closely allied than the hermit crab within a borrowed shell, for she had made the inner surfaces an extension of the soft animal that inhabited it.

Besides the big free-standing mirror by the washbasin, there were others, two ordinary, one oval wood-framed, the other square in red plastic, but the two older ones were collector's pieces. Their glass was bevelled and bright, one rectangular framed in brass, curlicued with renaissance dragons, the other large and round with art-nouveau florally abstract ornamentation on the top, also brass but a more coppery alloy than the first.

Most of her many books were coffee-table art books, many of them openly erotic in ways that have been unexceptionable in Germany for decades. On the walls there were unframed posters which she changed frequently – at the moment most related to Christo and the Wrapping of the Reichstag which would take place when summer came. A midi player system stood on the floor in a corner with CDs, vinyl and cassettes stacked more or less haphazardly around it, mostly jazz, some modern classical – Stockhausen, Górecki, Lutosławski, and some modern cabaret acts. No TV.

Clothes, including hats, were stacked neatly in another corner, apart from briefs and socks, which were strung on a line above the electric fan-heater, the same model as the one she had stolen for Kim. This was the only personal heating she had, though the shared apartment her room was part of was irregularly and inefficiently centrally heated.

No cooking facilities apart from the kettle, a tiny saucepan, a one-cup espresso flask, and a camping gas stove; no furniture apart from a long leatherette sofa, covered with kilims and a duvet with a kilim-type print, a wooden table and an upright chair.

Almost everything in the room had been stolen, most of it by Piotra herself.

The point was that, while living like this created problems, the hassle of moving to something, no not better but larger and with proper facilities, was, she reckoned, quite beyond her. So here she'd stay, in one fair-sized, but, with all her possessions, too-small room at the back of an old block east of Winterfeldtplatz. A long time ago it had been a squat, later legitimised as a sop to the radicals who infested the area before gentrification set in. She had lived there for almost half her life.

'Body and Soul' shifted into the very up-beat 'Who'. Gene Krupa beating out that rhythm on the drum. Her movements now included the sort of dance movements one only does when one is naked and is sure no-one can see you. Presently, using a small Zippo she lit a Lucky Luciano and, squinting through the smoke, began to dress. First briefs and socks taken from the line. She balanced the cigarillo on the edge of a tin Coca-Cola ashtray and pulled over her head an M-sized T-shirt, tight enough to make a bra unnecessary. The trousers were baggy, barely last year's fashion, but the waistcoat was old, once plum-coloured velvet, now faded to brick. She left it unbuttoned. Black Doc Martens. Finally a watch, taken from the shelf below the smaller mirror above the basin. It was slim, square, gold with a black face, white hands, no numerals. The strap was genuine lizard-skin. It was worth, or at any rate retailed for, one thousand nine hundred and ninety-nine marks, according to the tag on the box it came in.

Piotra stole as naturally as most people shop, but generally only small things like soap, books, coffee, briefs and socks, CDs from market stalls, cassettes and the like. She was almost never caught, and when she was she usually got off by pleading accident or pre-occupation with a personal disaster. Occasionally, when really pushed for money, she'd do an apartment, or a car where something inviting had been left on or under a seat, and on those occasions she followed a simple rule: only ever take one thing. Often that way the owner did not miss it, or could not believe he or she had been burgled by a burglar who left behind valuables that could have been taken. Consequently they usually did not report the loss, blaming friends or acquaintances.

But the watch she had not been able to resist. The buyer had brought it back to a shop at the top end of Ku'damm to change it – it didn't suit, whatever – and it was on the counter while he and the assistant looked at alternatives. And because it had been brought back there had been no electronic tag on it . . .

Irresistible, and she liked it, so, instead of taking it immediately to the fence she usually used, she kept it.

Half past twelve. She'd have to get a move on. BA 984 was due at Tegel at thirteen forty-five. She stubbed out what was left of the Lucky Luciano, drained cold espresso from a cracked cup, looked again in the washbasin mirror. Quickly she painted her lips with a bright vermilion stick, pushed fingers through her very short spiky sand-coloured hair, pulled on a baggy black leather fur-lined zip-up jacket, tight-fitting stylish black leather gloves and finally the high-crowned snap-brim bistre fedora with its black gros-grain headband. Her right index finger ran round the front rim easing it into a two-millimetre tilt over her left eye. Alain Delon in *Le Samourai*.

She mouthed the English words to her reflection: Here's looking at you, kid, pouted an air kiss, killed 'Nobody's Sweetheart', dropped a very large bunch of keys into her old, floppy, soft leather shoulder-bag, checked for lighter, Lucky Lucianos, and went.

Eloise Harman looked down through the window of the Boeing 757 at what appeared to be a huge flat snowfield.

There were even lines across it not unlike ski-tracks. Apart from them it was featureless for as far as the eye could see. Which, since they were twenty thousand feet above it, was a long way. The second pilot had just told them that Amsterdam was underneath. Brill, she thought. Brill. She'd always wanted to see Amsterdam. She coaxed a leaf of dayglo pink 'ham' on to a quite healthy-looking half of a brown bread roll. In Club they'd be eating boeuf bourguignon – probably not a lot nicer, but it makes you feel wanted, doesn't it?

Next to her Herbert Doe pushed his small soggy triangle of fruit flan to one side.

'You can have it,' he growled.

'I don't think so.'

'Well, I can't eat it.'

'Why not?'

'Fucking diabetic, ahn I?'

'I didn't know.'

'Nor I. Till I went to the sawbones 'n ahst why I was taking a leak all the time.'

'Is it bad? I mean, like injections and all that?'

'Nah, not that bad. Jus' 'av to keep orf sugar. Not easy, you know. Did you know they put sugar in bottled or tubed mustard? Now why do they want to do that? An' these airlines. They'll do you vegetarian. They'll do you pork-free – of course they bloody will, all the Arabs and Jew boys travel on them. But will they do you a sugar-free? Like fuck they will.'

Piotra slung the upright bone-shaker of a bicycle she had been riding against a six-storey wall of scaffolding covered with plastic and pointed a finger at it.

'Stay,' she commanded.

And it did. Because it really was a pretty crappy bike it would, at least until the municipal refuse collectors

decided it should go. And before that happened, it was
quite likely she'd be back for it.

She stooped, pulled the bottoms of her baggy trousers
clear from her socks, gave each foot a shake to settle the
turn-up over it, re-adjusted her hat, pulled down her
waistcoat, let her shoulder-bag fall against her hip, and
walked briskly up into Olivaer Platz, turning right out of
Lietzenburger Straße. She was now in front of a block
of old apartments which were being extensively and
thoroughly gone over, hence the scaffolding. On the other
side there was a patch of trees and grass with those
strange pink pipes which carry, above ground, water,
sewage, gas or whatever, round central Berlin. There
were cars parked along the kerb.

A '91 VW Polo would do, but what she was hoping for
was an '86 Mercedes TE estate that was often parked
here and which she'd borrowed before. Old though it was,
she reckoned, correctly, that Brits were always impressed
by Mercs. But it wasn't there. She walked all the way
down Xantener Straße to the corner of Brandenburgische
Straße and Ku'damm and back again without seeing it.
And by the time she got back the Polo had gone and the
only car she knew for sure she could get into was a milk-
chocolate '88 Peugeot 205 parked outside the entry to
Olivaer Platz 15. She delved into her shoulder-bag,
fingered the right key without pulling the whole lot out.

'Must be nearly there.'

They were in the cloud now, the cloud that had looked
like a snow-plain for most of the way. The wings shredded
it and, as El briefly glanced at her watch, woods and
lakes, dark, almost monochrome, beneath the ceiling,
appeared. Herbert glanced up from the *Daily Express* he
had bought at Heathrow and also glanced at his watch.

'Five minutes. Thereabouts.'

The usual announcements began to trickle out of the PA, and the forests, lakes and rivers, scattered with small villages and townships, rushed up to meet them. There was ice on the rivers and suddenly you could see the winter shabbiness of it all. El turned to her companion, offered him a slight smile, smoothed her cropped leggings and the wool of the fanny pelmet above them, then ran her fingers through her hair. It had grown a bit over the weeks, stood up now in a spiky mane.

Herbert Doe shifted his duty-free malt further under the seat in front of him, and grinned back, fastened his safety belt.

Piotra watched them come through immigration, customs. She was sadly under-impressed by what she saw. Would anyone seriously believe that they had cash, credit, clout? All right, the marks in a con have to be gullible and greedy, which maybe means they have to some extent be nerds . . . but this pair looked like the sort of people who save coupons off detergent packs, are pleased if they get a hundred marks back from the lotto. The girl wasn't so bad, though. Style. Cheap style, yes. But style.

She unglued her back, gave the bottom hem of her jacket a hitch down and moved towards them as they came through the automatic doors.

'Mr Sheen? Glad to meet you, sir. I'm Piotra Grabowski. I'll drive you to the hotel, OK?'

Her English was good, very slightly Berlitzy, mid-atlantic, but, Herbert Doe decided, good enough. They'd communicate. The Germans he hated were the ones who spoke like toffs, even better than the Queen.

'Sorry,' he said. 'Mr Sheen were a bit snowed under with business and such like, so he sent us on ahead. I'm Herbert Doe, and this here is Eloise Harman who is like Mr Sheen's PA. Personal assistant, if you take my meaning. She speaks German. I don't.'

CHAPTER 11

'As I see it, then,' Herbert grunted, 'none of us is actual principals. No thanks.'

He declined the Lucky Luciano Piotra was offering him.

'Don't mind though if you do.'

She fired it up. Between them, sitting across the end of the low coffee-table, El shrugged, re-crossed her legs, flung an arm along the back of the chair, turned her head away over it. Body language said it all: don't mind me, I'm just the help, don't give a toss whether you smoke or not.

Truth to tell, she was still a bit put out at having been so badly wrong-footed. At first sight, and then during the short drive in the crappy little car whose ashtrays overflowed with dog-ends, she had thought Piotra was a bloke. A not unprepossessing bloke, touch fey perhaps, could be gay, but a bloke. And then once they were settled in this hotel lounge-bar she'd taken off her gloves and revealed nail-varnish. Not enough in itself these days, but with the lipstick too . . . Thing was, El had been put in the back of the car, behind Piotra, and either she had not properly taken in the lipstick in the rather gloomy arrivals area of Tegel, or she'd forgotten about it. Something like that, anyway. If she was a bloke she was a tranny. But she couldn't be, could she? Men who were trannies wore women's clothes. Women – that is, wimmin – who wore men's clothes didn't do lipstick and nail-varnish. None of which seemed to bother old Herbert. But then one thing she'd discovered about old Herbert was that, while full of surprises himself, he didn't surprise easily.

She looked around. The hotel was sort of crappy too. At least not what she was used to – not a new building. This reception room larger than most she'd been in but tacky and tatty, like the paint was peeling in the corners, and elsewhere needed a wash, and the heating came from those really old-fashioned radiators that look like small dinosaurs. But the waiter came to you and asked you what you wanted instead of you having to go to the bar, and he wore an old-fashioned black tux, too. And outside, beyond the big windows, some fifty feet or more below them, there was a small lake and public gardens on the other side. Most of the lake was frozen over, but holes had been broken in it and a well-dressed lady, furs and a fur hat, was throwing breadcrumbs or whatever to the moorhens that swam in the holes.

She wondered what the rooms would be like. She excused herself and took a very old-fashioned lift up to see.

Herbert and Piotra had agreed that neither of them was a principal, but Herbert had surprised Piotra by declaring quietly but firmly that Sheen Associates, whom he represented, were not principals either.

'The way we see it is this. There's enough ammunition there to win a small war. Lodza small wars all over. But no one wants to be seen as the people who, like, caused a small war to be won. There has to be cut-outs. There has to be people who hold the stuff for a time, maybe only a few days. That's where we see our role is.'

He waited, see how'd she react.

'But that's much the way we see where we stand in all this.' Piotra leant back, narrowed her eyes through the smoke of her cigarillo. In the warmth of the room she'd taken off the leather jacket. The T-shirt beneath the unbuttoned waistcoat bore the slogan 'Dead Man Upright'. That oughta read 'Walking', Herbert reckoned. Not because he'd heard of the film but because he knew about Death Row in US jails. He'd lost a good mate on one of them.

'No,' he said. 'You're coming to market with something to sell. You represent the sellers.'

'So you represent the buyers.'

'No. Not the way I see it. Not the way Sheen Associates see it. We ain't buying. Nor selling. We're piggy in the middle.'

'Piggy?'

'Never mind. We're in the middle.'

'Not yet, you aren't.'

'Not yet,' he conceded.

Pause. She crushed out her cigarillo, thought about another. Not yet. She drank some mineral water and then lit one.

'So. My people sell to you—'

'No. We don't *buy*. We hold. Listen. How much you want for these four train-loads?'

'Six million. Marks.'

'OK. Call it four.'

'Six is not a lot for a war won.'

'Call it, for the sake of argument, four. It don't much matter. Four. Six. Ten. We ain't the sort of outfit can buy at that sort of rate.'

He looked around him. We'd be in the fucking Hilton if we was, was what he thought. Indeed, Piotra took the message.

'So tell me how you see this all turning out.' Not a question or a request. More a sort of command.

'What I think is . . .' Herbert leant forward, then cast an eye over his shoulder, not so much to check out the

room for potential eavesdroppers as to highlight that this
was the crunch. 'How we see it is this. We take title to
the goods. The paperwork is done to show we have title.'
Sam Pratchard's role. 'Then we pass on the goods to the
buyer. Come the fallout you're in the clear, your sellers,
that is, and we're no longer around or even visible.'

'And the money?'

'The dosh? We take delivery of that, and pass it on to
you. Less commission.'

'Ah.'

'Twenty per cent.'

'Shit.'

'But you're covered. We'll even launder it for you for
another five.'

'Five?'

'Per cent.'

'We'll need safeguards.'

'Like what?'

'During the time you have title, you could sell it off,
keep all that you get ... No, you can't. All you have is
paper. We still have the goods.'

Herbert leant back now and beamed at her. She was
getting the message.

'There are details,' he said.

'Yes. Of course.'

'First of all, you have actual buyers in mind?'

'There are Serbs. We know that. They made a play
already.' She resisted stroking her inner thigh. 'If there
are Serbs then there are Moslems and Croatians.'

'Could be an auction situation?'

'Could be.'

Herbert contrived to conceal just how pleased he was.

'And ...'

'And?'

'Like ... Well, we'd actually like to see the stuff, check

out it's real. Because if it ain't real the buyers are not
going to be pleased. So unpleased, in fact, as they're going
to want to snuff us. Not you. Us.'

'Yes.' Piotra leant in again. 'I guess we can arrange
that. That can be arranged.'

'Right, then.' Herbert slapped his thighs. 'Where can
we get hold of you?'

Piotra stubbed out her cigarillo.

'Not easy,' she said. 'I always use public phone boxes.
Safer, see?'

Herbert frowned.

'If this goes forward,' he grunted, 'I can foresee a situation where we might want you on the blower sharpish.
Maybe El can fix you up with a mobile.'

Piotra grinned.

'That would be nice,' she said. She stood, gathered
herself together, cigarillos, lighter, hat, coat, bag, but
leaving a hand free to shake his.

'Ciao,' she said.

Eloise's room was as unfamiliar as the rest of the hotel.
There was a telly, but terrestrial only and no in-house
videos. There was no mini-bar. There was a big bath with
funny old taps like her gran used to have, and claw feet,
but no shower. She unpacked what little she'd brought
with her, lay on the bed, which was big and soft instead
of small and bouncy, then, realising there was no remote
control for the telly, got off the bed, crouched in front of
the set and surfed the three channels. Finally she settled
on children's. Good old *Mr Bean*, would you believe it?
Dubbed, of course. It was even funnier dubbed.
'Brrrrbllbbble' dubbed was funnier than 'Brrrrbllbbble'
undubbed.

Twenty minutes later – an explosion.

She looked out of the window, not down over the lake

but into the suburban street of small apartment blocks.
The Peugeot 205 Piotra had used to bring them there
was a burning wreck, orange flames, black smoke. Then
the petrol tank blevvied – not a great event, 205s don't
hold a lot of fuel and this one was only a quarter full.
Still, it rattled the window. Piotra herself was on an
ancient bicycle, pedalling like a bat out of hell, a hundred
metres away, round the corner and out of sight.

Herbert had come in – their rooms had a connecting
door – was standing by El's shoulder.

'Well,' he said, 'I guess that shows us two things.'

El asked what.

'A, it's all real. B, that woman is street-wise. How else
wise remains to be seen.'

El thought for a moment.

'That explosion need not have been aimed at her.'

'Not to kill her, no. Warn her, maybe.'

'No, Herb. You're not with me.'

'I'm not?'

'No. That wasn't her wheels.'

'No?'

'She smokes those cheroot things. The ashtrays were
full of ordinary fag-ends. She nicked those wheels. She
could have blown it up herself. Had the bike on standby.'

'Why'd she do a thing like that?'

'Impress you?'

'She ain't got access to her own phone. I said you'd
organize her a mobile.'

El pouted.

'There you go,' she said. 'No wheels, no phone. She has
to do something to give the idea she's for real.'

CHAPTER 12

For the first time in her life Sharon King felt well off: that was the effect Brandenburg had on her. Sure the town centre, basically a long high street, much of it pedestrianised and the rest well and truly 'up' and under reconstruction, had the look and the feel of similar small towns in the west. The stucco on the houses had been repainted in pastel colours, the window-frames glossed with white, there were new street lamps, globes over candle-like bulbs (several of the globes had already been vandalised or stolen), the shops carried the names and goods you would expect to find in a small Wessi town like Oldenburg or Osnabrück. But once out of it you were in . . . not hell perhaps, but limbo, maybe, or one of the lower reaches of purgatory.

Of course, nowhere north of the Mediterranean looks good in February.

'Take a left here.'

A lad from the town police station was directing them, Sharon and Firat, to the address they had been given. The turn took them off a main road out of town into a long straight street. A yellow tram rumbled along the road they had left. On one side a school, drab prefabricated concrete, drab low bushes, on the other a seemingly unbroken terrace of four-storey brick-built apartments above a narrow, cracked pavement. The brick crumbled at the corners, needed re-pointing and the window-frames hadn't been treated for decades. The tyres rumbled over rectangular cobbles. There were no shops, no people about. Tiny snowflakes fell and melted to slime as they touched stone or concrete.

'He lives above a shop.'

That should not be difficult to find, Sharon thought, because there are none.

Their guide was in his early twenties, perhaps even younger, in the baggy, user-friendly, green uniform of the polizei. User-friendly, that was, until you stepped out of line. His skin was grey with bright red spots, so perhaps he was hardly out of his teens. Anyway, it made her feel glad that she was no longer in a uniform and hadn't been since EKHK Fechter had taken her out of the Burg traffic section and made her an Eco-cop. And how long was that going to last?

Behind her Firat shifted and grunted. He'd complained about a headache and occasionally rubbed the ear next to the small steel plate. It was strange, she thought, how before his injury he had been macho, chauvinist, sexually aggressive and had once, in a lift, harassed her quite nastily. Now he was irritable, ill at ease with himself, but harmless. She had to admit that she preferred the earlier version.

'This is it.'

And so it was. A shop, a corner shop, the first and only one for not far off a full kilometre. She pulled across the road and into the side-street, parked. They all got out, crossed the road. A bell jangled as they opened the door and went into the shop. Immediately the three of them filled, overcrowded, the tiny space in front of the counter. Sharon had never been in such a shop before. Firat had – but only in Turkey.

There were tired vegetables in crates on the floor but tilted against the base of the counter: beet with the leaves still on, a couple of sad cabbages, and other roots Sharon could not identify. On the counter, bread rolls, berliners and suchlike, in glass cases as if they were part of a museum – things dug out of Pompeii, perhaps? Behind the counter were shelves stacked with rubbish: chewing-gum, sweets in jars, cigarettes.

In response to the bell a woman appeared through a door behind the counter. She was ... nondescript. Literally. Instantly forgettable. Except that she smiled, offered them a welcome.

'Herr Furtwanger?' Sharon suggested.

'Yes. Of course. The polizei rang,' she indicated a wall-mounted telephone. 'He's expecting you. Please, come with me.'

She lifted the counter flap and they filed through. Sharon turned to the local policeman, who was almost treading on her heels in the tiny space.

'There's no need for you to come up.'

He shrugged, turned, tried to get past Firat or let the Turk through. Inevitably, a cardboard container toppled and spilled Chiclet look-alike gum strips over the floor.

The woman showed Sharon and Firat into a tiny, very dark hall with two doors and a narrow staircase. She then led them up the stairs, which were uncarpeted wood and very narrow. There were many smells: disinfectant masking urine, and the mouldy ones associated with damp and cold. The walls were varnished in a dark sticky brown to the dado, a sort of nicotiny cream above.

The landing echoed the hall. She knocked on one of the doors, but was answered from behind the other.

'One moment please', followed by a hacking cough and the sound of someone spitting. Then a toilet flushed and an old man came through the second door. Sharon had a brief glimpse of pipes and a cistern mounted above the pedestal crusted with rust and corroded paint.

Furtwanger was a square, solid-looking man with a barrel chest, short white hair, a red face with a drinker's nose. He was wearing a cardigan over a grey shirt, a muffler, grey trousers baggy and stained, woollen bedroom slippers. He smelt of kirsch-flavoured schnapps.

The woman turned, bustled past them and down the stairs back to her shop.

Sharon and Firat followed Furtwanger through the other door. On the threshold he turned on them.

'You don't look like police.'

They produced their IDs. He took the documents over to the window that looked down into the street, peered at them. They looked around them. The room was small, probably the same area as the shop below. It had a single bed, a couple of wooden chairs, a table with a gingham-patterned piece of plastic cloth on it. There was a paraffin stove, one of the old sort shaped like a small pillar. The glass port-hole near the base glowed blue. There were a few knick-knacks, some crockery, an electric kettle. No sign of the schnapps bottle.

'Firat Arslan? That's Turkish, isn't it? What's a Turk doing in the police, eh?'

He ignored Sharon, clearly pretended or hoped she wasn't there. Nevertheless she cleared her throat.

'Herr Furtwanger,' she began, 'we have to ask you a few questions about train movements in the month before you retired.'

Furtwanger took one of the chairs, fumbled about for a cigarette, lit it, coughed again.

'Carry on, then. As you can see, I'm not particularly busy today,' he said – to Firat.

'Your last position in the railway service was as acting superintendent of the marshalling-yard here at Brandenburg.'

'That's correct. And I reckon that's what I should have been pensioned off as. I've got the union on it, mind.'

'And you held that position over the ten days during

which freight trains left Brandenburg for the Polish border en route for Russia. The manifests described the loads as various forms of ammunition for light weaponry – assault rifles, mortars, pistols, machine-guns, grenade-launchers and so on.'

'Not ten days.'

'No?'

'Nights. Almost all unscheduled traffic is moved at night. All this is on record, or should be, down at the yard.'

'It is and we have seen it. It all seems to be in order. But as you will remember there was a query at the time as to whether or not the trains ever got to Russia or even Poland. And later it was thought that thirty-eight had got through but that four had not.'

The old man looked up, first at Firat, then, at last, at Sharon, then he carefully pinched out the burning end of his cigarette and put the half that was left behind his ear.

'Thirty-eight,' he said. 'There was only ever thirty-eight.'

'The paperwork says forty-two.'

'The paperwork is wrong.'

'How could that be?'

Furtwanger leant forward and down, made a slight adjustment to the milled wheel on a spindle that raised or lowered the wick of his stove. The fumes were stifling and the inside of his one window was streaming with condensation.

'The Russians came to us, borrowed the rolling-stock and loaded it themselves. We and they broke it up into forty-two trains. Then we looked at the schedules to see when we could move them and such, and we'd already quoted them a date by which it would all be out and we realised we couldn't meet that deadline, not with forty-two trains. So we broke up four of them and distributed them among the other thirty-eight. Understand?'

Sharon nodded. Furtwanger waited for Firat to nod, but Firat's headache was worse now, so he kept still but Furtwanger went on anyway.

'Right. Now the paperwork you've been looking at was probably the original contract, job descriptions and so on. But there is also on file a docket for each train. You count those up, you'll find thirty-eight of them.'

Sharon was confused, while Firat was now out of it.

'But the documents we've seen, and the Rzepin yard agrees, all point to forty-two trains. And the Russian military agree.'

'Military? They never know their arse from their elbow. I reckon that at the other end they were still expecting forty-two trains, and when they only got thirty-eight they beefed, but then they checked the manifests and what was in the trains and found it was all there, so shut up. But you can't make soldiers admit they made a mistake.'

It had all been too much for Furtwanger. He swung sideways this time and reached for the cupboard, opened a door, pulled out an unlabelled bottle and poured a couple of fingers into a cracked tea-cup. Down in one, the bottle re-corked and all safely back in the cupboard in less than ten seconds.

'You could be right,' Sharon conceded. 'Though it was the Polish controller at Rzepin who was the first to think four trains had gone missing. Or at any rate said that four of the promised forty-two had never turned up.'

Furtwanger was motionless for a moment, then turned watery grey-blue eyes on hers, at last making eye-contact.

'Maybe,' he said. 'But it makes no difference.'

'So, of course, you went back to records at Brandenburg, counted the manifests and found thirty-eight.'

'That's right.'

Renata got up from the executive chair behind her desk, walked over to the big window that looked down on the lawns that surrounded the Burg Regional Interior Ministry. The snow was only patchy now and had thawed from all the paths. She was wearing a dark blue, almost black, Nike tracksuit top, cropped woollen leggings, scarlet leg-warmers, and jogging shoes. Her hair was held off her forehead by a scarlet sweatband that matched the leg-warmers. She had just run, not jogged, the perimeter of the compound five times, roughly five kilometres, and her face was still a little flushed, though her breathing was back to normal and her heartbeat almost so.

To Sharon she looked fitter and younger than she had ever seen her. Renata, however, was still disgusted by the cellulite that had appeared at the top of her hips and buttocks during pregnancy and she was determined to get it back to healthy muscle.

'They were numbered?'

'Yes.'

'And in sequence?'

'Yes. The sequence was broken several times by unrelated trains carrying more conventional freight, but the sequence was complete. No manifests had been removed. We checked a week ahead of the movements and a week after for omissions or oddities and found none.'

Renata tapped her teeth with a fingernail.

'Surely,' she said, 'if the freight could have been made up into thirty-eight trains rather than forty-two, there should never have been any question of using four more trains than were necessary. Surely that would have meant waste of time, money, locomotives, whatever?'

Firat looked up from the notebook he had open on his knee.

'I asked about that,' he said. 'At first they said that

with thirty-eight trains they were very close to breaking the safety regulations regarding the length of trains carrying dangerous substances – they said they wanted to be sure they were well within the designated parameters.'

'But?'

'I pressed them and finally, well, they didn't exactly admit it, but it became apparent that, by pushing the number above forty trains surplus to normal schedules, they were qualifying for bonus payments and, of course, getting overtime for more of the people they work with – loaders, train-drivers, even signalmen and roster clerks.'

'Ossidom. Ex-DRB. Deutsche Reichsbahn.'

Firat shrugged his agreement.

'The general attitude we came across,' he went on, somewhat pompously, 'was that the railway existed to give them jobs and perks, rather than to provide a marketable service. Anway, a regional supervisor spotted the anomaly and made them reduce to thirty-eight.'

Sharon looked up, looked at Firat, and then at Renata.

'That's what they said at the records office. But it's not what Furtwanger said.'

Renata's eyes narrowed. 'No?'

'No. He said they had to cut the trains down to thirty-eight to fit the schedule they had originally contracted with the Russian military. There is slippage here. Between the two versions.'

Firat frowned.

'Furtwanger is a drunk. A silly old man,' he said.

Renata used the facility provided for senior civil servants and had a shower. She still found showering difficult, perhaps even more so now she was almost back to her pre-pregnancy lean, fit status. It was the act of caressing her own body that was the problem, of treating it tenderly, reinforcing her own self-esteem. It inevitably reminded her of Aldo Nerone and how his caresses had been about expressing his delight in her body and a desire to give her satisfaction, rather than a response to his own desire to possess it.

Bereavement struck in odd ways, would become, she realised, a habit if she were not careful. On the other hand, if she did not let it become a habit, that would imply a betrayal of his memory. Get a grip, she told herself. Basically, for all his gifts of tenderness, for all the pleasure he got from making her happy, he had, after all been a crook, a bent Wop pretending to be a businessman, accepting a role in a dangerous scam simply to get his aristo, crippled wife out of debt.

By now she was unrolling tights up her thighs, smoothing them into place. She pulled on a dark, conventional suit and pouted at one of the many mirrors. Would she ever have another lover? Of course she bloody would. But not, and she grinned at herself, Secretary Drenkmann.

'Secretary,' she said, ten minutes later, perched on the edge of the tubular chair as far from the big fat man's stinking pipe as it was polite to be, 'forgive me for asking, but if this is a cross-regional task force I am in charge of, why do I report to you rather than someone in Bonn?'

'Well, first, if you went off to Bonn once a fortnight someone might get the idea that your team is doing something other than what it purports to be doing. Why should an officer investigating the possible export of illegal waste from the Region of Burg need to refer back to Bonn? Secondly, since I am deputy chairman of the cross-regional committee you are serving, it is entirely appropriate you should report to me.'

He put the pipe into the copper bowl in front of him, together with the scraper he was using to clear it of clinker, and spread his podgy hands.

'Which makes sense, my dear,' he concluded, 'since, as you can very well see for yourself, I am here.'

This added up to something, but just what she did not yet know, could not guess. But one thing was clear. By making her report to him here in Burg in the privacy of his huge office, Drenkmann had created a situation whereby he could filter out information before passing it on. Or, and here the enormity of what had crossed her mind made her shudder inwardly, he could even *add* to it. Of course, if ever the shit hit the fan, she would have had her copies and résumés initialled by him as seen, but in the interim he could have got away with what he liked. Not for the first time she sensed a hidden agenda.

He picked the pipe up again and began to stuff it with moist silage.

'So, what have you got for me today?'

She decided to fly a kite, run a flag up.

'Nothing. And frankly I don't think there's anything there. Rzepin will take weeks, months perhaps, before their bureaucracy gets round to finding, let alone revealing, their records. But those at Brandenburg are clear enough. Forty-two trains were reduced to thirty-eight. All the ammunition went through to Russia, but on thirty-eight trains, not forty-two.' She explained why she thought this was so and concluded, 'No case to answer.'

Drenkmann looked a shade put out. He sucked flame into the loaded bowl. She was put in mind of howitzers in the Napoleonic Wars. Big bronze craters that could hoist a fused bomb hundreds of feet into the air. Then, peering through his half-moon spectacles he reached across to his left and hauled in a tray of papers. He shuffled them in the manner of a hustling poker-player, pulled printout from near the top.

'There are Bosnian Serbs in Berlin who, we know, thanks to our friends in the Federal Office for the Defence of the Constitution, are there to buy arms, and, one supposes, ammunition. They have been more than usually active in the last few days, and, just now, really' – he squinted at the bottom of the document, where small type gave the time, date and source of transmission – 'they blew up a car that had been stolen by a woman who returned from Rzepin only three days ago. She has accomplices . . .'

He droned on. What it boiled down to was that Renata should perhaps turn her attention to Berlin. The appropriate agencies there would give her every assistance.

'And the accomplices?' she asked, as she rose to go.

'It's not clear yet. A minor criminal who calls herself Piotra Grabowski – with a name like that one would suppose a Polish background – an English homosexual who uses the name Kim Kind but whose real name is Godfrey Newcombe and a group of English minor racketeers called Sheen Associates.'

'Shit.'

'What's the matter?' He looked up at her. Light glinted from his gold half-frames through the cloud of smoke.

'They're the people who found the missing radioactive waste from the Burghaven reactor. Nearly a year ago.'

'Oh dear me. So they are. I remember them. They were really quite helpful in the end, weren't they? Is that a coincidence?'

'Not until we are certain no other possible explanation can be found.'

CHAPTER 13

She heard the pistol-shot while she was still climbing the last flight of stairs. She stopped on the landing, hesitated. For a moment she wanted to bolt for it, scamper back to her room behind Winterfeldtplatz as fast as her borrowed bike would take her. But then she thought, hell no, I've got to find out what's happening.

The door to the sound-stage was shut but not locked. She pushed it open and the acrid smell of burnt cordite hit her nostrils before she was through. Kim was standing at the top of the stairs to his room and facing her. Three men were standing five metres in front of her with their backs to her. A fourth man was sitting on the floor holding his foot and whimpering. Blood was leaking out of the hole in the top of his shoe. There was a Makarov pistol on the floor beside him. All four men were so frightened they did not even look round to see who had come in, though they must have heard her.

Kim was holding the big Smith & Wesson, not levelling it at them but with the muzzle in the air and his left hand supporting his right wrist. The last haze of blueish smoke dissolved in the draught Piotra's entrance created.

He called down to her, 'Sweetie, are you all right?'

'I'm fine.'

'Good. They said they'd blown your car up. Gentlemen, please don't move or turn round. I didn't think they could have, since you haven't got a car.'

'Who are they?'

'The one in the middle has two very pretty black eyes.

I think he must be one of your gentlemen callers from the other night.'

'What do they want?'

'Darling, let's discuss that when we've, um, defused them. Would you mind terribly if I asked you to frisk them? Remove any hardware they might be carrying? There's a dear. Start with the thingy the chap with the sore foot dropped.'

She knew him well enough now to know that camped-up speech indicated emotion, anxiety, even fear.

He went on, 'You were quite right about tightening the screwy thing on my . . . my *piece*. It seemed to work rather well.'

She picked up the Makarov, checked the safety catch was off, dropped the magazine into her palm, pulled back the breech to eject the round that was there. The clunk it made on the wooden floor some three metres away from her echoed in the high big room. It spun and rolled for a second or two and she told herself she should remember to pick it up later. She replaced the magazine. Again she pulled back the breech and released it, so that the next round was under the firing-pin, and the hammer back so that the gun was cocked. The gun was now as lethal as it could be; all that was needed was the slightest pressure on the trigger for it to go off.

She walked further into the room so that the men could see her, but without getting between them and Kim.

'Look at me,' she ordered.

They did and she let them see the pistol.

When she went back behind them they were satisfactorily still. Indeed, one of them, the oldest, a short thickset man with cropped white hair, had broken out in a slight sweat. She took him first, felt hardware in his left armpit, through the leather of his jacket. They were all wearing black leather and jeans with CAT boots.

Almost like it was a uniform. She pushed the muzzle of the Makarov into the nape of his neck. He flinched.

'Take it out very slowly,' she said, 'and before it's clear hook your finger in the trigger-guard and then put it on the floor.'

This was a much smarter pistol, a Czech Česka Zbrojovka 85 with a double-column magazine holding fifteen rounds, and one in the spout on top of that.

The other two men yielded Walther PPs and a hunting-knife. She found no spare magazines or loose rounds, but later she and Kim found that all the guns were fully loaded.

'OK,' she called back to Kim. 'They're clean.'

'Darling, you've been watching too many movies, and all they prove is . . . Well, never mind. Now, could you move towards the windows but remain behind our friends while we have a little chat.' His eye ran over the four men, focused on the oldest one, the one who had had the ČZ 85. He switched to German. 'First, you can tell me how you got in. And tell it to me in a way I can believe.'

They, whoever they were, had been watching Kim and Piotra, had seen him buying new locks. They had then terrorised the locksmith until he sold them copies of the right keys.

'Now tell me what all this is about.'

'We know you are in a position to sell a large amount of Russian ammunition.' The voice was surprisingly soft and deep, carried well. 'We are prepared to buy from you at a reasonable price. What we are not prepared to do is allow you to sell the goods to anyone else.'

'And you poor sweeties thought you could achieve this by intimidation?'

The thickset man shrugged.

'We underestimated you.' He was philosophical. 'But we have resources. Beyond those we have so far deployed.'

'Is there any chance you might tell us who you are or who you represent?'

Silence.

'Oh, come on!' And almost casually he fired off another round. At four hundred and forty-three miles an hour and only three inches from his left ear, the displaced air gave the older man's cheek a slap before the slug smashed low down into the wall behind him. Piotra was so surprised her finger tightened involuntarily on the trigger of the Makarov, which also went off. The bullet plucked the leather sleeve of the man on the left of the oldest man.

'You know, darlings,' Kim went on, his voice fluking into a falsetto on occasional syllables, 'I've not had much practice with this sort of thing recently. I don't guarantee to remain within a margin of error you will find acceptable. Say something and at least make it credible.'

The oldest man's lips compressed and he wiped his broad, hairless forehead with the back of his hand. When he spoke it was quietly, almost inaudibly. He didn't want his voice to betray his fear.

'We are Serbs,' he said. 'From Bosnia-Herzegovina.'

'We represent the legitimate government of Bosnia-Herzegovina.'

'Ah,' said Herbert Doe.

Looking out of his window down into the street, where firemen under the eyes of nervous, watchful polizei were still spraying the Peugeot 205 with foam, although it now looked as dead and harmless as crushed can, he had seen them arrive.

He had been impressed. They had spilt out of three black and cream Cadillac Eldorados in front of the hotel's marquee. The Eldorados had diplomatic number plates. They were then driven away, but not, Doe supposed, very far. The men wore black fedoras, long black mackintoshes over dark suits, shades, black ties, white shirts. Two pairs remained outside, one at each end of the block. They had mobile phones, which they used as soon as they were in position and then again at about two-minute intervals. Meanwhile, reception phoned up and asked if Mr Doe was prepared to receive visitors. He had indicated that he was.

Since there were three of them and he had called El in, in case they needed her to interpret, his room was now uncomfortably crowded. They had the sallow skins of Turks – not dark, not even Mediterranean Levantine dark, but somehow not Caucasian either. The oldest, the boss, had silver hair immaculately cut and looked a lot like Omar Sharif a decade or so after *Dr Zhivago*. His smile was similar too: gap-toothed, open, exuding sincerity, inspiring trust. Well, for some, perhaps, but not Herbert. One of the few of life's lessons his father had been able to pass on to seven-year-old Herbert before his Wellington bomber was shot down over Burghaven had been that carpet-selling begins at Calais.

'And,' Omar continued, 'we are concerned that you might be planning to sell a large quantity of ammunition to rebel forces in our country.'

He spoke English, but with an accent that would have been comic had the circumstances been comic.

'Ah,' said Herbert again, 'and you are?'

'You can call me Kruno.'

With the nail of his right pinkie Herbert levered a shred of BA's pink ham from between his eye tooth and first molar, looked at it and flicked it away, thumbnail against fingernail. He waited.

Kruno's lips creased to a thin line.

'Don't,' he said.

'Don't what?' Herbert looked surprised.

'Don't sell to the Serb rebels.'

Herbert pulled his shoulders in. They were still quite massive. And he sighed.

'To whom, then, shall we sell them?'

The pointedly accurate grammar was probably lost on the Bosnian. El, though, recognised it as a sign that Herbert had made up his mind not to be put upon.

Kruno reproduced his bonhomous smile and added a shrug. 'That's your problem, not ours.'

'You're not yourselves in the market, then?'

'We have all the ammunition we need.'

'Assuming that your . . . rebels . . . don't get their hands on what we might or might not be able to sell them.'

The smile faded.

Doe went on, refusing to be intimidated. 'You know, the only way you can be absolutely sure that this ammo is not going to fall into your rebels' hands is by buying it yourselves.'

'Perhaps if we arranged for something very unpleasant to happen to you . . . and to the lady here?'

This was a dead giveaway. One thing had been bothering Herbert ever since the arrival of the Eldorados: what connection did these people have with the bombing of Piotra's car? Answer now: none. If they had done it, the obvious thing would have been to say so – a telling proof of their resources and ruthlessness.

His reply was robust. 'But that won't do you any good at all. You see, Mr Kruno, we don't actually have the ammunition or the trains. Our position in this is merely as middlemen. Agents. And, if you care to think of us as such, brokers on your behalf. But we don't have to be here. We don't have to have anything at all to do with it. If you do anything at all that I might construe as threatening towards me or my associates, we shall simply wash our hands of the whole affair and go back to England. And you'll just have to start all over again.'

He looked around at each of the men in turn. The other two, he decided, were just minders, heavies.

He went on, 'Since you are this far down the line, and you are talking to someone who may or may not be able to cut a deal on your behalf, why go back to square one? Now. Neither you nor I are principals. Why don't you go back to yours and make it clear that if they want to use us as a route towards getting these goods, or preventing them from going where you do not want them to go, then it's via money and nothing else. And then get them to make an offer and we'll see if the people we represent can accept it.'

'We'll have to know exactly what's there. And inspect it.'

'Sure. There are going to be a lot of problems of that sort along the way. But since it's in everybody's interest to sort them out, I'm sure we'll get there.'

Herbert watched from the window as the Eldorados circled back to the hotel's marquee. OK, they were fifteen years old at least, but they had style, loadzastyle and in another ten years, if they kept them well, their value would start appreciating. An investment. Without looking back he said, 'I did well, din' I, El? Tell me I did well.'

'You did very well, Herbert. Very well. But I think it's time we got Harry and Sam over here, don' you? It is . . . turning out quite the business, don' you think?'

'Yes, El. Get 'em on the blower an' we'll have 'em here in two shakes.'

'Of a puppy-dog's tail? Sure, Herbert. I'll get on to it right now.'

The fire brigade were pulling away from the wrecked Peugeot. The polizei too, just leaving a couple of guys with motorbikes to keep an eye on it until the municipal dustcart turned up.

'An' you know, El, I reckon it could all get a bit heavy, so why don' you give Jace 'n' Ash a bell too. Just, like, get them on standby.'

'I'll do that.' Her heart skipped a beat, then quickened. Moisture formed in the palms of her hands. 'An' Herb, I think you should look at this too.'

At last he turned from the window. He looked at her spiky mane, her Lana Turner lips and, God help me at my age, he thought, his heart skipped too. But it was the object in the palm of her hand she wanted him to look at. Black shiny plastic, half an inch by one and a half, small slice of magnetic metal on the back.

'Bastards! Where was it?'

'On the back of the radiator. I saw him put it there.'

'You're a good girl, El.'

'Buy me a decent dinner?'

''Course. An then, since it's allowed, we'll take the tube to the other side to the Staatsoper. Always wanted to do that when I was a squaddie at Checkpoint Charlie.'

'I did well, didn't I?' Piotra, up in Kim's room again.

'Darling . . . bloody marvellous! What was that about a car?'

'I borrowed this Peugeot. Just up the road from here in Olivaer Platz. To meet them. The Brits. As I came out of the hotel I saw one of them, you know, black leather jacket, the guys who keep trying to mess us about, getting out of it. He wanted me to see him. I'd already left a bike in the service alley, so I took that. Even so, I was close when it went off. Close enough to give me a scare.'

'That was what they were doing. The frighteners.'

'Well, it worked. For a time. Listen, you got any gelt?'

'Some.'

'I want ice, caviare, vodka. Then maybe grilled boar.'
'I'll go and get them.'
'Not eat out?'
Kim sighed.
'Not till I've changed the locks. Again.'

CHAPTER 14

Sheen and Pratchard arrived the next day, stayed in the same tired hotel overlooking the small frozen lake. There followed several hours of negotiations with Kruno in smoke-filled rooms, which suited Harry Sheen fine – most of the deals he had struck in a lifetime of deals had been made in smoke-filled rooms.

On the second day, squeaky Sam Pratchard went to Brandenburgische Straße. Kim, unslotting heavy bolts and manipulating double locks let him into the big empty hangar of a room but no further.

'Hallo, darling! You're just what we expected.' Kim stood back, head on one side, made a flowing vertical gesture with his right hand which seemed to contour Pratchard's round, balding head, his plump but sloping shoulders, the suit that was floppy in the wrong places and tight in the wrong places too, the shoes that were good but had never been cleaned, the document case that was large heavy and expensive, with red leather and gold-plate furniture. 'Lovely! Piotra Grabowski will be here shortly.'

He locked the door, chained and bolted it.

Pratchard felt acutely uncomfortable. He hated being cold, and he was cold. He was deeply homophobic and Kim, with his affected speech and discreet but evident mascara and lipstick, was clearly as gay as Paree, as camp as Brownsea Island. He didn't feel much happier for the forty minutes during which Kim withdrew to his eyrie at the head of the stairs, leaving him to pace up and down, rubbing his hands to keep them warm. Inevitably he needed a pee, had the sense to try the one door apart from the entry and the one at the top of the stairs. The toilet was cold, smelt of damp and disinfectant, but was clean.

At last Piotra showed up. A dike if ever he saw one. Still, business is business.

'First,' he said, 'here's the mobile we promised you.'

He handed it to Piotra.

She looked at Kim. 'Do you know how these things work?'

'Darling, of course I do. Life in Hamburg would have been utter misery without one. Trouble was, the one I had there was an Ass'n Jass perk and I had to give it back.'

Sam looked round.

'Look,' he said. 'Look, isn't there anywhere we can sit down?'

'Not really,' Kim replied with cod innocence. 'I mean, there isn't, is there?'

Realising that they were winding him up, and deciding the hassle or retaliation wasn't worth the candle, Sam sighed, propped his document case awkwardly on a window-sill and the icy radiator in front of it. He undid the catches, took out a mobile phone, a calculator and a leather-bound notebook. This was his routine when negotiating. Whether or not the trappings impressed the other side was not the point – they impressed him, gave his self-image the kick-start it often needed. Sam had few illusions about himself. He was short, fat, squeaky – and knew it.

'Problems,' he began. 'Always there are problems. Number one: question of proof contents are as described.'

Piotra tipped her hat back, stuck her thumbs in the arm-holes of her waistcoat. Kim sniggered.

'Does he have to be here?' Sam jerked a thumb at him.

'Oh, don't mind me, darling. I'll go and do my nails.'

Kim climbed the stairs, did a comic slip near the top which almost took him to the bottom, climbed again, mimed another fake slip and grabbed the handle to his door.

'Hasta la vista,' he cried. 'A bientôt, my friends.'

'One hundred and twenty containers,' Piotra said. 'Filled with boxed ammunition. Securely boxed. Your people want to check them all?'

'No. But a random check should be possible. Preferably against manifests.'

'Manifests? Where would we get those?'

'Mr Kruno does not believe these trains can be on Polish sidings without someone in Poland knowing about it. Somebody with authority. And such a person should have access to the relevant paperwork.'

'It was all burnt in a fire. Just over a week ago. Well, it would be, wouldn't it?'

'Nevertheless . . .?'

'We'll see what we can do. Next?'

'Number two: Mr Kruno wants the trains brought to Rybocice on the River Ilanka.' He opened his notebook and showed them a pencilled sketch-map. 'For transfer of containers to canal barges.'

'We'd expected as much. I mean, as regards the canal.'

Sam looked up at her sharply.

'You did?' he asked.

'Sure. In middle Europe the canal system is almost as extensive as the railway and far less thoroughly regulated. I mean, like on a road or autobahn, you don't have to keep a check of which boats are where to avoid collisions, the way you do on a railway. Now, up the Oder-Neisse—'

'The long way round is better. For big cargoes,' Sam

interrupted. 'The Oder–Spree canal connects with the Elbe, the Elbe with the Weser, the Weser with the Rhine—'

'And the new link between the Rhine and the Danube is in place and Belgrade is on the Danube. Lovely.'

'But not really your business. Mr Kruno will take delivery on the canal sidings at Rybocice. That is he will take delivery from Sheen Associates. Finally, price.'

'The third problem?'

'Let's hope not. The point is, Mr Kruno declines to put a figure on it at all until he has inspected the goods.'

'I think,' said Piotra, 'the people I represent, that is, the people who actually now control the trains, would like to know roughly the sort of offer we're looking at. I certainly can't guarantee an inspection of the goods without an offer.'

Sam began to put his gear back in his case.

'Let's say,' he squeaked, 'ten thousand marks per metric tonne.'

'Ten marks a kilo? You are not serious.'

Sam shrugged. He snapped the locks.

'Cash, bonds, whatever you like. And in any of the recognised international currencies you care to specify.'

Not złotys, new or old.

'Think about it,' he said, 'and let us know.'

As soon as he'd gone, she went up the stairs to the warmth of Kim's room and told him about the offer.

Kim asked, 'How many tonnes are there?'

'I've no idea. But let's say two per container, that makes two hundred and forty, two point four million marks. One mil sterling, give or take. Nothing like enough.'

'I don't get it. Sheen Associates are meant to be agents

and brokers, on ten per cent from each side. The higher the price, the more they get . . . Someone somewhere is pulling someone's mickey.'

'I'm sorry? Pull a leg or take a Mickey, but you can't pull a mickey.' Doubt shaded her brow. 'Can you?'

'Never mind.'

Sam did not go far, indeed just across Brandenburgische Straße and up a couple of blocks before making a right which took him to the Graf Leo Tolstoi, a café much used by Slavs and Serbs of all nationalities – but only ones with money. One of the Eldorados, with its green and orange CD plates, was parked on a meter nearby.

Inside it was very warm. There was a subdued hum of chat occasionally erupting into robust peels of laughter, with a background of chinking china and glass. Tall waiters with long white aprons moved round the tables with glasses of milkless tea on swinging trays or pushed trolleys laden with cream cakes. The air was heavy with black tobacco smoke and the fatty smell of *millefeuille* pastry. Kruno, flanked by two of his minders, was waiting at a corner table near an antlered coat- and hat-stand.

Sam squeezed into the chair opposite him.

'They want seventy-five marks a kilo. Eighteen million, give or take.'

He halted a passing trolley and the waiter used tongs to place on the plate in front of him a huge cream slice filled with strawberries. The cream on the top was crusty with caramelised brown sugar. He was pleased to see the price he had quoted did not seem to faze the Bosnian. He wondered even if he had pitched it a bit low.

'And she'll let us inspect the goods?'

'Of course.'

'When?'

'Soon as she can lay it on.' And he ordered a *Kaffee mit Sahne*.

An hour or so later he met Harry Sheen, El and Herbert in Sheen's room, which overlooked the lake.

'Kruno wants a view,' he reported.

'Of course. Bound to, wannee? I said all along.'

'All right, Herbert.' Sheen turned to El. 'Get it set up with that woman, man, whatever it was met us. Hang on.' He turned back to Herbert. 'He'll come mob-handed?'

'I reckon.'

'Then we'd better too. Herbert, get on to Jace 'n' Ash. See what they can come up with. El. Wait till we have Jace in tow, know what his requirements are.'

Herbert reached for the phone, punched nine for an outside line. Then forty for Hamburg. While he waited for someone in Ass'nJass to pick up the phone he hummed to himself *'Der Vogelfänger bin ich ja'* (on their trip, El's and his, to the Staatsoper, it had turned out to be *Die Zauberflöte*). I'm the bird-catcher, always happy, always . . . "Allo, mate. Could you get me Jace or Ash, please?' *Stets lustig, heisa hopsasa.*

Sheen dropped his voice, leant across to Sam.

'Get any figures?'

'Vague so far,' said Sam. 'I'm working on it.'

Seven o'clock in the morning and in the yard behind Ass'nJass Jace filled the boot of the the black BMW 318i convertible with ten short-barrelled 9mm Heckler and Koch MP5K machine-pistols, with ten thirty-shot magazines for each, and six 9mm Browning Mk3s with four fourteen-shot magazines for each. He then added a thousand rounds of the 9mm × 19mm ammunition which fitted both types of gun, boxed in hundreds. The guns were new, the pistols unused. It had not been difficult to arrange for them to fall off the back of a lorry during BAOR's final withdrawal from Krautland. He drove down Autobahn 24 with moderate care, knowing that a traffic infringement could just mean the fuzz might ask him to open the boot. He arrived at the lakeside hotel shortly before ten.

Not coming from a kissing culture, he gave El a squeeze on the shoulder as he passed her, but threw in a grin and a wink. Her heart did a handstand and Jace himself felt the sun had come out, although it hadn't. He booked in and then spent half an hour or so with Sheen and Doe in Sheen's room overlooking the lake before taking the S-Bahn at Bahnhof Westkreuz.

He got off the train at Hackescher Markt S-Bahnhof, which had been called the S-Bahnhof Marx-Engels-Platz the last time Jace was there, and straight into the Galway Irish Pub which was situated beneath it – next to the Kilkenny Irish Pub. From the outside it was impressive thanks to the late-nineteenth-century red-brick façade decorated with mosaics that went with the station.

Inside, well, that sort of place depends a lot on atmosphere, and in mid-February with a freeze-up which fucked concrete-pouring and consequently froze wage packets too, it was . . . sad.

In the summer, filled with construction workers with loadzamoney flashing their wads on a Friday night, with a ceilidh band and the girls in off Oranienburger Straße, it jumped. At such times the oak and pine bars and floors and railings, the simulated post-war advertisements for Guinness, which is good for you, think what toucan do, and Gold Flake for your throat's sake, all that tat, looked like fun – now they were a blown joke, a bust balloon, in a word, sad to have to say it again . . . sad.

In a corner by a CD juke-box playing U2's 'Where the Streets have no Name', two scrawny lads, in third-hand leather jackets and jeans, who you would have said were unshaven if their eczema had been able to muster more than a sparse crop of thin whiskers, chased tiny lumps of unidentifiable meat and potato round small bowls and complained in a brogue that owed more to Camden Town than Andystown that their mum never put cabbage in her Irish stew, anyway not much.

Jace leant on the counter by a square wooden pillar with simulated deathwatch beetle holes and asked for a pint of Original. The barperson was clearly German and a winter stand-in. The genuine colleens who personned the place from March to November were probably now performing similar functions in similar pubs in Sun City or Sydney – like swallows they followed the sun.

'Is Padraig about?' Jason asked, in German but giving the name the full Gaelic pronunciation.

'I think he's in today.'

'I'd like to see him.'

'Yeah, well. Why? That'll be six marks fifty.'

'Why is none of your business.'

'Who shall I say wants to see him, then?'

'Tell him the fucker who put a bullet in his hip in seventy-nine outside the De Valera Pub . . . Oh shit. You don't understand a word of that, do you? You'll fuck up. Why don't you just go and get him?'

'I can't leave the bar.'

'I'll look after it for you.'

The barperson, who was an unattractive fifty-something, gave a look which said all that needed to be said. Jace was beginning to contemplate mayhem when a rasping cough, followed by a weighty plop on the floor, made him look over his shoulder, then turn.

There's a myth about that the Irish are Celts. Some are, but those from the south are Saxons: Hengist and Horsa made it to Cork. There's a myth about that Saxons are blond. They're not. They have dark hair, ruddy complexions, weighty bodies, snub noses. Padraig's parents were from Cork and he believed he was an Irish Celt. He had been born and brought up in Belfast because that's where his Da' thought the work was. The fact that if you were Popish meant that there was no work had made them all Republicans. And that was why Padraig walked with a limp.

'Jace, you fucking bastard,' he said, 'keep away from me.'

After shooting him in the upper thigh, Jace had gone to the prison hospital to see how he was doing. Padraig appreciated the thought but not to the extent that they were going to remain life-long buddies. When Jace had excused himself by saying that, since there was a shoot-to-kill policy in operation, Padraig was fucking lucky to be alive, Padraig had made the obvious retort: 'You're just a fucking bad shot, that's all. I owe you for what?'

'Buy you a drink, Paddy?' Jace now offered.

'Perrier.' Padraig leant towards the barperson. 'But

charge him for a double Jameson's, which I'll have later.'
He turned to Jace. 'Bit early in the day for me. So. To
what are we indebted?'

Jace nodded towards a table set away from the bar
and the barperson, put down the extra twelve marks the
barperson asked for and took his Original and the Perrier
to the table. Padraig limped behind him, sat opposite
him, took a pack of Gauloise from his checked shirt
pocket, offered one, which Jace refused, shook one loose
and lit it.

'Come on, then. Let's be having you.'

Jace took a pull of the ebony ecstasy, wiped his mouth
and leant across towards the Irishman.

'I need some men,' he said. 'Five minimum, ten max.
Hard. Know what I mean? Two-fifty DM for one day,
maybe two days. And you're on ten per cent. All right?'

'Tooled up?'

'I'll see to that.'

'Yeah, from what I hear, you will.'

Jace was put out. Persons were not meant to hear, to
hear about him, not things like that.

Padraig went on, 'When?'

'Tomorrow?'

'Day after?'

'OK.'

'Where?'

'Hauptbahnhof. Ten-oh-seven train for Frankfurt an
der Oder. I'll have the tickets but they'll need their pass-
ports. Dress to stay warm outdoors. Like big warm
overcoats you can hide an MP or a Browning under.'

Twenty-four hours later Padraig rang the hotel and told
Jace four was the best he could do, but the good news
was that three were ex-army. Victims of defence cuts
often chose to come back to Krautland, the best billet

they'd had in twelve or fourteen years of service. The routine was six months on a retraining, bricklaying, concrete construction course in Blighty at HMG's expense, then back on the Harwich ferry with the old Cortina or if you'd been an NCO a Sierra. As often as not the wife and kids were happy to come along. They too remembered glitzy Cologne or Hamburg, had found Bog-, Clyde- and Tyne-side dismal and depressing in comparison.

El got on the phone to Piotra, and she to Kalinka. Sam contacted the Bosnians. It all looked good. The Bosnians were to take the autobahn which crosses the Oder four kilometres south of Frankfurt an der Oder at a village called Swiecko and drive to the Rzepin marshalling-yards where Kalinka would meet them. Piotra and the Brits would follow their previous routine, taking taxis in Słubice, led by Joe, owner of the ancient Opel, who knew the way.

Next day they all, that is, Sam, Jace, Herbert, Harry Sheen and Piotra, met in Harry's room to finalise the details. The crammed room was foul with cigarette smoke and the smell of the doner kebabs Herbert had brought in from an *imbiß* counter near the Bahnhof Westkreuz.

'Yeah, but what if Kruno tries to cut his own deal with Kalinka?' Sam asked, as the pieces were beginning to fall into shape.

'He won't.' Piotra was adamant.

'Why not?' Sheen asked.

'Who won't?' Herbert put in. 'I mean, which of them has a good reason not to cut us out?'

'It's not in either's interest,' she hurried on, tilting her trilby on to the back of her head.

'Why isn't it?' Sheen again.

'Well, in the first place we know too much. If they cut us out we blow them. And in the second place Kalinka knows he can't handle this on his own. Listen. He's a two-bit Polish bureaucrat, spent his whole life doing the paper for a marshalling-yard until he's the top, but he knows shit about anything else at all.'

'But he might be tempted,' Sam squeaked.

'No way. He's on to a fortune. Whatever happens. He needs x-plus million instead of x million? He knows this way we're handling it for him, all down the line, the currency deals, the cover. All he has to do is get the trains from where they are to Rybocice, then he can bank the loot in Zürich, get the next plane out of Kloten airport to Miami. Dealing with the Bosnians straight, he's exposed on all sorts of fronts. Trust me. He'll stay with us.'

They believed her. But Herbert Doe thought: The lady doth protest too much, methinks. For him Shakespeare rated almost as high as Mozart.

'And the Bosnians?' he asked.

'Takes two to tango,' she replied, 'and if Kalinka won't play they've got no one to play with but us. No. We're already too far in to be cut out now.'

They ironed out some more details.

'No metal-detectors at the border, no baggage search, patting you down, anything like that?' Jace asked.

'No. They open car boots, do a quick rummage in your luggage if you've got any. But the pedestrian traffic is mostly local – Germans going over to buy cigarettes and vodka to the allowed limit, jewellery, cover versions of Rolex or Seiko. The lads flog off a second-hand Walkman for złotys, use the złotys to buy the booze, end up with more marks than if they'd flogged the Walkman west of the Oder. Poles coming in pretending to do the same in reverse, but on their way to do a week or a fortnight as illegals on a construction site or demolition work, getting back before they're caught. That sort of thing.'

'Are there luggage lockers at Frankfurt station?'

Piotra thought for a moment, visualised the vaulted concourse. 'Yes.'

'Then here's what we'll do. We'll take the hardware in a couple of large cases. The lads can tool up on the train, in the john, whatever, then we put the empty cases in the lockers and pick them up on the way back.'

'Suitcases?' Sheen looked up. 'You're not using mine.' Nearly new Samsonite.

'We want three strong hold-alls, not too flash, and a loada newspaper so the gear won't rattle.'

They all looked at each other blankly.

Jace stood up. 'Well, I'll go and buy some. Come on, El, you can lend a hand. You've been here a day or two, you'll know where to go better than I do.'

Which wasn't really true – he probably knew West Berlin far better than she did – but she wasn't going to argue.

Not much later, at about four o'clock, they broke up and Piotra went back to her room off Winterfeldtplatz. There was a note in her mailbox. Kim wanted to see her. She got back on the old boneshaker she was using and took the bike lanes down Lietzenburger and Konstanzer Straße to the Brandenburgische junction, where she propped it against a plane tree outside a Lotto office.

Meanwhile Jace drove El up Kant Straße, round West Berlin's most famous landmark – the giant broken-tooth tower of the bombed Kaiser-Wilhelm-Gedächtnis-Kirche – into Tauentzienstraße where he parked the BMW almost straight away.

She liked that. He was, she could tell, the sort of guy who knew instinctively where a parking slot would appear when he needed one. They got the hold-alls in the best department store in town, the KaDeWe (Kaufhaus des Westens) – Berliners say it's the best in the world – and then he took her to the food hall on the sixth floor, which also has as good a cafeteria as you're likely to find anywhere. He fixed her up a large plate of sea-food salad, had a huge near-raw beef sandwich on rye himself, with double cappuccinos. Then he took her to the pictures, *Funny Bones* (OV), and she nearly peed herself with fright and laughter in the final scene when Lee Evans can't make up his mind whether or not to chuck Oliver Platt off the swinging pole a hundred feet into the circus ring below, and she had to grab hold of his hand. Back at the hotel he kissed her good night on the landing, warmly but not demanding; just right, she reckoned. Next time . . . maybe.

While El and Jace were still in the KaDeWe, Piotra climbed the internal stairs out of the studio and let herself into Kim's room.

'SHIT! What the *fuck's* going on!'

Fritz, tall, old and thin was standing in the dormer window, facing down the long, narrow room. But for that first moment all she saw were the high point of the forage cap, badged with the white circle with a black one inside, his face cadaverous with deep, dark eye-sockets, the high collar with its silver thread flashes, the greenish-grey jacket, the jodhpur-shaped breeches, the black boots. Worst of all, as she came in he snapped back the breech of an old Mauser HSc and apparently pointed it at her.

'Don't worry, darling, it's not loaded,' Kim murmured from the sofa behind her.

'Just testing,' he added as Fritz pulled the trigger and the firing-pin slammed into the air of an empty firing-chamber.

Nevertheless, she flinched.

'What the fuck?' she began again.

'Sweetie, he wants to go with you tomorrow. He's been listening through the wall, so he knows a fair bit about what's going on.'

She turned to the old man. 'Why?'

He smiled, revealing his broken brown teeth, but said nothing. He half turned, picked up a magazine case from the high window-sill behind him, slotted it into the butt, put on the safety catch, and slipped it, uncocked, into its black leather holster. All very small, very neat, almost a ladies' gun, and, for all it first came into service in 1940, very modern-looking.

'Why?' she repeated.

'Something about a train, he said. He was bothered by the trains we looked at. He's been telling me they shouldn't be there. They're a threat to his train, he says, the train he's meant to be guarding. So he's coming along.'

'Not in that uniform he isn't.'

'That's what I said. He said he'll wear his old overcoat over it all until we get there.'

Piotra slumped against the table, elbows on her thighs, face in her hands. 'I don't need this, you know. I don't need this at all.'

'It's very important to him, he says.'

'Why doesn't he talk to me? He always used to.'

'He doesn't trust you any more. Not since those four trains turned up near his train.'

'So what the fuck am I going to do now?'

'Ignore him. I'll come along and look after him. Just forget we're there.'

'Dear Kim, there's no need for you to be involved any—'

'Quite so, darling. You look after the wheeling and dealing and I'll look after Fritz.'

Later the old man curled up in his blankets in the window embrasure while Kim and Piotra lay on the sofa, head to feet, with their clothes on and under blankets. With the heater off, the cold slunk into the room and after a time, around midnight, Piotra turned herself

round. Kim put an arm under her shoulders and turned
her so her cheek lay on his shoulder.

'What is this train he's on about?' he whispered.

'Don't ask,' she murmured. 'Don't even think about it.'

She turned away, glad of his warmth but that was all.
He withdrew his arm too. He liked her, liked her a lot.
But not like that.

CHAPTER 16

Firat Arslan had at least three agendas. With the winding up of the Burg Eco-cops he needed a radical boost to his career. Preferably one big enough to take him out of Burg Regional Police and into one of the cross-regional agencies – perhaps something connected with organised crime in the immigrant communities. After all, his father had ended up as Chief Commissioner of Police in Istanbul and Firat himself had an impeccable record (Sharon had never reported his sexual attack on her in a lift). Surely he was well qualified. What was needed was an event involving individual initiative producing positive results which could be brought to the attention of the appropriate authorities.

But, too, he had to prove to them, and himself, that the gunshot wound to his head had not permanently impaired his faculties, his ability to make snap decisions, had not left him potentially confused, unmanned in the face of extreme danger – especially if fire-arms were involved. Counsellors had told him that this would, of course, almost inevitably be the case and it was nothing to be ashamed of: there were many avenues for advancement in the police which would not require him to face homicidal gunmen again. But this picture they painted of a newly constituted Arslan was not attractive to him at all: it simply did not recommend itself to a male with a millennium of Islamic, Turkish culture behind him.

And finally there was Sharon, Sharon King. She was the daughter of a US Army on the Rhine Sergeant and a

German waitress. Dad, of course, had buggered off back to the States, and she had been brought up German with occasional school holidays in Hoboken. At the beginning of the fifteen months during which Firat had worked with her, she had come across as a bimbo, plump, always wearing jeans and tops too tight for her breasts and buttocks, into Heavy Metal, sassy with it. He had treated her with deliberate condescension sinking occasionally into bullying. Finally he'd tried to feel her up in a lift and she'd slapped him. Well, hit him, really.

After that, and not just because she'd defended herself physically, but because of the way she had handled her end of the assignment they had been on, he had learnt to respect her – without losing any of the sexual feelings she provoked. And after the shooting she had actually visited him in hospital, brought him soft porn/performance-car magazines and even held his hand for a bit.

And then came rehabilitation, the slow return to work, monitored by doctors, brain specialists and psychiatrists, as well as counsellors, and none of it had been as easy as he had hoped. At work he fumbled small assignments, forgot things, made silly decisions or no decisions at all. And once or twice recently Fechter had been quite brusque with him.

Meanwhile, he'd taken Sharon out a couple of times – once to a good Turkish restaurant in Burg and he'd cocked that up. She'd never had Turkish before and nervously had asked not to have dishes with too much garlic. Not an easy request to satisfy. The old Firat would have cheerfully told her not to be so stupid, but enjoy what was put in front of her. The new one hesitated, consulted the waiter and chef, ordered one dish then changed it to another, ending up with lamb sofrito, chunks of leg on the bone, pot-roast with lemon juice, rosemary and . . .

garlic. Next morning, she had arrived at the office in a miasma of cologne and breathing peppermint.

'It's coming out of my pores, you know?' she'd said.

So: three reasons why Firat was driven to rehabilitate himself as a tough, decisive, brave male, the guy he knew he had been before that bullet sliced bone out of the side of his skull in the Schiller Park, Burg, ten months earlier.

Firat followed Sam Pratchard from the lakeside hotel to Brandenburgische Straße. There he spent nearly an hour in the freezing entry to a block on the other side of the road, pretending to read a newspaper, and occasionally stamping his feet and banging his leather-gloved hands together. Eventually Sam came out, and, head down against the bitter wind, trotted round the corner to the Graf Leo Tolstoi café – an indescribable relief. Outside Firat used his mobile to contact Sharon in the room Homicide and Organised Crime had made available to them in the Keithstraße station. Then he went in and took a table near the heavy glass door, sharing it with a fur-clad lady, thin, old and perfumed, and a black-leathered man who could not have been a day over twenty-five. They held hands, hardly said a word to each other, but drank Russian tea and ate cats' tongues macaroons. Firat ordered tea. Slav tea is like Turkish.

He put his dark blue felt hat on the table beside his gloves and undid his three-quarter-length matching coat, with velvet collar, ran his right hand behind his ear over the patch of skin which continued to refuse to grow hair, and gestured with a cigarette at the lady.

She signified permission and he lit a Yeni Harman with the new gold lighter he'd bought to replace the Zippo he'd left in Rzepin. For a moment or two the woman looked at him with approval, perhaps even more than she had shown the young man next to her. The fact was that Firat was sharply dressed and very good-looking in a sallow, Turkish sort of way. His father, the Commissioner, had sent him money after the incident in the Schiller Park, and the counsellors had suggested he should spend it on clothes, smart ones with designer accessories, bolster his self-esteem.

And his self-esteem was now high after the misery of the street. He was warm, in the sort of place he liked to be, and on a job of considerable national importance.

And then, just as he was stubbing out the Yeni Harman and wondering whether to light another and order another tea, the small fat Englishman got up from the table at the back of the room, shrugged on his coat again and began picking his way through the tables to the door. Panic and indecision. Firat felt cold sweat prick his forehead, the back of his neck, his throat felt suddenly dry and tingling. He reached for his hat, gloves, remembered he had not paid . . .

'Are you all right?' The woman let go of her boyfriend's hand, leant across to him.

Through a haze he saw Pratchard, only a yard or so away, pull back the heavy glass door – no gust of cold, the hot-air barrier on the threshold kept it out – and then what should have come automatically to him at last dawned on him . . .

No need to follow the Englishman – he and Sharon knew where he was staying. The men he had been talking to at the back of the café were the new leads, the ones he should now concentrate on. He leant into the leather-backed seat, and smiled.

'I'm fine, thanks.'

He ordered another tea, paid for it and the one he had had, so he could leave when he wanted, lit another cigarette.

He realised he ought to get a good look at the men

Pratchard had been talking to. He knew he wanted to take a pee. He was sure that if he went back out into the cold the need would become an intolerable imperative — a minor disorder rising from his injury was that when such needs occurred they had to be satisfied. And the *Herren*, behind a heavy wooden door on the other side of the hat-stand Pratchard had taken his hat and coat from, was close to the table. All right then.

He stubbed out the second, hardly started cigarette, carefully left his hat on his seat and his gloves by his glass and set off for the toilet. He had a brief glimpse of the men Pratchard had met, took in that they were well-to-do, middle-aged, and, he realised, quite possibly Turkish, wearing dark suits, dark ties and white shirts. When he came out of the very well appointed gents, having fastidiously washed his hands and used the hot-air dryer, they were gone ... Their table was empty, a waiter held stacked cups and glasses in one hand while he skilfully wiped the surface clean with the other.

Firat rushed back through the room, knocking tables, causing anger and consternation, snatched up his hat and gloves and ploughed out on to the street. Just in time to see the Eldorado pulling out of its parking bay. He looked wildly around for a taxi. Of course, there weren't any. Turned, saw one on the corner of Hohenzollerndamm, three black leather jackets piling out, surely that meant the taxi would be free, but no, as he rushed up they closed round him, seized his arms, twisted his right fist into the small of his back, jerked it up towards his shoulder blades and bundled him in. His mobile clattered on to the pavement. The taxi pulled away, leaving his hat rolling in the gutter.

'Mr Secretary, this *is* serious. I cannot tell you how serious.'

Holding the phone to her right ear while bob-bobbing
Karl-Rosa up and down on her left hip, Renata detached
the phone from her ear and put the mouthpiece close up
to the bawling baby's mouth. Under her breath she
counted to ten, slowly, then put the phone back to her
own ear and mouth.

'Are you still there? Mr Secretary, I say, are you still
there? Yes? Good. Now you know just how serious—

'Yes, yes, I know,' she said slowly with heavy emphasis,
as if speaking to an idiot – shit, she *was* speaking to an
idiot, 'I know small babies can cry for quite long periods
without physically harming themselves, I know that, but
the time they can cry is probably longer than a reasonably
sensitive human can put up with them crying without
going mad.

'No. No. I don't want the health visitor, or the midwife
or whatever, I want Carmen. Now . . . Why not?

'Yes, she does have a permanent address' – slow again,
to an idiot – 'her permanent address is Siegfried Weg 12,
apartment 6 . . . Yes, believe it or not, Mr Secretary, I do
know that that is where I live. It is also where María
Carmen López Ortega lives. And, for the matter of that,
Karl-Rosa Fechter, though I wouldn't bet on how long he
survives here if we don't get Carmen back here pretty
damn soon. I mean very soon—

'Look, I don't give a shit whether or not Carmen bothered to notify her change of address. Indeed, are you sure
she has to? Spain is in the EU, you know. Yes, I know
that, of course I know that, that IDs have to be brought
up to date if there is a change of permanent address . . .

'Just hang on a moment. Let me get this straight. You
are saying that if I go down to the Rathaus, with my own
ID, and vouch for Carmen then they may— Yes, I thought
that was what you said. And who the fuck is going to
look after Karl-Rosa while I do that? . . . . No, I am not

going to get a taxi and take him with me. Because it's
freezing outside, he's still not quite two months old, and
the taxi-driver will almost certainly have an accident if
Karl-Rosa goes on making this row while he's trying to
drive.'

Shit.

'Yes, Mr Secretary, you're right. He has shut up. He
may be dead, but I think he's asleep . . . In the morning?
OK? I suppose so. In the morning. Sorry to bother you.'

She hung up.

Karl-Rosa in his pale blue Baby-Gro had collapsed into
the crook of her elbow. His face was still flushed, a frown
still creased his brow, but his thumb, on which he sucked
voraciously, seemed to be fulfilling his most urgent needs.
With his tiny quiff of damp black hair on his forehead,
he looked like Napoleon. Like Aldo Nerone. Renata
breathed a huge, heavy sigh. Then, against all the odds
she smiled, grinned, felt warmth rush through her. It was
the first time, possibly not the first time but certainly the
first time since she had come home from the maternity
unit and handed him over to Carmen, the first time her
son had gone to sleep in her arms.

It's nice, she said to herself, when a guy you . . . you're
learning to be fond of, goes to sleep in your arms. Now,
could she do it? She moved as if on well-oiled wheels into
Carmen's room and gently, ever so gently, laid him in the
basket-work bassinet with nineteenth-century broderie
anglaise trimmings. Should he be on his back or his side?
Shit. I'll look it up in the book. Not on his front, anyway.
On his back will do now. She laid the padded coverlet
with appliquéd snowdrops over the baby, pulled it up
to his chin and checked the temperature setting on the
thermostat. Eighteen degrees. As little as that? She
notched it up to twenty-two. After all it was cold outside.

The phone rang.

She ran back to her living-room. Desperate to cut off the noise, she knocked over a small table with a white porcelain Japanese vase holding one blue silk lily. It crashed to the floor.

'Sharon? Yes? Oh shit, shit, Karl-Rosa is screaming again. What? Yes? No . . . The silly man. Our fault. My fault. We should never have let him out on his own.'

Firat Arslan had disappeared.

He didn't know Berlin well enough to know where it was they had taken him, but it was in fact an alley off Reichenberger Straße in east Kreuzberg, with the Landwehrkanal running across the bottom of it. The black leather jackets spoke among themselves in a language Firat could not understand. They paid off the taxi, pushed him through an entry, one of them unlocked the first door on the left and pushed him into a large bare room. A bare bulb hanging from the ceiling came on. There were old newspapers on the floor, a dark patch of what might have been urine in a corner, and not much else. They shut the door, bolted it, closed shutters and pulled down blinds. Firat noticed that one had a pronounced limp, and another had ugly inflamed sores in his neck, painted with purple disinfectant. They looked like toothmarks.

Then they began to kick him. They were wearing CAT boots.

After a time they stopped and went through his pockets, finding his police ID. This puzzled them. How come a guy with a Turkish name is a policeman? What is a policeman from Burg doing on an assignment in Berlin? And he was a Moslem, yes?

Yes. But no fanatic.

But before he could explain that his religion was a matter of form rather than conviction, they began to kick him again, but with more dedication than before. He got the impression they had a thing about Moslems.

Then they brought a bent-wood chair in from another room, pulled his trousers and pants off and tied his ankles to the legs and his hands behind the back. There was no seat to the chair and they used a carpet-beater on his testicles. The oldest of them, short with close-cropped grey hair and a deep voice, began to ask questions. The questions became specific. They wanted to know where the four trains loaded with ammunition were.

Firat did well for twenty minutes. Then the one with the toothmarks in his neck, who had also been taking an almost personal delight in attacking Firat's genitals, noticed the small patch of skin behind his ear where no hair grew.

He touched it. Firat flinched. He pressed it. Firat bit his lip till it bled. His torturer put his left hand on the other side of Firat's head and his right fist against the patch of bare skin and pushed. Something moved in front of his knuckles. Firat screamed, and dumped a load of runny shit on the floor beneath him.

He talked. He told them as best he could where the trains were. Somewhere in the Rzepin marshalling-yards was as good a guess as he could make.

CHAPTER 17

During the night the weather shifted, fronts moved in from the south and west. When Kim woke and stood straddled over still-sleeping Fritz to look out of the dormer window, big puffballs of snow were dropping out of a leaden sky, as big as tennis balls. They melted as soon as they touched the roofs opposite, and, he guessed, the street below. He could envisage, even though he could not see, the build-up of oily, wet slush. And as he watched the tumbling snow, he heard a throaty rumbling in the roof behind his head and then here he came, cruising in from across the spaces above the street, sickle wings braking, tail spread – he, because he was smaller than the female who was calling for him, very like a hobby but without the red flash underneath. Yes. A male peregrine.

'Piotra, he's here. He's arrived.'

'Who's here?' Grumpy, slow, annoyed to be awake.

'A boyfriend for Périe.'

He went back to the sofa, sat close to her. They listened. The traffic sounds from below were muffled by the snow. They could hear scraping noises, a tiny clatter of feathers, then a scolding 'rek-rek-rek'.

'Maybe she's not enjoying this,' Piotra said. There was a hard note in her voice.

'Oh, she's just playing hard to get,' Kim crowed. 'We girls always do, it's expected.'

Fritz grunted, sat up, pulled out his Mauser, pointed it

at them, shook his head, put it away again.

An hour and a half later they were again on the platform at Hauptbahnhof, under the big, high, black and grey roof.

El introduced Piotra to Jace. Jace shook her hand and then turned to Kim, slapped his shoulders.

'OK, mate? How's tricks, then, in little old Berlin?'

'I turn a few Jace, a few.'

'Brought your cannon, have you?'

Kim slapped the bulge beneath his coat.

'You won't want one of mine, then. Good to have you along, Kim.'

'Who's he?' El asked, indicating the old man. He was wearing a long black coat, mittens and a woollen hat. He carried a plastic bag. The black boots he was wearing didn't seem to fit with the rest.

'He has an interest, but not in anything we're doing,' said Piotra. 'Don't mind him. He won't be a nuisance.'

I hope.

'Mr Sheen and Mr Doe not coming, then?' she added.

'Mr Sheen has an ear infection,' El said. 'It often flares up after a flight. Mr Doe stays with Mr Sheen. It's his main job, looking after Mr Sheen. And Sam Pratchard reckons this sort of do isn't his scene – i.e., he's scared shitless. I'm empowered to negotiate with the buyers if you'll handle the sellers.'

Four men who had been standing in the background moved forward. One, with short ginger hair, not tall but compact, fit body and limbs, wearing a donkey jacket over working jeans and serious, builder's boots, not designer, spoke for them.

'Jace? Jason? Padraig sent us. I'm Andy, this is our kid Jimmie.' The accent was Tyneside. Jimmie's hair was more yellow than red and he looked a touch slighter, younger. 'Northumberland Fusiliers. Heard about yer, bit of a legend in the Province. Pleased to help you oot. And this is Daffydd. I know he's a nigger, but don' hold it against him – he's as Welsh as Caerphilly cheese. Ex-First Para, so he's all right.' Six foot three and built like Frank Bruno. 'Last and least, Alec from Southampton. He's just a brickie, but he reckons he belonged to a pistol club. Once.' Another big guy, reddish hair, wearing specs, for Chrissake. 'We'll take half now and half when we get back, OK?'

Jace peeled high-denomination notes off a wad.

The train came round the bend beneath the arc of grey light and snow at the end of the platform. The wind-screen-wipers on the front of the locomotive cab pushed wedges of snow this way and that. As it came to a squealing halt, Jace swung two heavy hold-alls on to the step above him. In spite of the newspaper padding inside them, they clanked dully. They all piled into a compart-ment where smoking was allowed, and most lit up straight away.

As the train moved out, heading east into the gloomy, decayed industrial suburbs Piotra and Kim had seen only five days earlier, Alec, the brickie from Southampton, pulled a worn deck of cards from the breast pocket of his brown bomber jacket.

'Game a cards, anyone?' He pushed his specs on to the bridge of his red nose. 'Three-card brag?'

'None of you silly buggers is wearing the sort of clothes I asked for,' said Jace.

Kim smiled hopefully if shyly at Jimmie and got a very cold look in return.

Since the MP5Ks were only just over a foot long and the Brownings just eight inches, they managed to conceal them to Jace's satisfaction, either in deep inside pockets or stuck in their belts under thick jackets. Jace made them distribute spare magazines through different pockets. Daffydd, the big black Welshman could only carry an MP5K – with a pistol in his plaid jacket as well, the cloth hung crookedly. Alec got a pistol only, never having handled a sub-machine-gun, and so did Piotra. El declined – she'd never fired a proper gun in her life. Fritz went to sleep almost as soon as the train pulled out of Hauptbahnhof and they let him be.

Alec took a hundred and fifty-eight marks off Daffydd and young Jimmie before the train pulled into Frankfurt an der Oder an hour later. Andy felt pretty sure the cards were marked.

After Kim had explained how the border crossing worked, with kiosks for both states on the German side, the nine of them crossed the bridge into Słubice without incident. The snow was now falling heavily and settling on the rubble-like ice of the river, though still melting on the tarmac. Down in the tired, wide square Joe was waiting in his ancient Opel with a mate who drove an equally old Audi and another in a Lada. Jace, Piotra and Fritz went with Joe; Andy, Jimmie and Kim took the Audi, which left El, Daffydd and Alec in the Lada. El was fed up that she wasn't with Jace but understood: Jace went in the front vehicle as leader, and Piotra went with him as the speaker of Polish. She wasn't jealous or anything like that – fat chance of Jace wanting to get off with a middle-aged dike – just annoyed that she wasn't with him.

The sticky snow falling in a steady thick curtain was almost more than the windscreen-wipers could cope with and their progress, especially once they had left the main road, was slower than it had been before.

At the gate into the forest Joe muttered to Piotra. She translated.

'He wants us back in an hour. If the snow doesn't let up, he'll have to put on chains.'

Jace took over.

'Rules of engagement,' he said. 'We're here in the first place to protect El. It's her lot are paying you. Then the lady in the trilby and the tall guy with her. Piotra and Kim. Finally ourselves. You don't open fire until I say so – unless they take me out first, then you can do what's needed to get El and yourselves out. Is that clear? Right. We march open order, ten metre gaps, weapons concealed but ready. Me then Daffydd in front, then El and the other lady and her mate, Jimmie and Andy in the rear. Alec in front of them. I understand the old guy knows the way better than anyone, so he can show us.'

This time the snow beneath their feet did not crunch, it splashed sloppily. All of them had adequate footwear except Alec who was wearing loafers. He complained bitterly. Jace was short with him.

'You were fucking told what to wear,' he growled.

Once, on the way, El saw a small herd of five deer a couple of hundred metres away, browsing off holly beneath a stand of mixed birch and pine. Most of the falling snow was caught in the branches above them so they were quite visible. They lifted their heads and were gone before she could point them out to Jace, who was in front of her with the big black Welshman between. The deer made no noise. She sensed he might not believe her if she told him she had seen them. Fritz dropped behind for a moment, then he strode up past them, head high, arms swinging.

'Christ,' said Jace.

Fritz was now wearing his forage cap and had undone his coat, revealing the uniform beneath.

'What the fuck is he up to?'

In spite of his age, and although he stumbled occasionally, the old man pushed on ahead, was soon a tiny figure almost obscured by the falling snow, before he took the left turn off the ride and disappeared.

When they got to the sidings, the Bosnians were waiting with Walery Kalinka. No sign of Wisa. There were eight Bosnians including Kruno, the Omar Sharif look-alike, all wearing heavy coats and fur hats and banging leather gloves together to keep their hands warm. They were not overtly armed, but then neither were Jace's Brits.

Kalinka came up to Piotra. 'The old man just went by,' he said, speaking Polish. 'He's mad. Wearing that uniform.'

'But harmless. I think.' She gave a slight, almost indiscernible, shudder, remembering the Mauser.

'Here are the keys.' Kalinka coughed, spat into the snow. There was a trace of blood in his sputum. 'You might as well keep them. You can't move the trains without my say-so.'

He handed her a ring with eight chunky brass keys.

'I'm afraid you'll have to fiddle about a bit finding the right ones for the right padlocks, but those will in fact open all of them.'

He pulled off a glove, pushed a thin claw of a hand deep beneath the lapels of his coat, pulled out a sheaf of printout.

'Most of the containers also have combination locks. These are the numbers stencilled on the containers and beside them here are the numbers of the combinations. Sell it all for what you can get. I don't care how much. I'm not greedy but it's going to cost me to get it all shifted to Rybocice. Several payouts. But ten million marks will cover it. Anything above that is all yours. You'll have to find the barges though – that's not my responsibility.'

He shook her hand briefly, nodded at the rest, singling out Kruno especially who flashed his gap-toothed smile. Then he was off, swaying down the single line track into the forest, presumably back to the Rzepin marshalling-yards.

Piotra turned, and translated what he had said into German, but left out the bit about ten million marks.

'Where do you want to start?' she asked when she had finished.

Kruno walked down the first line of containers, passing three of them before turning back to the first and nearest.

'With this one. Why not?'

Why not indeed. Piotra understood his reasoning. Nine people out of ten would not choose the first waggon, just as you would not expect anyone to choose the numbers one to six for the National Lottery. Except, of course, many hundreds do every week and have done so since it started. It's a fourteen million to one chance, just like all the others.

She fiddled about with the keys, got the right one on the third go. Then she went for the combination lock. Nothing happened. She turned to Kruno.

'It's an electronic lock. Maybe the battery has run down. Or the cold . . .' She shrugged.

He frowned. Marched off down the line and stopped at the fifth container.

'This one.'

They all followed him, Piotra up close, the Bosnians a loose, informal ring round them; Jace and his Brits further off, all standing or moving with elaborate non-chalance, none too bunched up, three of them now smoking. The ex-soldiers knew what to do. They not only watched the Bosnians; their eyes wandered over the black trunks of the nearest trees, searched through the tumbling flakes behind them.

Again Piotra found the key without too much difficulty and this time the numbers on the tiny display lit up when she punched the right buttons. At a signal from Kruno one of the Bosnians hauled back the sliding door. It moved easily on recently oiled runners.

The interior of the container was stacked with wooden cases stencilled with numbers and cyrillic letters. Each was about two metres by one by fifty centimetres. Two more of the Bosnians climbed up and hauled out four cases – clearly they were very heavy. Then, going to the row behind, they pulled out a fifth. Whatever else they might have had in the way of weaponry beneath their coats, they were concealing short but serviceable jemmies. They broke open the case and revealed a series of oiled heavy-duty cardboard boxes. Again they went below the top layer to the one underneath. They lifted off the lid, revealing rows of cartridges.

Kruno lifted one out, produced a set of calibrated calipers. He read off the measurements. 'Diameter five forty-five. Length fifty-six fifty. Case length thirty-nine fifty. Rim diameter nine fifty.' He hefted it in his hand, and his innocent smile broke accompanied by a disclaiming shrug.

'I don't have scales. But I guess it weighs about right.'

'For what?' Piotra asked.

'An AK-74, five forty-five mil. In 1974 it replaced the original Kalashnikov. Russian scientists had shown that a smaller calibre gave better first-round-hit probability. NATO followed in 1980 with a five fifty-six. What was that?'

It could have been a branch snapping under the weight of the snow. But the fusillade of shots that followed it could not.

CHAPTER 18

One shot took off the top of Kruno's head, and another removed Piotra's felt hat. She hurled herself into the open container and squeezed herself, just, between the boxes and the steel side. She pulled the Browning from the inside pocket of her leather coat, cocked it and waited. Presently she realised that a container filled with live rounds was perhaps not the best place to be during a fire fight, but there was nowhere else to go. She found a paper handkerchief in the outside side pocket of her jacket and used it to wipe a teaspoonful or so of Kruno's brains and blood from her shoulder. Then she waited, to see what would happen, who would win. Indeed, who was fighting whom.

At the first gunshot Jace seized El's arm with his left hand, pushed her head down with his right and launched her, as if she were on wheels like a supermarket trolley, round the end of the waggons, and then even further on, before giving her a push which sent her flying between the third and fourth sidings. Her knee took a nasty knock from the rocky ballast, but her spirits soared in spite of her fear and the pain. She had been his first consideration – he cared. She'd forgotten that protecting her was what he'd been paid to do.

The shooting lasted less than two minutes. Then silence settled like snow back over the clearing.

Jace returned. His HK MP5 was in his right hand, held pointing upwards so naturally that it looked like a cybernetic limb, as much part of him as Edward Scissorhands' blades. With his left hand he helped her to her feet.

'You all right?' when he saw how she limped.

'Fine. You?'

'No problem.'

One single shot. Loud.

They rounded the end of the first siding. A thickset man with very short grey hair straightened above the body of one of the Bosnians. He had a Kalashnikov in his left hand, and the ČZ 85 Piotra had already seen in his right. At his feet the last of the Bosnians twitched and died.

'He was not as dead as I would have liked,' the thickset man said, in bad German. 'My name is Vojislav Milošević. No relation.'

El looked around her. There seemed to be bodies everywhere, and blood, much of it sinking into the snow. Snow was already settling on the clothed parts of the bodies but melted on hands and faces. Her head swam, her knees went to jelly, she thought she was going to faint. Jace caught her round the waist and got her on to the edge of the open container. He pushed her head between her knees. Piotra appeared above them, stooped, picked up her hat. She looked at it for a moment then twirled it with her finger in the bullet-hole before putting it back on. Then she walked round El and stepped lightly down into the snow. She looked around, eyes narrowed beneath the brim of the hat. One of the bodies nearby got up, knees first, brushed snow from the front of his long coat, straightened, grinned.

'Kim,' she said. 'You're all right.'

'Fine. You too, sweetie?'

'Fine.'

One by one men began to appear, rising like Kim from the snow, from between the waggons, from behind trees.

Only Kruno and his Bosnian Moslems stayed down with four of Milošević's men. The one whose Kalashnikov on automatic had killed Kruno and nearly killed Piotra had been killed by Andy. That was the only shot the Brits had fired. Once in cover, the three ex-soldiers could see that neither of the factions was shooting at them, and the people they had been told to protect were in cover. Mindful of Jace's rules of engagement, they had held their fire.

No sign of Alec.

Jace bellowed into the cold air, 'Al? Alec? Come out, wherever you are.'

It was a minute or so before he appeared, coming down the track that had brought them to the clearing. He had further to come from than the rest of them.

Milošević looked around, recognised Piotra and Kim, scowled.

'You speak for the sellers, yes?'

Piotra nodded.

'How much?'

El pulled off the woollen cap she was wearing, shook her bleached mane and coughed. 'Kruno was buying through me. I represent Sheen Associates.'

The Serb looked down at Kruno's body, then back at her. 'Fock off,' he said. In English.

Without lowering the machine-pistol he held pointing upwards in his right hand, Jace brought his left hand across and cocked the weapon. Andy, Jimmie and Daffydd did likewise, assuming unexaggerated postures of readiness.

Alec looked nervously from each to each and back to the eight remaining leather-jacketed Serbs, three of whom were now smoking.

'Need a slash,' he said, brushing a snowflake from his

glasses. Without bothering to wipe them he set off back into the forest.

Milošević smiled uneasily.

'So,' he said, turning to Piotra, 'the people who control these waggons talk to you, you talk to the English woman, and she talks to me?'

'Yes.'

'Too many focking people in the middle.'

'Insurance for all of us.'

'Maybe.' His eyes turned icy, year-old ice, and in spite of herself she shuddered. 'At least I don't have to talk to you again.' He turned to El. 'How much?'

Her head swam. Fucking bastard Pratchard should be here. But she got a grip. Think of a number and double it. No. Then pressure on her elbow. Piotra eased her out of whispered earshot of the rest. Snow squeaked and she stumbled on an almost hidden rail.

Piotra steadied her, whispered, 'It's no longer negotiable at our end. Twelve million marks. Cash or negotiable financial instruments. That's it.' A million each for her and Kim.

El knew what she meant. Euro bearer bonds, that sort of thing. The fact you had one in your hand meant you owned it, like a banknote. But bearer bonds come in bigger denominations.

'What about your ten per cent?'

'That's included.' Except it was now twenty. 'Whatever you get out of that murderous bastard above twelve is yours to keep.'

They came back across the tracks.

'Eighteen,' said El, and she made it sound like the double beat of a bell. Piotra ran her finger round the brim of her hat, pushing it back, raised her eyebrows, and let a low slow whistle emerge through pursed lips.

Someone else was whistling too.

Fritz came into view, coat swinging above his uniform, hat high on his head. He was whistling the Horst Wessel song, the official song of the movement, *der Bewegung*. El put English words to it: 'The future belongs to me.' Not to you, old chum, she thought.

Fritz came to a smartish halt in front of them, croaked in his high old voice, 'Chap in a leather jacket got too near my train. So I shot him.'

The breaking branch that had started the war.

Milošević brought his cold eyes to bear on El. She met his stare, did not flinch, but she did push her platinum hair back off her forehead. Strong fingers with painted nails pushed it up into a spiky spread. Christ, I must look a fright, she thought. But frightened I'm not. Not now.

'Eighteen? Poof!'

'Not negotiable.' She managed to indicate the nearest body that had stayed face down in the snow. 'They'll be back. And they have a lot of money behind them.'

Islam.

'So,' she went on, 'you'd better be quick. And no more . . . arm-twisting, eh? We have our army too.'

Footsteps squeaked in the snow, two sets, one out of the forest, the other up the track. Al Keegan was back, but so too was Kalinka.

Kalinka stopped ten metres away, took in the scene, eyes panning from left to right.

Alec pausing to pick his nose. The big, very black Daffydd scratching his cheek with the sight of his MP5K so that his stubble rasped. Five or six Serbs trying to look cool but failing, because somehow, very casually, the three other Brits, who all looked so at ease with their weapons, had spread themselves around them, so that although there were more Serbs than Brits, the Serbs looked surrounded, contained, vulnerable, almost like sheep in a pen. Then the two women, one with a long dark woollen coat and bright hair that glowed above a cupid's bow of a mouth, the other in a black bomber beneath a trilby with a hole in it. A small thickset Serb, older than the others, Vojislav Milošević, the only one of them who looked at ease. And at the back the two who did not fit: the tall Brit wearing a grey floppy beret above plucked and lined eyebrows, whose long coat was open to display an antiquated and large revolver stuck in his belt, and, the strangest of all, the old man who looked like the Grim Reaper and wore a uniform Kalinka's father had told him, when he was a very small boy, he should learn to respect. And the bodies, and the blood.

Kalinka felt the phlegm rise, thought of Wisa and a beach in the Caribbean, coughed and spat.

'What the fuck,' he said, 'am I going to do with three Cadillac Eldorados?'

CHAPTER 19

On the train back (they made the five o'clock from Frankfurt an der Oder, after picking up the hold-alls from the luggage lockers) Piotra faced Kim in window seats. She looked out at the darkening fields and woods, the drifting snow, and was glad of the tobacco-laden warmth of the train. Presently she leant forward and tapped his knee.

'There's an English word I can't get my stupid brain to remember,' she said. 'It describes someone who is . . . plucky? Brave? Under difficult circumstances. Sort of . . . jolly too.'

Kim pulled back under the dull, anonymous lighting and grinned.

'Game?' he suggested.

'No . . . I know why I can't find it. It has a sort of . . . male, almost rude connotation, and . . .'

'You're thinking of a woman.'

'Yes.'

'Spunky.'

'Ah.'

She glanced across the gangway to the window seat corresponding to Kim's. El too was watching the white fields slip by, but her face was reflected in the glass. She caught Piotra's stare, and smiled briefly but a touch wanly and without turning her head from the pane.

Kim leant forward and squeezed Piotra's knee.

'You're falling in love,' he said, without a trace of mockery or feyness.

'Yes,' she said.

'Good luck.'

'I'll need it.'

'You will.'

Opposite El, Jace leant across and offered her a Marlboro. She held his wrist while he lit it for her and her hand shook as she pulled back.

Piotra sighed. Kim was not surprised to see the sudden sheen in her eyes. Been there, done that. Or rather too often . . . didn't.

When he'd finished his cigarette, Jace sent Andy and Jimmie to the ends of the carriage to check that none of the women inspectors was about to come in. He collected Daffydd's and Al Keegan's guns and magazines; then he swapped them round and collected from Andy and Jimmie. If any of the other occupants of the carriage noticed what was going on, they gave no sign of it. Nor would they have done if it had been plastic bags full of white powder or hard currency. Most of them were Poles involved in their own contributions to Germany's black economy, and a fuss was the last thing they wanted.

Fritz slept, again, mouth open, chin on his collar bones – only the high colour of his cheeks indicated he was alive. His thin, claw-like hands clutched the plastic bag that contained his hat.

Al Keegan suggested cards but no one took him up.

On the platform at Hauptbahnhof Jace paid up their second instalments.

'We'll likely need you again,' he said. 'For a week, check in the Galway each day about five o'clock. I'll have left a message with Padraig if there's anything on.'

Kim and Piotra took Fritz back to Brandenburgische Straße. Fritz said he wanted to go home. 'Home' was in the roof behind the board. While Piotra took out the holding screws Kim made ready-mixed packet soup, which they made him drink before he clambered back into the black hole.

'Did you have a good day?' Kim asked him.

Fritz looked back over the steaming mug. His eyes were rheumy, distant.

'They were all there,' he murmured, a soft voice describing the panoramas hidden behind the eyes. 'All present and correct. Of course, I didn't have time to count them, but they were all there. Oh yes.'

Back at the hotel El told her associates what had happened.

'I told them,' she said, 'eighteen million. That makes us six mil, what's that, more than two mil sterling?'

'Two point six,' Sam said. He wasn't pleased. It wasn't the deal he'd been putting together. The profit fell short by one point eight mil marks. And the way it was going, it left no opportunity for him to sideline any away from the rest for his own personal use over and above what they'd divvy up at the end of the game.

Harry Sheen moved his fag from his mouth, ran a finger over moist lips.

'But the Islamics'll be back, won' they? The auction's not over yet,' he rasped and then coughed into a handkerchief. He looked at what he'd brought up and found nothing there to worry him.

'If they do there'll be another war,' Jace said, back to the old boarded-up fireplace, elbows on the mantelpiece. 'Whoever loses the auction will fight it out. Or indeed they may decide to fight first, winner takes all and no auction.'

'Reckon Milošević's lot will have worked that out for themselves,' said Doe. 'They've regained the initiative, they won't want to lose it. He'll be back PDQ if you ask me, try to get it sorted before the other lot can regroup.'

El suddenly started to weep. Jason put his arm round her shoulder and took her back to her room.

'This afternoon was horrible,' she said. 'I didn't mind a year ago, when it happened in Burg. Those men had been horrible to us and they would have killed us if you hadn't killed them. But today it was different.'

'Yes,' he said.

'Jace, I don't think I can be on my own tonight. Will you stay with me?'

'If that's what you want.'

'But ...'

'Hands off? OK. I can live with that.' He risked a grin. 'Just.'

'You're a brick.'

And she kissed him, and then suddenly clung to him and let the tears go.

CHAPTER 20

'Secretary?'

'Fechter.'

'KOK Firat Arslan has disappeared. In Berlin. The last we knew of him was that he was following Sam Pratchard, a member of Sheen Associates. I have to go to Berlin.'

'Of course.'

Pause.

'So I suppose María Carmen López Ortega will shortly be here to look after Karl-Rosa.'

'Who?'

'Herr Secretary, post-natal depression is a recognised clinical condition.'

'Yes, I know that.'

'Then you will put it down to post-natal depression when I tell you to stop wanking and do something.' Renata slammed the hand-set down.

Carmen was on the doorstep within twenty minutes.

Three hours later Renata joined the two remaining members of her team in Berlin. They were in their room in the Homicide and Organized Crime headquarters (LKA 4113) in Keithstraße between the Tiergarten and Kurfürstenstraße. Renata talked it through with Sharon.

'The police here were able to give you the address of Kim Kind, aka Godfrey Newcombe?'

'Yes.'

'And Firat was keeping it under surveillance?'

'No. He was at the Seehof Hotel, watching Sheen Associates. He followed the man called Sam Pratchard to Brandenburgische Straße where Kind lives—'

'How was he keeping in touch?' Norbert Eintner chipped in.

'By mobile to here. This is an outside line – it doesn't go through the LKA 4113 switchboard.'

He indicated the handset on the desk at Renata's elbow. He also anticipated Renata's next question.

'He was outside the Brandenburgische Straße block for just over half an hour. He rang in when Pratchard left to go to the Graf Leo Tolstoi café to say that was where Pratchard had gone, and that was that. After that . . . silence, disappearance.'

He passed his white palm over his bald pate, readjusted his spectacles. He was, Renata decided, fitting almost too readily into his new role. He clearly liked systems, order, routine, but he was enjoying the disorderly aspect too, the sorting it out and so on. Clearly he had the personality that makes a happy desk policeman, and he must have been as miserable as hell on the beat or in a patrol car. A happy policeman, she reflected, is not necessarily a good policeman. She gave herself a shake, pushed on.

'You've made enquiries at the Tolstoi?'

'Not personally,' Sharon answered. 'I felt it would be better if these were carried out by officers who knew the patch and were known on the patch. If Firat has been kidnapped, there's no sense in exposing ourselves. EKHK Lietze lent us two operatives.'

'You were right to think of that. Well done.'

As her estimation of Norbert became more and more compromised, that of Sharon continued to rise. For all her American gum-chewing, her sexily tight clothes, her too-open manner, she was turning into a good policeperson, never jumping to conclusions, always adaptable to events as they happened, prepared to listen. Maybe not happy, but good.

'I briefed them. They've drafted reports' – Sharon tapped printout – 'which they may want to go over, but I told them it was urgent. All things considered, they did rather well.'

Renata speed-read them. The waiter remembered that Pratchard had come in and sat at the back with four or five very well-dressed men who he guessed might be Turks. He remembered Firat sitting near the door. He knew the woman, Frau Wilma, who had been at the same table, because she was a regular customer, and well, they, the people who worked at the Tolstoi, all knew her relationship with Edgar, her latest boyfriend, was not going well.

Frau Wilma, described as a well-to-do retired couturier, was visited and had also been helpful. She had seen, from her table by the door of the Tolstoi, that Firat Arslan had been bundled into a taxi by a group of men in leather jackets. Yes, she agreed, he had not wanted to go with them. Force had been used.

Why did she not report the event?

No answer given, but Renata could imagine the look Frau Wilma gave the questioner.

Renata went to the window, looked out at the plane trees, across Keithstraße to the Tiergarten on her right, the traffic lights at the Kurfürstenstraße junction to her left. It still snowed with heavy wet flakes but none of it settled, though black slush collecting in the gutters held up the dispersal of surface water. The sky remained iron-grey.

Norbert Eintner coughed. It was the sort of cough that says: speak to me. Or I want to speak to you. She turned. He had gone back to the sheets of printout stacked concertina-wise on his desk, was looking up from them, moon-faced and with a happy smile.

'I think,' he said, 'I've rumbled something of what's going on here. Anyway, a definite series of anomalies.'

'Yes?'

'Can't be sure.' He took off his glasses, gave them a polish on a tissue. 'Can't be sure till I've been back to Brandenburg and had another look at their records. And maybe had a chat with Furtwanger.'

'No way can we take you there. Not till this Firat business is cleared up, anyway.'

'I can go on my own. Catch the train. It's only half an hour or so from Charlottenburg. Or the Hauptbahnhof.'

There was something almost manic in his voice which Renata recognised as typical of computer nerds when they feel they're on to something.

'You want to go now?'

'Yes. Yes, I think I do.'

Without waiting for her say-so he began bundling the printout into a briefcase.

'All right, then. Keep in touch.'

After all, it wasn't as if he'd be much use in the search for Firat – indeed, he'd probably get in the way.

Half an hour after he had gone there was a knock on the glazed door. Renata turned from the window, saw EKHK Karin Lietze through the glass. She signalled for her to come in. Lietze was a tall, handsome woman with blonde-streaked hair stylishly cut. It wasn't clear whether the streaks were natural or not. She was a year or so older than Renata. They knew each other slightly from conferences and so forth – inevitably, as not many women reach or go beyond their rank in German police forces, or any others for that matter. They were a touch wary of each other, the way one is with a comparative stranger in situations where one feels expected to form an immediate alliance. But now it was clear from Lietze's face that she was the bearer of bad news.

'We think we may have found your man,' she said. 'He's dead.'

He was still in the ground-floor room of the apartment near the Landwehrkanal, and he was still strapped to the bent-wood seatless chair above the faeces he had let go. The smell was awful. He was a mess, not identifiable from his face. The *coup de grâce* had been a 9mm parabellum bullet fired upwards into the back of the neck, smashing the upper vertebrae and the base of the skull, exiting through the bridge of the nose. The exit wound had taken a lot of facial bone and cartilege with it. Identification had already been confirmed through his thumbprint. Although his documents had been removed, KOK (provisional) Kalle Jokisch, who had been conducting the search for LKA 4113, had asked for modem-ed versions from Burg the day before and they included Arslan's thumb-print. Jokisch was a short, jolly-looking man with a ready smile, though on this occasion all he could muster for his boss and Renata was a wan grimace. As he was an ex-Ossi policeman, his rank was still provisional, pending clearance of Stasi involvement beyond a tolerable minimum.

They stood in the doorway and watched the forensic team going through their familiar routine.

'I've done a preliminary interview with the landlord,' Jokisch said. 'When I'm through here we'll take him to Keithstraße and see if we can't jog his memory further.'

Lietze glanced at Renata. Renata had gone pasty white, and now suddenly a red flush was rushing up her neck and into her cheeks. Her fists were tight clenched. Lietze recognised the signs – horror, pain, yes, but overriding these, anger, fury. At all events, her colleague was in no state to ask or answer questions. She turned to Jokisch.

'Who were they?' she asked.

'The landlord can't or won't say. He's Hungarian Volksdeutscher, has owned the apartment for a year only. He admits he let the room on a daily basis to the tenants and that no contracts were signed, no ID asked for or recorded. He knows that means he's infringed regulations and he might cough a bit more when we hold that over him.'

'So what did he let out?'

'The actual tenant was a short, thickset man with short, whitish hair. He spoke German badly with a marked accent.'

'The actual tenant?'

'There were several men with him. They all wore black leather jackets, jeans, boots, that sort of thing. He took them for laid-off construction workers. There are a lot about just now.'

'Thousands. When exactly did this tenancy start.'

'Two days ago, lunch-time. The tenant paid for two days but said he'd be back. Today is the third day. He didn't return. The landlord used his own key to get in. Then he phoned the police.'

'Where does the landlord live? Didn't he hear anything. Didn't the other tenants hear anything?'

'He says no. We haven't got round to the other tenants yet, though we have told them to stay in their rooms.'

Lietze sighed.

'They heard plenty,' she said. 'They heard him scream, they heard a shot. And they just hoped it would all go away without touching them. Illegals. No valid papers. Deportation if they got involved.'

Sensing a new presence behind her, she turned. Sharon King had just come back in from the street. Her complexion too was pasty beneath her capuccino skin. She was wiping her mouth with a handful of tissues and her eyes were filled with tears, not those that shock or grief cause – they would come later – but those one sheds when one has vomited suddenly, uncontrollably.

Renata seized her hands in both her own and squeezed violently.

'Sharon, we'll get the bastards. I promise you, together we'll get them. I don't care what it takes, we'll get them.'

CHAPTER 21

'Hi, Fred, saw your car parked down the street. What you drinking?'

The small, tubby man, almost bald apart from a fringe of black hair circling his head round the back from ear to ear and almost long enough to reach the collar of his pin-striped blue suit, lifted his low backside on to the bar stool.

'Shit, Karl, what are you doing here? Since you ask, a coffee.' Fred looked at his watch. 'Maybe a little later I'll have a Beck.'

Karl, as his accent betrayed, was a Münchener, and as such had no qualms about drinking at any time of day. He ordered a half-litre of Löwenbräu from the tap.

Fred was tall, had white-blond hair cut very short, had put his long grey mackintosh, grey snap-brim trilby on the counter next to his grey gloves and pack of Philip Morris. Although different in stature and actual clothes, the two men had a lot in common. They shared with minor salesmen the belief that sharp but subdued clothes were part of the job, and like minor salesmen let themselves down in detail – shoes down-at-heel, a frayed cuff, fingernails not scrupulously clean. They were not, however, salesmen, they were private investigators working out of two small rival establishments.

It was not so much a case of curiosity overcoming discretion as a mutual awareness that sharing the job if the jobs turned out to be the same job would lead to mutual benefit. It took no time at all for them to realise that they *were* on the same job, namely, attempting to keep the four members of Sheen Associates, together with the youngish and certainly very tough-looking man who seemed to have moved in with them, under surveillance. Not only that, but they were also meant to identify any visitors they had.

'All of which is bloody impossible,' Karl concluded. So they shifted about a bit, Karl moving to the end of the small bar from which he could hear most of what the receptionist said on her phone, while Fred concentrated on the stairs and lifts. They agreed that Karl would follow the first Sheen to leave, and that if they were separated they'd meet here at the bar at nine o'clock in the evening to collate their results. The one question neither asked was the identity of the other's client.

The first visitor was Vojislav Milošević, accompanied by four of his entourage. Fred reacted slightly when he saw him and Karl correctly guessed that this might indeed be Fred's firm's client. Karl meanwhile overheard the receptionist's end of her conversation with someone in the Sheen Associates' suite. Mr Milošević could go up, but on his own. He remonstrated, and the receptionist went back to the phone. Sheen Associates were adamant. Milošević's face flushed, the flush faded, he shrugged massively, told his men to wait, stubbed out his cigarette and stamped angrily over to the lift.

He came down twenty minutes later, looking pleased. His men fell in round him and they went.

'Know them?' Karl asked Fred.

'Sort of.' Fred thought for a moment. If this temporary association with Karl was going to work, he had to keep his side of the bargain. 'Like I'm pretty sure they're our clients. The secretary back at the office will tell me their names, or as much as they've told the boss.'

Half an hour went by, during which Karl got stuck

into his second half-litre of Löwenbräu but resisted a schnapps chaser, while Fred had the Beck he'd taken a rain check for. Then Sheen, Doe and Pratchard, all in outdoor clothes, the last clutching his grand document case, came out of the lift. They asked the receptionist to order them a taxi and they smoked while waiting for it to arrive but said nothing. Karl sighed, finished his beer, nodded to Fred and went out ahead of them, got into his car, and waited for the taxi to arrive.

He followed them up Kant Straße through Charlottenburg to Savignyplatz, where the taxi took a left and eventually pulled in beneath the awning of a definitely up-market post-modern apartment block with an oriental carpet shop on one side of the entrance and a smart boutique on the other. Self-taught to be good at such things, Karl spotted that at a nod from Harry Sheen, Herbert Doe pressed the top right-hand bell-push. Karl parked his car, an old but well-kept Ford Cortina, and came back to read the label by the bell-push. Deniz Enver. It provoked him to puff out his cheeks and let out a small whistle of excited surprise.

Back at the hotel Fred had almost another hour to wait. Then, close on half past eleven El and Jace came down the stairs, holding hands – which Fred thought was rather sweet. Jace handed his room key to the receptionist and, putting his arm round El's waist, led her to the door, fumbling out his car keys with his other hand. Fred, pulling on his coat and hat with, as it were, three hands, made it to his own car in time, but only just.

This was a longer journey, first down the whole length of Kant Straße, under the railway bridge by Zoo Station, round the Kaiser-Wilhelm-Memorial Church, past the Europa Center, leaving it on the right, the Mercedes building with its revolving sign, three more blocks down Kürfurstenstraße and then a left into Keithstraße. The

black BMW pulled in on the right-hand side and Fred
was even more surprised than Karl had been. El and
Jace, still hand in hand, trotted up the three or four steps
of Keithstraße 30, which, since he had worked there for
ten years, Fred knew very well was the headquarters of
the Organised Crime and Homicide squads in central
West Berlin.

Fred parked fifty metres up the street towards the
Tiergarten and wondered how the hell he was going to
find out who the two Englanders were seeing. He did not
have to wait long. KOK Ernst Prützmann came down the
pavement towards him.

Prützmann was in his thirties, and had been an athlete,
a shot-putter of not quite national standard. He was
large, had a big red face beneath cropped ginger hair,
wore snazzy suits which could not quite keep up with his
steadily growing girth. He was addicted to *Weissbier* and
Weisswurst. His hands were huge and as red as his face.
He used them to beat his broken wife and two small
children, who hid on the rare occasions he came home
before their bed-time. Fred hated him but wound down
his window.

'Hi, Ernst.'

'Fred. Fucking Fred.' The big man pulled up, bent
down, stuck his head close to the window. 'What are you
doing here? Want your job back? You can't have it.'

His breath, the moisture in it condensing in the cold
air, was sour with sausage and beer.

'No, Ernst. But I am following an English couple who
have just gone into HQ and I want to know who they're
seeing and why.'

'If you think I'll tell you, you're out of your fucking
mind.'

'I've five hundred marks says you will.'

'Five c now and five when I come back with the goods.'

Fred fiddled a wad out of his inside pocket. Spare no expense, he had been told – but only if you get a result. He was pretty sure Prützmann would be back for more.

CHAPTER 22

Deniz Enver was famous in Berlin, even throughout Germany. She was getting to be well-known in Paris and London too. Born fifty years ago in Izmir, the daughter of a raisin merchant, married to a German chef in Köln for long enough to establish an up-market Turkish cuisine restaurant there and her status as a German citizen, she had then gone on to build up an import business specialising in Turkish products and artefacts. Starting with kilims, and Bursa pottery she had moved on to rugs and carpets, silver and copperware, faïence and turquoise. She bought already good vineyards near Ankara, put in Australian wine experts who developed fashionably fruity wines that sold cheaper than their Australian or New Zealand models. She set up a factory there too which matured sheep and goat cheeses to a quality that matched those from the Pyrenees and La Mancha. She was also reputed to trade illegally in antiquities and some even said opium derivatives.

At all events she was one of the wealthiest women in Germany.

A German PA, 1.85 metres of athletic blonde womanhood, cropped hair, scarlet nails, purple made-to-fit jumpsuit opened the door to Sheen Associates and led them over marble floors to a large drawing-room with views over the university to the Tiergarten beyond. There was absolutely nothing visible in the apartment that could be described as Turkish or even oriental. The walls were hung with paintings and etchings by Beouys, there

were maquettes by Oldenburg and a couple of late de
Koonings, hard-edged colourful abstracts. Even the rugs
were modern – textured loosely woven tawny affairs,
clearly the work of a designer weaver.

Enver herself, though, was Turkish all through – small
with iron-grey hair in a bun, corseted beneath a black
dress that made her look like a Mediterranean matriarch
even though the label was Christian Dior. She waved the
three men into deep armchairs. The PA offered them
Diplomat cigarettes from a silver box and asked if they
would like Turkish tea.

There were two other men in the room and Enver introduced them.

'Mr Sheen, I'd like you to meet Mr Hamdija who is the
Bosnia-Herzegovina consul here in Berlin.'

Her English was very good; indeed, all three spoke the
language better than the Englishmen. Hamdija was thin
with waved silver hair, eyes that looked in different directions, one blue, one green. In all other respects he was
your typical European diplomat.

'And this is Mr Mehmet Sayeed.'

Sayeed was dressed casually in a woven silk and wool
mixture jacket, open polo-neck shirt, dove-grey slacks and
Ferroguamo loafers. Doe, always the best-informed of the
trio, recognised him as a famous Palestinian exile and
millionaire. All Sheen saw was class, class out of his class.
It made him feel resentful. Pratchard hung on to his
document case with both hands as if it were a life-belt
and he'd drown if he let go.

As soon as the athletic PA had served the milkless tea
in elegant tulip-shaped glasses, Deniz Enver got straight
down to it.

'Mr Sheen, we understand you are acting as agent or
broker for people who control four train-loads of ammunition at present in sidings near Rzepin. You were dealing

with General Kruno of the Bosnian army and had arranged that they should be sold to him—'

Sheen glanced at Doe and interrupted. 'Didn't know the poor geezer was a general, did you, Herbert?'

Doe shook his head. Enver sighed, the way a nanny sighs at a recalcitrant infant.

'You must of course tell me if I have been misinformed about anything, but otherwise please let me continue. This morning the bodies of General Kruno and five of his associates were found on the German bank of the Oder about three kilometres upstream from Frankfurt an der Oder. They had been shot. There was evidence that they had been carried across the ice. We believe they were ambushed in Poland by Serbs led by a notorious criminal called Vojislav Milošević?'

She ended on a question and her thick but well-shaped eyebrows rose. Sheen nodded but said nothing. She went on.

'It now seems likely that the Serbs have made you an offer for these train-loads. Mr Sheen, no matter what their offer is, you must refuse it and accept ours – which will be five per cent greater than anything they have come up with. The cost will be shared between Mr Sayeed, myself and' – she nodded towards Hamdija – 'the Bosnian government. So the first thing we have to know is how much these murderers have offered you.'

Pratchard coughed, leant forward, his podgy fingers drummed on the lid of his case.

'Mr Milošević has offered twenty million marks. Fifteen of them will go to the seller's agent. In the circumstances, I do not think a five per cent mark-up is sufficient to persuade us to renege on that deal.'

Colour rose in Enver's cheeks and in her lap her knuckles whitened, but even so she spotted Herbert Doe's reaction to what Pratchard had said – a quick sideways glance and eyebrows furrowed in a frown.

'You have something to say, Mr Doe?'

'Yes, ma'am. Sam here knows darn well he's fibbing. We're asking for eighteen and twelve goes to seller's agent. How they divvy it up ain't our concern.'

Pratchard looked as if he might explode. Sheen looked at his fingernails and raised his eyebrows, but said nothing.

'Thank you, Mr Doe. I think my colleagues and I can go up to twenty.'

She glanced at Hamdija and Sayeed. They nodded agreement.

'There is one thing, though. A condition which you will have to fulfil.' She cleared her throat, pursed her lips, sucked in breath. 'We have made enquiries and we understand that you too sent a party to Rzepin yesterday and, while they did nothing to save General Kruno and his colleagues, your men conducted themselves admirably.'

Sheen flinched. The thoughts flashed through his mind: how'd she know that? Who she bin talking too?

'The condition is this. You will appear to let the deal go through with Milošević, but once you have his money your little private army must liquidate him and his little private army. Do you understand?'

Pratchard brightened up considerably at the thought that they were playing for double. Sheen continued to worry – the only people this woman could have been talking to were the sellers' agents: the dike with the Polish name or the English queer who seemed to be a mate of Jace's. If that was the case, there was a serious danger Sheen Associates could be cut out of the whole deal. Indeed, it suddenly came clear to him that they would be, unless they provided an army and started a war. That could well be what this woman was actually paying for – revenge for the murder of Kruno and his guys.

Doe had something else on his mind. Two things.

He leant forward out of his armchair.

'Ma'am,' he said, 'we had five men out at Rzepin yesterday. I wasn't there myself but we got a full report. One of them was a dud, which leaves four. We need odds. We need enough firepower to be sure not just of winning but enough to win without casualties. I reckon we can get in more but it'll take a day or two, maybe three. Number two. These men of ours are not killers. They'll go along as minders and they'll shoot to kill to protect the lives of those they're minding. But they won't start the war.'

Silence for a moment. Deniz Enver seemed to contract, then pull herself even more upright than before, and finally expand again.

'Something can be arranged,' she said. 'I'm sure. I'm sure something can be arranged.'

Renata had been in two minds over whether or not to embrace El when she came in. Their association eleven months earlier had been friendly, as well as useful to both, and they had embraced when finally all the details had been cleared up and El was on her way home. But she sensed El's tension, distrust even, and she had to remind herself that even the most innocent of people feels nervous when summoned to a police station with no good reason given. Instead she shook hands briefly, but she hoped with warmth, backed with a sympathetic smile, and indicated she should sit in the utilitarian but comfortable arm-chair to the side of her desk.

El indicated Jason. 'Can he stay?'

'Of course.' Said quickly without hesitation, attempting to achieve if not rapport, then at least trust. In any case Renata remembered very well who Jason was. He, with his twin brother, had killed, in self-defence, two ex-cops, both particularly evil, both resisting arrest, according to Sharon, who had been there at the time. Renata sat behind her desk, but angled her chair so as not to make a barrier of it.

'I'll be as plain with you as I can,' she began, speaking German, knowing that both El and Jace were fluent. 'First, I must tell you that I am leading a special group whose task is to locate four missing train-loads of Russian ammunition that disappeared somewhere between Brandenburg and Moscow. I'm pretty sure that Sheen Associates are involved in a scam whereby these trains, amounting to some one hundred and twenty containers, possibly sited in the Brandenburg area, possibly in or near Rzepin in Poland, are to be sold to the highest bidder. I suspect that the bodies of six Bosnian Moslems which were found this morning on the west bank of the Oder near Frankfurt are connected with this business. I know that a member of my team, KOK Firat Arslan, has been brutally tortured and murdered, possibly by Serbs, while carrying out his duties connected with this case. I want to find those trains and I want to bring to book the men who killed Firat. I think you can help me.'

El glanced at Jason. He looked down at his hands, then raised his head and grimaced. She liked his hands. They were good hands, strong but tender. She knew. She also knew where her first loyalties lay.

'I'll do what I can,' she said. 'But I won't compromise my associates.'

Renata thought about this, thought about the tone El had adopted. Thought she had the measure of it.

'You want your associates to remain in the clear? Free from prosecution?'

El's stony silence suggested that there might be more.

'That they should get their rake-off from the transaction?'

El cleared her throat.

'Frau Fechter,' she said, 'I do not think Sheen Associates are involved in anything illegal. Certainly not knowingly. We are broking certain goods from an agent acting for the owner on behalf of whoever will pay the best price.'

Renata was suddenly irritated, almost angry.

'The owner,' she said, 'is the Russian government.'

El was quick in reply.

'And who is to say that the man whose agent we are talking to does not represent the Russian government?'

Renata almost broke the pencil she was toying with. Shit, she thought. Why did no one think of that? Not the Russian government itself, of course, but people high enough up its ladder to be able to dispose of unwanted arms, taking a hefty rake-off, but able to give the affair a veneer of legality.

El ran her fingers through her bleached mane, then put her hands on her knees.

'I won't tell you where the trains are.'

'Won't' not 'can't'. Both registered the distinction.

'But in every other respect I will do anything I can to help you catch the murderers of your colleague.'

Renata stood, walked to the window. No snow. It had stopped at last. There was even a patch of blue sky. She turned back.

'Miss Harman, there is one other thing. Do you believe in coincidences? That they really can happen?'

'Sometimes.'

'Do you not think it is an extraordinary coincidence that we are meeting like this again, less than a year after the affair in Burg?'

'Yes. It is odd. I hadn't thought about it before. But

then it was only when you rang the hotel this morning that I knew you are . . . on the case.'

'Whereas I have known almost from the start that Sheen Associates are involved. I've had time to think about it. Eloise, when did Sheen Associates first become interested in these trains?'

El thought for a moment.

'Right back in April last year Sam, Sam Pratchard, our accountant, brought it up. We were in the Burg hospital visiting Herbert. Sam said Jace here had heard of Russian ammunition going missing and that it might be worth looking into.'

Jace looked up.

'Just read it in the newspaper,' he said.

'Nothing came of it,' El went on, 'and we all forgot about it, then we heard there really were four trains unaccounted for. We came back to Hamburg and asked Jace to look into it. Three weeks later he reckoned he had a line on them and we came back again—'

'It wasn't quite like that.' Jason intervened. He went on. 'Sam had heard a whisper that these trains were still around. I told him that thirty-eight were accounted for, but it seemed maybe four were still off the record.'

Renata faced both of them.

'Where did Mr Pratchard get that information from?' she asked.

They shrugged. Renata pushed her fingers through her hair, breathed in.

'All right,' she said, and she firmed up her voice. 'You can go now. Keep out of trouble. I shan't be able to help you if you don't.'

She sat down again, swivelled her chair into the desk, opened her diary, picked up her pen, tapped it on the desk.

El and Jace looked at each other, grimaced, and went.

Renata sat back in the chair, arms spread. She'd been a fool. She knew it. Moved by Firat's horrible death, she had acted impulsively, pursuing any line open to her to get to his killers. She felt suddenly cold, alien. Used and abused. There was far more going on here than she knew of. Two things were for sure. The involvement of Sheen Associates was no coincidence. And El's promise to help her catch Firat's murderers was hollow, since she refused to divulge any details about the trains. Suddenly bereft and lonely, she picked up the phone again, dabbed numbers.

'Carmen? How's Brat? How are you?'

Carmen and Karl-Rosa were fine. But Karl-Rosa would like to see his real mummy again quite soon. Renata did not believe her, but chose to try to.

She considered her options and realised she had none. Already the Sheens were under discreet surveillance by agencies other than hers, and Lietze's homicide squad were using conventional if well-tested routines – there really did not seem to be much more she could do.

Even before El and Jace had left the building, Prützmann had earned his second five hundred marks.

He bent down, stuck his head through the window of Fred's car.

'They're seeing an EKHK from Burg called Renata Fechter. She's here with a small team, cross-regional, investigating four missing trains filled with Russian ammunition. One of her blokes came to a sticky end down in Kreuzberg. She's pissed off about it. So is Karin Lietze. Consequence is everyone in the building's yakkety-yakking about it.'

Fred peeled the five notes off the wad his boss had given him. He didn't feel anyone would complain – he'd clearly got close to what the clients were interested in.

Shame, though, that it all had to go to a bastard like Prützmann.

CHAPTER 23

Norbert, in his heavy black raincoat and black, wide-brimmed fedora, glasses twinkling, bulging briefcase under his arm, took a taxi to Charlottenburg station, climbed the stairs, watched the indicators, caught the right train. As soon as he was on it he wished he'd taken the taxi the whole way, or got one of Lietze's staff to drive him out to Brandenburg. This was no inter-city express, but a local train with carriages not much different from a tram and half-filled with youths, male and female, students or unemployed, who smoked the whole time, drank beer from tins, wore leather and had spiky hairdos. This was a world Norbert tried to keep clear of. He looked out of the window at the melting slush and watched the drab allotments with their little summer houses, the canals and rivers on which chunks of melting ice still floated, the ugly parade of Ossi industry flow by.

There was a brief moment of past glory, well-preserved or restored, the domes both palatial and ecclesiastical of Potsdam, but then, a touch more rural now with stunted forest and rank prairie-farmed fields, the drabness returned. He allowed himself an uncharacteristic shudder – he'd be glad to get back to Wessi-land, the tidy, prosperous world of Burg.

Twenty minutes later the little train cruised into Brandenburg. He had not been with Sharon and Firat on their visit, but, bespoken by phone from Keithstraße before he left, the same young policeman who had driven them around was waiting for him with a car on the windswept concourse circled by small trams and buses. He took him the short distance to the offices, sited in prefabricated concrete huts, from which the regional freight traffic was controlled.

Here Norbert followed, as Firat and Sharon had done, step by step but with a more serious eye for detail and time-lapses than they had, the processes whereby forty-two trains had been booked, the forty-two had been cut to thirty-eight, though one set of documents still put the number at forty-two. He had with him copies of the manifests for each train which he had been going over minutely in Keithstraße. He knew how each container had been loaded, what its capacity was. He knew precisely how big the crates and boxes of ammunition were, saw how each container could have been loaded, should have been loaded. And now he checked what he already knew against the real documents, the real files. Because he already had a good idea of what he was looking for, it only took him two hours and a bit to confirm his suspicions.

The clerks in the offices watched him with barely concealed suspicion, if not hostility, but did not impede him.

When he was through, he asked the young policeman to drive him to the block where Furtwanger's room was.

The faceless, forgettable woman who ran the shop below had news for them. Herr Furtwanger had moved out three days ago.

'Moved? Where to?'

'Not far. Just round the corner.' She gave the policeman an address.

Literally just round the corner. This time Furtwanger had a proper flat, on the ground floor – two rooms with a kitchen and proper bathroom, nicely if cheaply furnished, with proper if old-fashioned central heating. And Furtwanger himself was not there. He was across the road, standing among dead sunflower stalks, sproutless sprout heads in front of a typical Ossi summerhouse, a clapboard construction, painted yellow and pink. Just big enough to stand up in inside, with small windows with frames cut like those of alpine chalets from plywood, it no doubt held gardening tools, patio chairs, and maybe even a TV and a fridge.

The policeman called to him and he came through a little wicket gate, crossed the road, let them into the flat.

Furtwanger sat them round a small table with a lace cloth on top, put out three shot glasses and a tall bottle of schnapps.

They toasted each other briefly, then the policeman said, 'You've gone up in the world, then, Wilhelm.'

'You know bloody well I have.' The old man winked broadly at Norbert. 'Not much they don't know about us all down at the police station.'

'Herr Eintner here would like to know what happened.'

'Got my just deserts, didn' I? They up-graded my pension. To that of Assistant Controller.'

Norbert leant forward, suddenly confident that his suspicions were correct.

'Although you'd only been Acting Assistant Controller?'

'That's right. They'd promised they would. They said if I did my duties to their satisfaction that's what they'd do.'

'For how long were you Acting Assistant Controller?'

'For six months.'

That surprised Norbert. But then, thinking it over, it was likely the whole thing had been planned well in advance.

'And towards the end of that six months they wanted you to do certain specific things, things connected with the shipment of Russian ammunition back to Russia.'

'That's right.'

'Who were these people?'

'Well, the bosses, of course. The Regional Director. I thought it might all be a bit dodgy, so I checked with the regional union boss. He said I was right to go ahead with it. Lucky to have the opportunity to do something for myself at the end of my career. In the end I got a lump sum too. They said it had accrued to me over the years according to some Deutsche Reichsbahn insurance scheme everyone had forgotten about.'

Norbert, flushed with his first success as a detective, leant back in his chair. It creaked. He looked around him. In all truth the flat was not that much better than the room described by Sharon. But it was tolerably clean, and the smells were of cabbage and pork rather than damp and schnapps. Maybe Furtwanger read his thoughts.

'Let myself go a bit, when what they promised never came through. Didn't know how to handle it, see? Get what I was due to. But it came through in the end. Just been buggered up in the offices and all that. Bureaucracy. Well, I've been living with that all my life, haven't I?'

'Did they tell you to . . . um, keep quiet about this?'

'Sort of. Told me not to go shouting my mouth off about it.'

'But you don't mind talking to me.'

'No. Why should I? They told me there was nothing illegal, against the law. Indeed, they told me it was all in the service of the state. What I don't understand is why you don't go and ask them about it, instead of me.'

'Well, of course I or my superiors will do just that. One last question. What exactly was it they wanted you to do?'

'Mess the records up so it would look to anyone who got hold of them that all that ammo went out on forty-two trains instead of thirty-eight.'

'There only ever were thirty-eight?'

'That's right. And never any need for more than thirty-eight. That's what I kept telling that black girl and the Turk you sent before. Drop more Schnapps?'

Back at the Brandenburg railway station Norbert found a payphone. He rang Keithstraße and got Fechter, told her what he thought he had discovered, briefly, of course, without all the reasons and evidence.

As the journey back re-wound itself and he sat clutching his briefcase he surrendered to a small glow of self-satisfaction. The plot to make people think there had been four trains more than there actually were had come from the top. At least one lowly official in what had once been the Ossi Deutsche Reichsbahn had been discreetly bribed. What it was all about he did not know and could not guess, but at least what he had found out would assist Frau Fechter – probably more than anything else that had so far come up during the four-week investigation. Yes, he really was at last beginning to enjoy police work, or at any rate the side of it where his particular skills were brought into play.

Darkness was closing in when he got off the train at Charlottenburg. He would, he thought, report back to Keithstraße, then phone his wife in Burg, then he'd go and have a real blow-out on rump steak and red wine at the Churrasco steak-house near the lodging-house he'd been put in. But as he got to the foot of the stairs two men closed in on him. Large men, dressed conventionally but already flashing IDs at him.

'KOK Norbert Eintner?' It was a statement more than a question. 'We are officers of the Bundeskriminalamt and we would like you to come along with us.'

They took his briefcase off him and bundled him into the back of a black Mercedes 200.

CHAPTER 24

They sat under the roof in the long, narrow, hot room above the ex-film studio, listened to the water running in the gutters, smoked pot. Kim was in the chair with his elbow on the table but facing not the sound-proof window with its blind, but the sofa beneath the part of the roof that sloped into the red-painted boarding. Piotra was on the sofa, flipping through a glossy magazine, long legs stretched out so her ankles just rested on the arm at the other end. They were waiting. Waiting for El or Jace or someone from Sheen Associates to get in touch on the mobile, tell them that a deal had been agreed on the buying side. When that happened, Piotra would get in touch with Kalinka and set up the transfer.

It was an awkward, irritable time. Kim toyed with bits of fish, tiny squid, prawns, pickled herring he had actually bought at KaDeWe together with crisp small loaves coated with poppy-seed and a bottle of vodka. There was also a small tin of caviare that Piotra had hoisted while he was going through the check-out. They hadn't really enjoyed any of it as much as they had expected to – the marinades seemed too vinegary, they couldn't get the vodka cold enough. It had become the sort of situation, mid-afternoon, too hot with the fan-heater going, when, if she had been an attractive male, or a male Kim was fond of, he would have knelt beside her and started sex-play. Next best thing were the spliffs they were smoking.

She read his thoughts, dropped the magazine to the floor without letting go of it.

'You can stick it up my bum, if you want to,' she said. 'Might put you in a better mood.'

'Piss off, darling.'

She wrinkled up her top lip, lifted the magazine again, pulled her knees up, rested it against her raised thighs.

'Only trying to help. Put some music on.'

'Oh, for Christ's sake, I don't know. Something cheerful.'

He chewed on an olive, spat the pit so it clanged on the heater.

She turned her head towards him again. 'If this is domesticity, then thank God—'

And she was cut off by the burbling of the mobile which was lying on the floor beside her. She hoisted the aerial.

'It's not working,' she said.

'Press the dinky button with a picture of a telephone on it.'

'Oh yes.' Then: 'El? Yes. . . . Yes. . . . I think so. Look. I'll get on to him and phone you back . . . *Not* on this? Public phone? Oh, all right. What else? . . . Yes . . . I see. Well, I suppose I see.'

She pushed back the aerial.

'And the telephone-thingy button again. So the little light goes out. Otherwise the battery runs down.'

'I know how it feels.'

He hoisted himself forward, put big hands on the knees of the 501s Piotra had 'found' for him in the Winterfeldt-markt. He doubted they were genuine.

'So?'

'So. She'll have the twelve million marks by the day after tomorrow in negotiable financial instruments.'

'I beg your pardon?'

'A negotiable financial instrument is currency or anything that can be exchanged for currency with no hassle. The fact you have it in your hand is proof of ownership.'

'I'm with you. Like diamonds, or gold, or enriched uranium—'

'Or bearer bonds. I'm certainly not taking enriched uranium.'

'Bonds can be forged.'

'Kim, you're pissing me about. You knew all along what a negotiable financial—'

'Sorry, darling. Go on. The details. Les détails. Or should that be détaux? Go on, anyway.'

But she had stopped, was looking up at him from the sofa. There was a grin on his face like a Cheshire cat's. The muscles in her own cheeks were beginning to ache too. It was the thought of the million marks each they would take away from the deal. Round aboout 430K in sterling. Enough. They were both getting off on it, higher than the vodka and pot would ever hoist them.

'The details. The canals and the Oder are thawing. They won't freeze again. The buyers want the trains shunted to the container port at Rybocice by noon the day after tomorrow. They'll provide the barges. Kalinka has to organise the loading. Once the barges are loaded, the containers cease to be his, or ours, they become the Sheens' and the Sheens hand over the twelve million. We give Kalinka ten, keep our cut—'

Kim started singing, bass-baritone: 'Freude, Freude, ray of mirth and rapture blended, tochter aus Elysium—'

'That will do. This is not a football match. There's something else, though. Two things. If I have to get in touch with the Sheens I'm to do it by payphone and make sure I'm not followed on my way to it. The same when I phone Kalinka, which I must do this evening. Secondly, if the Serbs contact us and ask why the delay, we're to say it's because Kalinka needs the time.'

'So the Serbs are the buyers.'

'Looks like it.'

'But they're shits. Bastards. Look what they did . . . to you, to Kruno . . .'

'I know. But I think the Sheens are up to something. There's more going on than El said on the phone.'

The high euphoria was shifting gear. Still there, but cut with danger.

'I'll take my cannon.'

'Please.'

'And what about him.' Kim jerked his head towards the blood-red boarding.

'He's been there twice this year. He won't want to go again.'

Kim collapsed back into his chair, Piotra on to the sofa. They grinned at each other again, the grins getting broader. He passed the vodka across and she took a pull while he rolled another spliff.

'How about the music, then?'

He put on a Schubert trio. The one you hear in *Barry Lyndon*.

'What the fuck's that? Play Lou Reed. Play "Walk on the Wild Side".'

He sang along. Doo-de-doo-de, de-doo-de-doo-doo. What the coloured girls say.

'Take your clothes off.'

'No. You.'

He did.

Later, when it was almost dark and they were watching his video of *Casablanca* and he was trying to persuade her that the relationship between Rick and the French policeman was not as innocent as you might think, he suddenly broke off.

'There are coincidences here, you know.'

'There are?'

'I arrive in this room. A few days later Jace and Ash

get in touch and ask me to find out if anyone knows of four train-loads of Russian ammunition in Poland. And then I find I'm sharing the premises with a weird old guy *and* a dike who both seem to have an in to these trains. One way or another.'

'Don't worry about it, darling.'

'Darling?'

'Just the way *you* call people darling.'

'Ah.'

She reached forward, killed the video.

'Play it again, sometime,' she said. 'Now listen. I've got to go out and phone Walery. I want you to come with me, check I'm not being followed, that I'm clean.'

'Walery?'

'Kalinka.' But a swift blush rose up her neck as she pulled on her outside clothes. She went on hurriedly: 'For a start we'll go out through the roof.'

Kim looked at her back for a moment, his face suddenly serious. Then he shrugged. Even though he felt certain now that there were deep structures supporting the whole affair which were completely hidden from him, there was no reason to suppose that the loot, the pay-offs, would not be genuine.

He took out the screws, lifted out the board. Piotra followed him down the narrow tunnel to the lift-shaft. They went round it into Fritz's tiny lair, following the pencil-beam of Piotra's torch. The old man stirred in his nest of blankets, coats and so on, but did not apparently wake up. Piotra led the way down the passage beyond the lift-shaft for about the same distance again, before taking a ninety-degree turn to the left. They could now stand fully upright, going as it were down a central aisle. Only where there were chimney-stacks did they have to duck into a side passage up against the steeper part of the roof. Kim realised they were walking above the rooms that looked out on to the courtyard below and backed on to the block next door. There was a lot of dust and grime, signs of mice and occasionally the swift skittering of fleeing claws, but few cobwebs and none around their actual route. Kim guessed that this was because Fritz, and perhaps Piotra too, used this way in and out quite frequently.

Presently Piotra ducked to the right under low angled timbers. The torch showed a small triangular door. She pushed it open on to darkness. On the other side there was a short but steep flight of stairs down into a long corridor.

'Herberge Mannheim, Mannheimer Straße,' Piotra whispered. 'Cheap hotel. Pension really.'

The hotel occupied the top two floors, the next two were offices much like those in Brandenburgische Straße, the ground floor a small supermarket on one side of the entrance, an electrical goods shop on the other. Piotra walked a block down on to Berliner Straße. Kim hung back. It seemed pretty impossible that she should have a tail and after she had crossed the wide boulevard, walking east away from the Wilmersdorf cemetery and crematorium, he was pretty sure she hadn't. She crossed back to telephone booths close to the Blißestraße U-Bahn entrance and he waved a hand to signify she was tail-free. The call to Kalinka, *Walery* Kalinka, took a full ten minutes.

CHAPTER 25

In his office in Burg, Herr Secretary Drenkmann dismissed his PA for the evening, used rheostats to lower the lights in his huge office, poured himself classic cognac from Waterford cut crystal into a smaller vessel, also Waterford cut crystal, the set a present given at an EU Dublin conference on security two years before. Then he put aside his pipe and slowly prepared a Romeo y Julieta. He took it from the humidor he had inherited from his father, clipped it with cutters, sucked the end with relish. He used remote control to bring on Bruckner's Fourth, the 'Romantic', and then lit the cigar. It, with twenty siblings, had been a present from his opposite number in Dresden – the GDR had after all been privileged in many ways barred to the West, and Cuban cigars had been one of them. Tons of them had been chilled as soon as re-unification was on the cards.

The lush music and the heavenly smoke filled the room.

All this was so he could calm himself and get his head together. The whole plot, complicated from the start, had become impossibly over-complicated. The committee as a whole had been desperately over-anxious to foresee every possible snag. Discipline and order. Every cushion correctly placed at the back of the chair or sofa and correctly dented. Back-ups there if something went wrong. Thoroughness. The half-dozen men who had put it together under his chairmanship had competed with each other to think out every tiny detail, foresee every eventuality. Since Frederick the Great had won battles by putting men in double or triple lines, and made them march in step and fire their muskets all at once, even when round shot was tearing them apart, their culture and upbringing had demanded that this should be so.

But the committee was also a collection of individuals, each of whom wished to leave his imprint on what happened – thus none wanted to be blamed for neglecting some possible eventuality, and all could reap praise and promotion from their masters when it all worked out right.

And now it was out of hand, getting away from him. There were too many strands, too many people involved. Fechter had gone ballistic over Arslan and now she was in orbit over this Norbert Eintner. Drenkmann realised he should never have involved her. But the committee had ruled that there should be a competent and wholly incorruptible police officer on hand at the end who would, if the whole affair finally leaked into the media after all, testify that the final conflagration was an accident, the result of a wholly different operation regarding missing trains filled with Russian ammunition. And since they had been at pains to convince everyone that four trains had gone missing, it would be reprehensible of them not to put in motion an investigation targeted on finding them.

Kalinka, Walery Kalinka, had turned out to be a far cleverer person than any of them had suspected, and greedy with it. Perhaps his sister, Wisa, was the brainy one – anyway they made a formidable team. Piotra Grabowski it now seemed might have been involved right from the start – they should never have accepted her apparently fortuitous intervention so readily. And of course, though the Bosnians, both Serbs and Moslems, had turned out much as they had supposed they would, the Serbs had been more ruthless than they had expected, and the Moslems more resourceful where raising money was concerned.

Of course he was sorry about Firat Arslan. And at this point in his cogitations, Drenkmann pulled his big fat palms down over his flabby cheeks – he really was genuinely sorry, for there would be no more holidays with Firat's father, ex-Commissioner Nur Arslan, on the banks of the Bosphorus nor in his delightful Black Sea villa. No, it was more than that. He really was sorry, dreaded having to make the phone call the situation demanded to a bereaved father. And mother.

The other consequence was that all the agencies available were now interfering and doing their damnedest to uncover Arslan's killers. And if he wasn't careful, they'd be doing the same to find out where Eintner was.

He put aside his cigar, put Bruckner to sleep, picked up the phone.

'Frau Fechter? I can assure you KOK Eintner is alive and well and in the custody of the Bundeskriminalamt. No, I am not going to say why. Oh, you know why. He phoned you ... Where from? ... I see. Well in that case I'll arrange for him to rejoin you tomorrow morning. Yes. Yes ... I do concede there may be more to this than ... Oh, very well, yes? Frau Fechter ...?'

For a moment his face went white then flushed. His blood pressure tablets? But no, the moment had passed. Admittedly he had heard a phone ringing at the other end on another line. All the same. It was twenty years since anyone had hung up on Herr Drenkmann. And that had been a woman too. His first wife.

The telephone buzzed before he could restore Bruckner to life and salvage his cigar.

The voice in his ear told him that a María Carmen López Ortega had rung from an apartment in Siegfried Weg. She and a baby called Karl-Rosa were about to be taken to an unknown destination. They would be killed if the investigation into Firat Arslan's murder was not put on hold for forty-eight hours.

It was too much for Herr Secretary Drenkmann. And on top of everything else his half-smoked Romeo y Julieta had gone out. One never relights a good cigar.

The phone again. He looked at it. It could only be one person. In the last few minutes the kidnappers would have been in touch with EKHK Fechter.

He stood up, pushed back his huge chair, wove his way across the Aubusson carpet, and, the phone still ringing in his ears, let himself out.

CHAPTER 26

During the next thirty-six hours all the principal parties made plans or adjusted their plans according to what they knew. None of them knew enough.

Through Fred and Karl, the Serbs knew that Sheen Associates were still in touch with Moslem money, and that El and Jace had visited the female leader of a special police group investigating the missing trains. They were not too bothered about the first. They still had an army and as far as they knew the Moslems did not. If the Brits who had been on the scene before showed up, they reckoned they could handle them. And Renata Fechter they had sidelined by kidnapping her son and his nanny.

Deniz Enver and her associates also knew that El and Jace had been in touch with Fechter and that the Serbs, anyway Vojislav Milošević, had visited Sheen Associates but that had been before Sheen Associates came to Enver's penthouse apartment. Enver believed her offer to top whatever the Serbs could pay would look after that aspect. As far as Fechter was concerned, well, Enver made enquiries and was pretty sure that El and Jace had been called in to be questioned about Firat's murder. According to her source, that was now the prime concern in Keithstraße.

Kim now felt pretty sure that Piotra was far more deeply involved from the beginning than he had ever suspected. There was nothing he could do about it except ride with it and hope. He was bothered about Fritz, though. Piotra knew this but was not sure how deep

Kim's suspicions were or how much the prospect of a
million marks would outweigh them. She hoped that the
physical intimacies they had at last shared would cement
the bond that already existed between them – he had
seemed pleased enough at the time and although he did
not ask for a repeat she felt there was a sense of collusion
between them, a shared conspiracy that went deeper than
it had.

Renata Fechter knew now that the Russian ammunition had gone back to Moscow or wherever in thirty-
eight trains, not forty-two, and that probably, certainly
possibly, the German government had arranged or colluded with the deception that left everyone looking for
four missing trains. Just why, and why she had been
asked to find the non-existent trains, bothered her. She'd
worried at this like a puppy with a bone all through the
evening. She knew that all the activity they had stumbled
on, or got a sense of, was not about nothing. The torture
and murder of Arslan proved that, the bodies of Moslem
Serbs on the west bank of the Oder. And then, at ten
o'clock, had come the news of her son's kidnap together
with an anonymous phone call telling her that if she
backed off the case for forty-eight hours, he and Carmen
would be all right.

Her first reaction had been a powerful mixture of anger
and despair. She spent an hour with Karin Lietze,
shouting, sobbing, finally talking it through. At the end
of the hour, towards midnight, and with the backing of
the senior police officer in charge of the Berlin Regional
State Security Section, she had conceded two things. One.
That there was nothing she could do about the kidnapping. The appropriate departments, in Burg and Berlin,
would already be taking all the necessary steps following
established and well-tried procedures. She knew very
well, but Karin had to make her reaffirm her faith again

and again, through coffee and the cigarillos Karin smoked, the same brand as Piotra's, that the first aim of these procedures was always the welfare of the victims; denying the kidnapper's demands and apprehending them always came second. Other countries might have less civilised approaches to these sorts of problems, but not Germany.

Nothing she could do about it. So. Two. For the forty-eight hours she must take a back seat. She, Sharon and Einstein–Eintner must stay overtly out of touch with the police and the authorities, in the public rooms of her hotel. As Karin kept insisting, this was no dereliction of duty: the four trains Renata had been told to find did not exist.

The fact that Piotra and Karin smoked the same brand of cigarillo was the only genuine coincidence in the whole affair.

First thing in the morning of the middle day Jace went back to the Galway Irish Pub. Problem. With the thaw the contractors were taking on hands again. Since the first-in, last-out routine, prevailed he found that only Daffydd, the ex-para afro from Cardiff, and Alec were immediately available. The Tynesiders, Andy and Jimmie, both of them steel-fixers, were already, with a score or so of their mates, weaving vast trellises of steel rod for an underground carpark on the Checkpoint Charlie development. Jace drove the short distance south across the Unter den Linden leaving the Reichstag and the Brandenburg Gate on his right, and then got badly snarled up with all the construction work on Friedrichstraße. Never in his life had he seen such a mess, as the thirty or forty sites struggled through slush and mud to get going again.

Forced into several detours he eventually managed to

grab a space between the British Bookshop and the glossy offices of the Checkpoint Charlie Bauprojekt Gmbh. He crossed the road to a wooden walkway above a huge square hole in the ground just north of the signal-box-like watch-tower that had once dominated the checkpoint. He'd spent some of the most boring hours of his life in it. Were they going to keep it as a memento of evil times, or had they just forgotten to pull it down?

He looked down into the hole. Not easy to pick out Andy's red hair or Jimmie's yellow under the hard hats below, but quite soon Andy spotted him, came over, looked up, shielding his eyes against the sky with heavy-duty rubberised gloves.

'I need you tomorrow, mate,' Jason bellowed, above the noise of machinery.

He couldn't hear the answer above the cacophony of turning machinery, dumper trucks and the clang of steel rods dropped. But he could lip-read it.

'No chance.'

He turned, and saw a round little man with dark hair almost to his shoulders turning away to look at a display in the bookshop window featuring Britain's Queen of Crime. Jace crossed the road, took him by the elbow. Yes. The same guy who had spent a lot of time yesterday at the hotel bar. Gently but firmly he led him across the narrowed road, then backed him into the timber fence. With his left hand he grasped his collar and tie, and with his right he got hold of his scrotum. Then he hoisted him on to the top of the fence. He let the round little man sense the thirty-foot drop beneath him.

'If I ever see you again,' he said in German, 'I'll make sure they come away in my hand.'

He dropped him on to the walkway.

'As it is,' he went, 'you'd do well to count them when you get home.'

Private eye Karl turned to the fence, supported himself on it on his forearms and let out a soundless scream. Well, with all the noise, it seemed soundless.

Jace walked away, but somehow got the feeling that the old lady whose photograph was the centre of the window display (he had no idea who she was) was looking at him with stern disapproval. Often the way with old ladies, as far as he was concerned.

Jace found a payphone and rang his twin in Hamburg.

'Ash? We need a couple of bricks. The real thing.'

'Eight men? Actual squaddies?'

'Not squaddies, Ash. I want them hard. Milk-trays. The genuine article.'

'You got to be joking. When?'

'I want them here this evening in their own cars, or by train, not more than two travelling together. They find their own accommodation and phone in to me at the Seehof.'

'How much?'

'Well, you come too, that'll make ten, let's say we split a million ten ways. Marks, of course.'

'It's beginning to sound possible. They won't be tooled up, though. I mean they can get off the base all right, but not with hardware.'

'I reckon I've got enough here already.'

'How long is this going to take?'

'They can be back on base tomorrow night. If they want to be. No one need know they've gone.'

'I'll try, Jace. I'll try.'

The payphone wasn't tapped, but by then Ass'nJass was. Twenty minutes later Drenkmann was reading a trans-lated transcript of the conversation off his desk-top VDT. The translator had even worked out that a milk-tray was a member of the SAS and had put a translator's footnote to explain why. Seemed far-fetched to Drenkmann, but he was prepared to write it off as an example of English humour. He thought it all through. It took a pipeful of Whisky Flake. Then his floppy jowls relaxed into a sort of grin and he reached across to his personal scrambled phone. His podgy fingers dabbed in the numbers for the first of several calls, the last of which was to the Chancellery in Bonn. It could, he reckoned, work out well. The people he spoke to agreed with him that it could.

'Poof, it's stuffy in here.'

Piotra threw open the tiny dormer window.

'Hey, look at this.'

A swift shadow passed across the top of the window frame. She rushed on.

'He or she, I don't know how you think you can tell the difference when they're not together, but I guess it must have been Mum ... with a twig in her beak. Isn't that marvellous? Isn't that great?'

There was something unsatisfactory in her enthusiasm. Lacked, Kim thought, the ring of confidence. She rushed on.

'I mean, it must mean they're building a nest, mustn't it?'

She turned to stop him before he could come any nearer. She was fully dressed in jeans and black leather bomber. He was still in briefs and a black T-shirt decorated with Saul Bass's story-board for the shower scene in *Psycho*. She picked up her trilby, snapped the brim down.

'Anyway, I'm off out for a bit.'

'Where to?'

'Nowhere in particular. Have a look at my room, make sure everything's OK. That sort of thing.' She moved towards the door. 'One thing,' she said. 'I'll go out the front way. You can watch from the studio window and see how many tails I pick up. Be a laugh, really.'

'Hang on.' He pulled on his black 501s, struggled with stiff buttons, pushed in the shirt, tightened the alligator belt. Both belt and shirt had also been 'presents' from her. She admired but felt little desire for his lean, muscled torso, hips, thighs and bum which she knew were tough and tight in spite of the slight bagginess of the jeans. He pushed fingers through his long hair, looked round for a band to tie up his ponytail.

'You're not coming with me,' she said, as he thumbed his heels into loafers.

'Oh. All right.'

'I said, watch what happens from the window.'

He followed her down the stairs, undid the locks he had put in for her. He suddenly wanted to ask her how long she'd be, but he knew that that sort of question arouses suspicion. He re-locked the doors behind her, went to the window, two floors below the dormer, where Pratchard had rested his document case on the window sill and radiator, looked down into Brandenburgische Straße below. The snow had gone but everything still looked damp and shabby, most of the cars, even the Porsches and larger BMWs, still streaked with black below their fairings. Come the weekend, perhaps their owners would clean them up.

Piotra crossed the street, came into view. She didn't look up or wave, but already he sensed movement, reaction, along the sidewalk. Then without a pause in her stride she swung her leg over the cross-bar of a very old beige-painted bike, with a basket in front, and pedalled off down the bike lane like a scalded cat. It would be an exaggeration to say the street erupted, but to the knowledgeable – and Kim, who had spent days in OPs in the Falls Road area, was knowledgeable – that was what it was like.

Two guys in leather jackets, crewcuts, pounded down the lane after her and sent a courier with long hair and knee-pads arse over tip into a litter bin, a green and white polizei car did a U-turn in front of a double-decker bus, two men in long raincoats and trilbies folded up their newspapers, shrugged and walked away in opposite directions. And an old man with a high, beaked nose, in a shabby black coat and a soggy, floppy woollen hat, who had been prodding the litter bin with a short stick, hoisted his obviously weighty supermarket carrier over his shoulder and set off in the opposite direction from Piotra. Fritz.

Kim went back up the stairs, pulled back the sofa, pulled out the screws, picked up a torch, stuck his Smith & Wesson in his belt and made his way down the narrow, low passage. The peregrines above him mewed to each other, not at him. As soon as he got round the lift-shaft he knew that Fritz was not simply out but had flitted. Some blankets and rags still remained, and the old musty smell. But everything else had gone, including the uniform. The only other thing that remained was the skull, the skull they had jokingly named Martin Bormann.

Then he heard them. Two men, he reckoned, in the studio below. Climbing the stairs to his room. Talking low in a language he could not understand, though he knew he had heard it recently. He turned off the torch, moved on the balls of his feet down the passage towards the glimmer of light. As he got to the end he realised the language they were speaking was Polish. Question was, would they understand German? Or English?

They were quiet now. Although he had made no sound they must have guessed he was on the other side of the oblong hole in the wall. A sudden scare might give him the advantage. He got within two inches of the hole, could see well into the room, his shelves of books in the alcove between the chimney-breast and the inner wall, took careful aim at a shelf balanced uneasily on bricks which had already fallen down once, and fired. The noise in the space was deafening, books and shelves satisfactorily tumbled about the place.

He came through the gap with a horrendous war-cry, and with the revolver weaving between the two men. One was on his knees with his pistol out but pointing high. He fired and the bullet crashed into the ceiling above Kim's head. Kim fired and smashed his wrist. The second man was through the door and tumbling down the narrow stairs outside. He took part of the banister with him. They were the two men, leather-coated with crew-cuts, who had followed Piotra down the bike lane. She had given them her keys.

'Raus,' Kim shouted. 'Come on, you evil bastards, raus!'

Then, seeing the man he had shot was bleeding and in pain, he picked up a T-shirt of Piotra's and tossed it to him.

'Raus,' he repeated. Bastards could do their own first aid.

The wounded man descended the stairs very gingerly and joined the other in the main part of the studio. Kim waved them on. Halfway across the floor the unwounded man dropped to his knee, came up with a gun. Kim fired but ... nothing. The hammer clicked on to the second chambered round but ... nothing. And at that moment the wounded man, trying to get to the other side of his companion and briefly coming between them, trod on the cartridge that had been left on the floor during the Serbs' second visit. Skidding, he scythed the unharmed man's legs from under him and the battle was over.

Kim took Piotra's keys from them and their guns, pushed them out, re-locked the doors. He went back upstairs and examined the Smith & Wesson. He knew some of the rounds were British with harder caps than American. He knew he had adjusted the main-spring tension to compensate. He could see the tension had been slackened. He was bloody lucky the first round had gone off. Lucky, but saddened too. Only Piotra could have been responsible for slackening the screw. Correction. It might, just, have been Fritz.

Twenty minutes later he was at the lakeside hotel talking to Jace.

'I don't know what the fuck is going on,' he said, 'but it's got right away from me. Mind if I hang out with your lot now?'

'Come aboard, old son, come aboard. We're not as mob-handed as we'd like to be, so you'll be an asset, a real asset. Even if you were a fucking rupert.'

'Cut the shit, Jace. On this op, you're the rupert. I'll just do what I'm told.'

The port of Rybocice, a kilometre upstream from the small town, did not look as if it had ever thrived much, certainly not since the demise of the Third Reich when no doubt it had had its place in the web of transport systems that sustained the Wehrmacht on the eastern front. Set in prairie-farmed fields but with dense forest close by, it was little more than a couple of quays on a river that had been turned into a canal. There was a handful of derelict sheds and warehouses, windows broken, set back from the quays. A railway line ran between them and the edge of the quays and between it and the water there were six derricks in working order. They had been adapted to lift stacked timber as well as standard containers. On the cracked flags and cobbles through which the stunted brown stalks of burdock, willow herb and wild lupin poked, a litter of oil drums, broken gear, were reflected in puddles swollen by the thaw, sheened with rust and oil.

Blown bullrushes fringed the opposite bank, which was lined with heavily pollarded willows in front of a large field, newly harrowed and perhaps with a spring sowing of rye or barley already in – here and there dotted over it were bird-scarers of various sorts, conventional scare-crows interspersed with posts carrying strips of flashing, clattering foil. It gave the place the look of a bleak, post-modern sculpture park.

Back on the north side, the single railway line curved away from the buildings and derricks across another patch of open meadow and disappeared into mixed forest, mostly larch and fir but with stands of beech and birch too. Just outside the forest, and still close to the railway, about three hundred metres upstream, there was a bascule bridge, almost exactly like the one Van Gogh painted near Arles, presumably there to carry farm carts and machinery from field to field across the river.

Between the derricks and the brown water below, some ninety or so containers had already been stacked. There were sidings behind the station buildings. One was occupied by a freight train of thirty trucks, each still loaded with one container. At the front, behind the buildings, as though it had just pulled the train in, a steam locomotive, big, black, still fired up, occasionally clanked and pushed gouts of purplish-grey smoke into the air. The smell was a nostalgia trip if you were over fifty.

The morning dawned with thick mist hanging over the river. The weak sun did little to dispel it, though later a breeze and then rain out of the west dispersed it. The trees dripped and the last tranches of snow held in their boughs slithered sloppily to the ground. Although it was no longer freezing, the air was raw and the damp got through to you.

That's what the first men to arrive discovered. They began to filter in in twos and threes from about ten o'clock onwards: four, who had taken the 0907 train from Hauptbahnhof, came in a couple of taxis from Słubice; three who had hitched from Berlin, leaving at dawn, and then walked the four miles from Swiecko, on the Polish side of the autobahn bridge; and four who had hired a VW Golf and a small Opel in Berlin and driven the whole way. The Brownings and HK MPs had been split up between them together with most of the spare ammunition – on the basis that if they lost one group, they could still manage with three, and to lose more than one would be very unfairly against the odds. In the event, all got through. It had, of course, although they did not know this, been arranged by the authorities that they should.

All wore dark clothing, the sort that looks nondescript in a street – jeans, dark shirts, jerseys or leather jackets blue or black, dark woollen hats – but against black earth, rusting metal and tired brick, served well as camouflage.

At just about this time two incidents happened elsewhere. The only genuinely old part of Burg, the only part that had not been firestormed by American planes smashing it to bits with high explosive during the day so that all the timber was shattered and exposed for the RAF incendiaries at night, is close to the railway station. The railway station had of course been a priority target, but was missed. The buildings have medieval brick shells, are narrow and tall and are now among the cheapest housing in the city. Who wants to live in a real old house when a very genuine restoration with all mod cons can be had in the city centre? It was in the attic of one of these old shells that Karl-Rosa's and Carmen's kidnappers hung out. It had most essential utilities but one thing it lacked was formula. Milk-powder for infants.

The two youths, lean, weedy specimens who had been recruited for the job off the street – they hung out on the street most of the time – and had been paid more marks for the job than they had ever seen, spoke almost no German and certainly no Spanish. They had fled from the Moslem village they had previously ethnically cleansed, when it was retaken by the Moslems, and somehow or other they had ended up in Burg. Neither would have been able to put a finger on a map and say: that's Burg.

Karl-Rosa had just been fed when they put their foot in the door of Siegried Weg 6, and fed well, so it wasn't until the next morning that his screams became really insupportable. The lads realised that milk was what was needed. What they could not understand was why Carmen didn't get on and feed him. After all she was hung with containers that looked big enough for quads. At last, one of them, maddened by the baby's howls, took the baby out of her arms, not without a struggle, and tore her cardigan and dress open.

That was enough. Ignoring the knife and the gun they waved at her, Carmen smashed them into unconsciousness with what came to hand, a double electric ring mounted on enamelled iron.

In ten minutes she was at the Central Police station, and within five more Drenkmann out in Gründorf knew she was free and Renata's baby was safe. It was with him but the work of a moment to decide it would be better if Renata continued to believe her baby was under threat for a few more hours at least. With things coming now to a very delicate head, he really did not want another, and often unpredictable, element getting back into the scene.

The men stood around in the lee of one of the decayed buildings and smacked gloved hands together.

Ash called for their attention.

'Right, lads. We've got two hours before the opposition turn up so I'll give you a sit-rep, then we'll look at the small print and finally we'll shake out—'

'Hang on a mo, Ash,' Jace was bustling about the boot of the Opel. He pulled out and set up a four-ring Camping Gaz stove. 'First things first.' A chopping-board, mushrooms, tomatoes, bacon, black pudding, eggs, fresh seeded rolls. A large Kitchen Devil knife flashed over the lot. 'Full English. You need it on a morning like this.'

In her hotel in Kurfürstenstraße Renata Fechter suddenly felt weariness and worry shift again into frustrated

anger. She, King and Eintner were sitting in a wide
lounge. It was low-ceilinged but because the sweep of the
curved window filled half the wall and they were on
the second floor, so that the outlook was over the tops
of the trees in the Tiergarten, it was light and airy. With
potted palms and swiss cheese plants in ceramic holders,
low tables with low-slung chairs, waiters who glided
about as if on wheels to a Mozart-based adagio muzak,
it was an ambience designed to ease the stress of executive lives. In fact it was driving her mad with its slick
banality.

Ten o'clock. The three of them had had German break-
fast, which is like an English one but cold, and were now
sitting in a triangle at a round table. Eintner was reading
the sort of glossy monthly computer nerds love, picking
his nose, and occasionally liberating bogies on to the
underneath of his seat. Sharon, for once wearing a suit,
black with a pencil skirt, over a flame-red silk shirt, was
getting out of her soft leather black bag the things she
would need to do her nails. Emery board, tissues, cotton
wool, acetate, lacquer to match her shirt, gloss. I must,
Renata thought, put a stop to this. She pulled a set of
car keys from her purse, and leant across to her.

'Sharon, I want you to take the Audi, drive to Rzepin,
find out what's going on there. I'm sure Rzepin is the key
to the whole business.'

Sharon King's face lit up in the first big smile she'd
managed since Firat's murder. Moving very briskly, she
put all her gear back into her bag.

'I'll go and change. Won't be a sec.'

Eintner blinked nervily across the table.

'Do you want me to go with her?'

'No, Norbert. We sit this one out. Together. Though how
we're going to pass the time I do not know.'

He looked relieved, hoisted his state-of-the-art lap-top on to the table, clicked it open.

'I've some good games might interest you.'

Oh God. The best, the least awful, will be chess.

'Mah Jong?'

For the first time in their short acquaintance, Renata had discovered something likeable about Norbert.

Walery Kalinka and Wisa joined them just as they were scraping the last traces of food off their plates. He looked down at them, hunkered as they were about the stove and supposed he liked what he saw. But he shuddered. These ten – no, eleven – men, most of them between twenty and thirty, the rest not much older, were as tough, as mean, a lot as he'd ever seen in one place at one time. It was their hardness, their fitness that was so striking. Not an ounce of wasted flesh, not a torso or a limb that wasn't muscled to a perfection that combined strength with agility. Of course he could not see all this but lean, square faces, solid necks, easy, lithe movements, strong, capable hands, said it all. There were a couple of older ones whose heavy moustaches held some grey, and a fair-haired lad whose forelock almost tumbled over his eyes. He was quick and skittish, wired up on the adventure, like a puppy. What it most put him in mind of was a first-class football team, with Kim the odd one out, the goalie perhaps. He was wearing his long black coat, a grey scarf and his floppy beret, and did he? Was he? Yes, painted lips, a hint of blusher, a touch of mascara failing to mask a rather wan, sad look. Yet the others treated him with respect.

Ash called them to order. Almost, but not quite, immediately they settled down, some sitting on the ground with knees pulled up, others hunkered, one or two on the periphery leaning against the nearest trees, facing at least half outwards into the unknown. Walery understood that these had their ears cocked as their eyes wandered into the distances behind them.

'First of all,' said Jace, 'our friend here, Walery Kalinka, will tell you what you need to know about the general situation. Unfortunately, he does not speak English so the lady who is with him will interpret.'

In English it came out like this, in Wisa's high, nasal voice: 'We are selling the contents of these containers to some very dangerous people who should arrive here at midday. The containers become theirs as soon as they are loaded on to barges. The buyers will provide the barges, I think about fifteen of them. They will pay for the goods barge by barge, each barge holding eight containers stacked four on top of four. As I said, these are dangerous people and we have asked you along to make sure that they do not renege on the arrangements or offer any sort of violence or threat. That's what you are here for. Your man in command will tell you how he wants to do it.'

'What's renege, Sarge?' asked the puppy.

'He's so bloody ignorant,' one of the older ones said. 'Go on, Sarge, tell him.'

At nine forty-five Piotra found the '86 Mercedes TE estate she'd wanted to use when meeting Herbert and El at Tegel. Her bunch of keys let her in and she drove it round to the lakeside hotel. There she picked up El.

Once on the Stadtautobahn, the inner freeway box, still uncompleted, she lit a Lucky Luciano and glanced at El's profile. She was more smartly dressed than before, real smartness now, in a really good coat, but her profile remained severe because of the bony largeness of her nose.

'Shouldn't Sam Pratchard be doing this?'

'Maybe.'

'Kitchen too hot for him?'

'Something like that. Yes. He's just too shit-scared to come.'

'Do you think you're up to it?'

El glanced back, her eyes cool, serious, but not worried.

'I've spent several hours with him going over all the known ways of forging high-denomination notes in the principal hard currencies, the more stable of bearer bonds, and so on. He's put all the conversion tables he thinks I might need in this—' she indicated an electronic notebook she held in her lap – 'and I'm not to accept slack beyond one point two five per cent . . . and so on.'

'That's all right, then.'

But it wasn't what Piotra had really meant.

Just before Tempelhof airport she took route ninety-six to the Rangsdorf autobahn access and driving at a steady hundred and twenty kilometres an hour on the autobahn she got them to Rybocice shortly after eleven. On the way they overtook Sharon in a small Audi. El thought she recognised her but, since it was only a glimpse as they swept past, decided to say nothing.

At one o'clock the remaining Sheen Associates, Harry, Herbert and Sam, took a taxi and then the lift to Deniz Enver's apartment.

Meanwhile, at the little river port and rail terminal itself, activity continued to build. Ash gave the men roles, and hardware to fit their roles. Four of them were to remain in the forest edge – in the first instance to counter any cover operation the Serbs might have planned, in the second to provide a reinforcing wave if the inner core got into difficulties. Ash led this outer group. The next four, three regulars from the NATO Special Services lines near Hamburg, plus Kim, were placed in cover around the quays, each given a very specific area to control, to mini- mise the risk of direct or ricocheted friendly fire finding the wrong target.

Finally Jace and the two oldest men from Hamburg were to remain in the open and overtly armed. It was clear that the Serbs would expect an armed presence – if there was none visible they would be suspicious. All the men, apart from Jace, painted up hands and faces in black and grey displaced pattern camouflage. The only serious worry they had was that they might be over- whelmingly outnumbered and outgunned.

More Poles filtered in, about eight of them. They were clearly workmen, presumably railwaymen, who acknowl- edged Kalinka as their leader. For the most part they wore oilskin peaked caps, heavy-duty jackets in the same material, heavy canvas trousers, boots oil-stained and heavy. They were all at least forty years old, some a lot older. One wore a red star in the band of his cap, another a tiny hammer and sickle. They were, Kim thought, dinosaurs, strange survivors from a previous era, the Iron Age. It had had a good run, more than two thousand years, but now it was over.

They threw heavy switches and diesel generators spluttered into life, they swung the derricks so that the giant hooks and claws pendulumed slowly out over the river and gently clanged above the almost still water. Moorhens feeding off the remains of eleven English breakfasts scuttled for the far bank, leaving silvery arrows behind them, a little grebe closed hatches and dived, a heron hoisted itself on slate-coloured wings and, trailing spiky feet behind its tail, flapped lazily away into the mist.

The SAS sergeant coughed discreetly behind Jason's back.

'You know, Jace, what we could really have done with is a couple of stun grenades.'

'Maybe.' Dismissive. But to himself: I should cocoa. We're taking no prisoners today, thank you very much.

The slipways north to Frankfurt an der Oder and south to Eisenhüttenstadt and Cottbus, a sign: Staatsgrenz – Polen (Swiecko) 4km. From the high embankment they could see the spires of the big brick churches, the monolithic tower blocks from the days of the GDR.

Piotra let her gloved right hand fall on El's knee.

'Nervous?'

'A little.'

'You should be. But you took it well the other day.'

'Nothing happened to me. Just a badly bruised knee. Where did you get this car?' It had been bothering El ever since she got into it, remembering the little Peugeot filled with cigarette ends that weren't Piotra's, remembering how it had blown up.

'Xantener Straße.'

'It's not yours.'

'No.'

'Won't the frontier police spot it's stolen? From the licence plate?'

'It won't be reported stolen until five o'clock. By then I'll have it back where I took it from.'

El pushed her painted nails through her platinum mane, pursed her Lana Turner lips, let her fingers run across the black fur lapels of the charcoal-grey suede jacket Jace had bought her, and finally made a decision.

'They're going to kill the Serbs,' she said, keeping her voice level, trying not to hurry it. 'Jace has got some real soldiers in from Hamburg. The deal is, all the Serbs get killed. Pay-off for the other day. Paid for by these Moslem millionaires. So there's going to be shooting. I thought you ought to know.'

Piotra glanced at her, then shifted down a gear as the tail-back to the bridge came into view.

'Passport time. You did bring one?'

El smiled. 'Of course.'

The car came to a halt. Piotra stretched her legs, lit a cigarillo, wound the window down.

'Of course,' she said, blowing smoke out, 'I knew there was a strong likelihood that things might turn nasty. But it's another thing to know, know for sure that they're going to.'

And again she patted El's knee. El wished she wouldn't.

They reached the quay twenty minutes later. Piotra parked in the vehicle park just below the sidings, got out and looked around. Four other cars already there, Polish railway workers, no soldiers that she could see, but then she rather supposed that was the point, wasn't it? As she looked around, the air briefly stirred and the mist across the meadow shredded before re-forming. A cackle of crows lifted from distant treetops and settled back. Head up, she sniffed.

'Change in the weather,' she murmured, and pulled her trilby down more firmly over her cropped hair.

Walery Kalinka and Wisa stepped out from beneath one of the low cast-iron and broken glass porches that covered the land-side entrances to the buildings. With the warehouses they formed a sort of small square or plaza. It even had a well in the middle with wrought-iron hoops above it. Piotra walked briskly, almost trotted, over to them and embraced them warmly, Wisa first.

Very warmly, Kim thought. He was standing in the corner of a first-floor window in the three-storey warehouse next door. Of course, she doesn't know I'm here watching her. She thinks I've been killed by the two Poles she sicked on me. Up till then it hadn't got to him how deeply betrayed he felt. Perhaps, though, trying to cheer himself up, they were just there to incapacitate me or make some sort of a prisoner of me. Ah well. Whatever. A learning experience.

He'd been looking down. Now he looked out. An HK MP5k stuck in the deep pocket of his overcoat, as many magazines as all his other pockets would hold, and his Smith & Wesson in his belt, and suddenly he knew Ash had made a fundamental mistake. As he moved off to find him, clanking in a muffled sort of way as he did so, he reflected that the thing about learning situations is — you learn from them.

At ten past twelve, just when they were beginning to look at their watches and wonder, they heard a distant ticking chug of diesel and then saw nosing round the bend, half a kilometre to the west and with the quickening breeze behind it, the first of the barges. It was twenty metres long, three wide, had a snub bow that lifted just a little higher from the water than the rest and cut a white cicatrice out of the grey water below the hieroglyphic-like marks of its loading-lines. It was followed by three more. Six or seven armed men were cramped into the very small cockpits at the stern of each barge. The final barge flew a stained, threadbare flag from its stern – mucky though it was, it was clearly a Swiss white cross on a red background. Its name, in floriated capitals, was *Friedrich Dürenmatt* and it was registered, in modern sans serif, in Basel. Which, Kim recollected, has a free port on the Rhine and is at the heart of Europe's waterway system. No doubt the Serbs planned to get the containers illegally bonded – if they could, they would be able to get them an awful long way before anyone felt the need to open them.

At the back of the quay Jace waited, his arm round El's waist. The two SAS sergeants stood in front of them, half shielding them, with Wisa, Piotra and Walery in the rear. Walery was struggling not to cough.

CHAPTER 29

The leading barge, towing the second and third, nudged into the quay beneath the derricks. The fourth, under its own power, seemed to drift across the stream to the other bank. A man at the bow leapt across the small space on to the grassy bank on the other side, made a painter fast to one of the pollarded willows and then caught the automatic rifle one of the men on the barge chucked to him. He ducked behind the tree bole and Kim heard the double click as he folded out the butt and operated the cocking mechanism. An AKS 74, Kim reckoned, 5.45mm and very similar in design to the old Kalashnikovs except that it was far more accurate on single shot and had a higher rate of fire on auto.

Covered by him, three more men crossed on to the southern bank and took up similar positions in reasonably protective cover. One of them carried a much longer weapon than the others. Kim recognised it as a Dragunov sniper's rifle but without the telescopic sight – unless the guy who carried it was about to find one in the black webbing rucksack he had on his back. At fifty metres, which was about the distance that separated the sniper from the men on the other side, you'd only have to leave half a cheek and an ear, the ball-and-socket joint of your shoulder, exposed and he'd have you out.

These, Kim thought, are not street-fighters, ethnic cleansers, bully-boys like the ones we've dealt with or seen in action. These are the real thing – men who have been trained for open-country infantry combat, and probably seen it as well. If the whole contingent is like that, we're in for a high old time.

But that was not the case. The twelve or so men who disembarked under the derricks and closed round the compact figure of Vojislav Milošević with his silver crewcut were, for the most part, the gang who had murdered the Moslems in the forest behind Rzepin, though Jace, facing Milošević but letting his calculating eyes flicker briefly over the rest, reckoned there might be three new faces.

Like the Brits they were dressed in a mixture of darkish clothes, leathers and denim predominating, though there were quilted waistcoats as well – the sort of thing which in winter would not draw attention anywhere where men might be found working outside. They carried duffel bags and as soon as they had landed briskly took from them an assortment of weapons, some of which had to be assembled. There were Yugoslav versions of the old AK 7.62mm automatic rifles, Zastava M85 sub-machineguns and Zastava 9mm parabellum pistols. Milošević himself had a chrome-plated Zastava revolver built to use .357 Magnum. Who does he think he is? thought Jace, Dirty Harry?

As far as he could see, no grenades or grenade-launchers. Which was a relief. Unless the bastards on the other side of the river were tooled up with them.

Milošević opened his palm by the side of his leg and said something in Serbo-Croat. A man behind him put into it the handle of a large, old-fashioned, rigid aluminium document case.

'Procedures,' he said, in English, but slurring or lisping on the sibilants.

El pushed herself forward.

'Nothing elaborate,' she said, her voice cool. 'You give

us the money, we check it, then we put the containers on your barges.'

He smiled at Jace, small piggy teeth, many capped in some grey metal, added a shrug, made it male complicity in the face of feminine naivety.

'See nothing wrong with that,' Jace growled.

They haggled for half an hour. First Milošević wanted to make random checks that the containers contained what he was there to buy. Jace and Walery argued that if that happened more than three or four times they'd not be through by dark. Walery produced sheets and sheets of printout, manifests for the four trains, the one hundred and twenty containers. Each container was numbered, and the manifests said what was in them. The document- ation was in German, Polish and Russian. Milošević had with him a railway worker from Belgrade who was used to such documents and could read Russian. From the first tranche of containers he picked three. El intervened. Before any containers were opened, she wanted to check the authenticity of his negotiable financial instruments. Milošević said, sure, to the value of three containers. Kalinka pointed out that if the Serbs were going to check every round of ammunition or whatever in every con- tainer, and El was going to check every scrap of paper, it would take a week and the Polish authorities would be helping them do it before the week was up.

They could check the three containers they had picked. After that, since each barge could carry eight containers, four on four, Milošević would hand over NFIs in batches to the value of four containers as they were loaded. El would check them. And, Piotra added, out of each batch hand over to her what she was owed, which she would then pass on to Walery and Wisa, less her agent's fee.

Jace insisted on one final condition. All Milošević's men would remain within a carefully subscribed area between the quay, the first of the derricks, the main building and the first of the warehouses, that is, in the square-like space round the well. If they crossed those perimeters the deal was off. If they showed any sign at all of hostile behaviour or of trying to get behind Jason and his two bodyguards, they'd be fired on. Milošević glanced up at the empty window-frames that looked down on the area, out into the carpark, at the still clanking and hissing locomotive. A shadow where no shadow should be, an empty car that rocked a little – he chewed his lip, and nodded.

They got down to it.

Sharon parked the Audi at the barrier Walery had taken them to before, a kilometre or more from the main mar-shalling-yards. There was no one about. The red and white counterbalanced barrier was not locked and tipped up with satisfactory ease when she lifted it. She walked into the area, looked around. There were a few old waggons standing in sidings like old cart-horses hoping they'll never be called upon again to move. A couple of diesel-shunters also, it seemed, trying not to be noticed. Not much else. The forest was a dark presence all round but alive, almost tingling, as the last snow and frost slipped to the floor and branches shrugged and shook as they got free of them. Everything dripped, was wet, but, on a breeze, a brief beam of sunlight made it all shine and glitter for a moment. Then the gloom returned, thicker, it seemed, than before.

She drove the Audi up to the steps of the two-storey shoe-box which Kalinka had taken them to before. Two of the metal-framed windows and the rough stucco around them were blackened. She went up the stairs. The red paint, rubberised cement, whatever, was even stickier than before.

The room where Kalinka had said the records of freight
through Rzepin were kept had been gutted, and not just
by fire. The steel cabinets had gone, apart from a couple
that lay on their sides on the floor with hanging files
spilling out like the innards of eviscerated animals. A
filing-cabinet, also on its side, with drawers in-out, in-
out, in-out, looked like a sow imagined by Tanguy. Chairs
were smashed where they had not burnt – indeed, and
Sharon was after all a policeperson, they looked like
chairs that had been smashed so they could be burnt.

Among it all, on a table, she found Firat's Zippo. She
knew it was his: it had a red crescent and star on it, had
been a gift bought from Kizilay, Red Moon, the Turkish
equivalent of the Red Cross. She put it in the breast
pocket of her sheepskin jacket and knew she would
keep it.

She went to one of the glassless windows overlooking
the yard. She could see that a single line led off into the
forest, and – her eyes were good – that the counterbalanced points-shifting system had recently been greased.
She checked others. They were red with rust.

Sharon went back down the stairs, checked the Audi
was locked, and set off down the single-line track – the
rails gleamed here and there or were black rather than
red. They took her into the forest. She did not have far
to go. What she was heading for, though she did not of
course know this, was a spur off a spur off the main
marshalling-yards of Rzepin. After walking down the
middle of the track for less than ten minutes she found
herself in another clearing. This was where the four
freight trains had been parked, where the Serbs had
massacred the Moslems and the Brits had looked after
themselves – but Sharon knew none of that, and now the
whole area, the sidings and the rest, was empty. But she
could see again that steel wheels had recently gone back

and forth over the rails and the points had changed, probably quite often, that the track had been used recently. She felt certain that four, five? three? but why not four? trains had been parked here recently and then moved out. Where to?

She scouted about a bit more, the black boots she wore over thick black woollen leggings squelching in the mud or awkward on the heavy-duty ballast between the rails. Back the way she had come was the obvious answer – but at the furthest end of the clearing she realised that the linking line of track that passed across the top of the sidings wound on into the forest and that, though the rails themselves were rusty, there were still footprints in the melting slush on the ties between the rails. OK, she said to herself, let's see who's been here before me.

Fritz was who.

As she stepped into a long crescent-shaped clearing, and briefly had time to take in the presence of a long train of bleached wooden waggons, suddenly lit again by sunshine, almost white against the black of the forest, she heard a twig snap.

'Please to put your hands on your head.'

He spoke in heavily accented English – because she was black he did not expect her to understand German.

For a couple of hours it went well. Milošević checked three containers from the first twelve and was satisfied with what he found. El scrutinised the paper he gave her, high-denomination banknotes and Euro bearer bonds, issued to finance hydroelectric schemes in north Italy, the building of a new container port five miles from Swansea, that sort of thing. They certainly met the criteria Sam Pratchard had given her. Using her calculator and the financial pages of that morning's *Frankfurter Zeitung* she valued them and parcelled out Piotra's share. As she did this, on the greasy floor of a clapped-out canal port some-where in Poland, she began to experience a steadily increasing glow of euphoria. It was incredible, crazy, out of it. Here she was, slowly putting together six million marks for Sheen Associates, two and a half million quid, all to be stacked in cases she'd brought from the hotel, now in the back of Piotra's hoisted Merc estate. Even after expenses they'd clear two mil sterling. And that was without what the Moslems would pay . . .

And then, and her heart fluttered at the thought, but more with a terrible anticipation than real fear, there was the battle to come. Occasionally she looked up at Jace, at the two SAS sergeants beside him, and she realised that they too were hyped up, were getting high on the same anticipation as she was, their faces a shade paler beneath the bronze tans, their knuckles showing white where they gripped the stocks of their Heckler and Koch machine-pistols, a sheen of sweat forming on the backs of their solid, bull-like necks.

There was a plan. Presently, when she had a stack of paper big enough to warrant it, she would excuse herself, go back to the Merc and come back with a case. And when that case was full she would take it back to the Merc, saying she intended to bring a second. But this time, once she was by the vehicle she'd walk briskly across ten yards of open ground to put the furthest warehouse between her and the quay, and as soon as she was out of sight Ash and his eleven men would take what he called pre-planned pre-emptive action.

It did not work out like that. Battles never do. By two o'clock, when the ninth to twelfth barges were being manoeuvred alongside the quays, the breeze briefly gusted and brought with it out of the west a sudden sharp squall. The heavy drops, almost hail, pocked the water with white and broke in tiny shell-bursts on the greasy flags and cobbles. Milošević snapped his case shut, straightened, pulled up his collar, cursed. Then, as the rain stopped almost as suddenly as it had started, he walked out from under the mostly broken glass and cast-iron porch and stood for a moment on the edge of the quay, looking along it to the stern of the twelfth barge.

'What's he up to?' Jace muttered.

The Serb watched as the two derricks, the last in the line, hoisted two containers and swung them over the barge, and again a sudden gust came out of the west. The nearest container lurched a metre or so, and its end thumped the end of the next one. They clanged . . . a hollow sound. Milošević was already still, motionless, as if, El thought, he had changed for a moment into a statue.

'Make your move to the car. Now.'

There was no disobeying that tone of voice. El raised herself on to her toes, briefly brushed Jace's cheek with her lips, stopped, locked the case, picked it up. The euphoria had gone, emptied out of her. In its place, sick dread.

'Take care,' she said, and walked.

Behind Jace Piotra took in what was happening. She pushed open a door, part-glazed with cracked, frosted glass, and almost pushed Kalinka and Wisa through it. As she did they all jumped, literally, as two pistol-shots came almost together but with the thunder-like reverberation of rattled sheet iron mingled in.

Milošević had leapt into the barge, gone round the other side of the first container, which had now been lowered on to the decking, and shot off the padlocks. The sliding door was well-greased and easy to open. The container was empty.

Jace had to wait until El was in cover. She had the sense to make straight for cover, rather than follow the plan and his instructions, which would have taken her via the Merc. Nevertheless she hesitated before breaking into a run, and Milošević fired the first shot in anger at her. Concealed from Jace by the end of the container, he loosed off his Zastava Magnum, holding it two-handed. At twenty-five metres at a moving target he did well. The bullet, made, like the gun, for the American export market, smashed the upper right side of the rear of her pelvis, just below her kidney, and she went down like a bird blasted out of the sky. The lock on her case burst and paper worth thousands began to drift about the yard as the rain came again and the battle got under way.

CHAPTER 30

It did not last long. A scarecrow was the decisive factor. Over in the big field on the other side, Kim straightened his lolling head against the upright of the beanpole cross he had made, brought his arms down from where they had been hooked over the crossbar, pulled the HK machine-pistol from the deep pocket of his coat. It was set for three-round bursts. He left the man with the sniper's rifle to last – his was not a rapid-reaction weapon. The other three, at fifteen, twenty and twenty-five metres away from him, were out of it in three seconds. Then he dealt with the sniper, who was now on his back, facing him at thirty yards and sighting a 9mm pistol on him. He got off one round, only just wide of its mark, before Kim squeezed off his fourth burst. The bullets raked the sniper's body upwards – his balls, his stomach, his throat.

Kim ran forward. With half an eye on what was going on the other side of the screen of willows, he went down the line. Only one of the men was outright dead. He killed the other three with single shots to the head – whichever way was easiest. Then he rolled the first man's body out of the way, picked up his AK rifle, and lined himself up against a treetrunk, looking for targets on the other side.

In all this, training lasting ten years took over his mind and body as completely as a devil is said to possess the minds and bodies of witches. Although it was almost four years since he had been cashiered, it came back as if he had never been away.

He was now upstream of the quays and the leading barge, and the derricks beyond obscured his view. He could hear short bursts of gunfire and the screams of at least one man in pain. Or woman. Bent double and swerving wildly, he raced down the line of willows until he was almost opposite the last barge. There were four men on it, using the containers as cover, standing with their backs to the containers and looking out across the river in his direction. Possibly they were wondering why no help had come from the other side. Then much nearer to him, on the middle and unloaded barge, he caught a movement, and very briefly saw Milošević's silver head flash above the low gunwale. The shooting stopped, and, after a moment or two the screaming too.

For perhaps five seconds there was no noise, just the creak of mooring ropes straining against the slow but heavy current, the sigh of the wind in branches or the latticework structure of the derricks. Then it came: a long-drawn-out wordless cry, starting low, rising slowly to a terrible crescendo, and suddenly there he was. With one mighty leap Jason had hurled himself from the quay on to the top of the container. He stumbled a little on landing, recovered, and emptied the thirty-bullet magazine of his HK MP into the heads of the men below him. In the two seconds that that took, Milošević got to his knees and loosed off just the one round of Magnum before Kim shredded him with a full magazine of 7.62 FMJ. Jason, shot in the ribcage below his raised left elbow, hit the roof of the container, tried to rise, died.

All the Serbs had been killed. The only British dead were Eloise and Jason. The 'puppy' had been nicked in the upper arm, the humerus possibly chipped, and he had shat himself. The sergeant told him there was no shame in shitting himself, but he'd been bloody stupid to allow himself to be hit. Ashley and the three men with him, came in from the other side of the carpark. None of them had had to fire a shot. When they lifted Jason's body on to the quay all Ashley said was 'Put him by the girl.' He then walked briskly back into the forest, put the muzzle of a Browning HP in his ear and pulled the trigger.

Kim re-crossed the river by the Van Gogh bridge, walked into the space and looked around. There were bodies of Serbs everywhere. He supposed that, in a way, he was now in charge. Certainly the Brits, faces almost closed apart from a hunted, appealing look in their eyes, clearly expected him to do something. He was, after all, a fucking rupe, wasn't he? Situations like this, you need a rupe.

Two things happened at once. Coming out of the west, still several kilometres away and still in German airspace, the sound of at least three large helicopters. Coming out of the main building, in front of the quay, Kalinka, Wisa and Piotra. Wisa and Piotra began to gather up the loose currency and bonds that were still blowing about. They stuffed them into Milošević's case. Kalinka came over to the soldiers, looked round, shook his head, called for Wisa. She translated.

'We are sorry you have suffered casualties. I believe you were to be paid one million marks for what you have done today. Here are your marks.' And she lifted a large bundle of high-denomination currency. 'You have your cars here. You can return now to Hamburg. You will not be stopped nor questioned. Please forget about today's events and do not talk about them. Thank you.'

The helicopters were nearer. They were German military but marked as on ambulance duty with red crosses. The Brits looked at the weapons they still carried, shrugged and, Kim included, piled them neatly close to the well. Then they began to drift away towards the carpark.

One of the sergeants stopped in front of Kim.

'Coming, squire?' he asked.

Kim shook his head.

The sergeant shrugged, moved off, turned back and suddenly emoted.

'It's a fucking shame,' he said, 'a fucking stupid rule. You're fucking good, sir.'

Kim knew what he meant – the rule that banned homosexuals from the British Army. But he'd had enough of senseless killing in the Gulf, and even now felt recurring waves of self-disgust at the way he had responded during the last few hours. And before. But not only self-disgust – the devil in him was pleased he'd done so well. Talk about mixed up.

Kim moved over to the warehouse and leant against it.

'Sarge,' he called, 'have you got a smoke I could use?'

The older man came back with a slight swaying swagger and a big grin beneath his grizzled moustache. He pushed up a German-made Senior Service and lit it for him. Kim caught his wrist.

'I bet my mascara's all over the place,' he murmured.

The sergeant thumped his biceps, playfully.

'Bastard,' he said.

The helicopters landed in the meadow but close to the carpark just as the first of the cars left. An officer in field uniform, DP fatigues, peaked cap over shorn blond hair, bright brown leather boots laced up above the ankle, holding a clipboard, talked earnestly with Kalinka. Paramedics checked the dead, zipped them up in black bags. When they came for Eloise, Kim sought out Piotra. Throughout the few hours they had been there, they had ignored each other. But now they made eye-contact, and then Kim chucked his dog-end and went over to her. They held each other and looked over their shoulders as the paramedics lifted the body. The plume of bleached hair momentarily brushed the cobbles. One of them folded her charcoal grey suede jacket, trimmed with glossy black fur, over her chest. Then she was gone beneath the black tide of zipped plastic.

Piotra pulled away. Kim held on to her arm.

'Just tell me,' he said, 'what all this has been about?'

'Don't ask,' she said, 'don't even ask. And don't try to find out. They'll give you a lift back.'

She meant the helicopters.

He watched. He saw that she rejoined Kalinka and Wisa. He saw that, after getting together a few things, including Milošević's case, they walked out into the tiny marshalling-yard and up to the front of the train. The first container was open. They got into it. Four of the railway workers who had operated the derricks joined them, though one of them first unhitched the first four trucks from the rest of the train. The engine blew off some steam, sounded a high whistle. Shit, thought Kim. A million of that is mine. He broke into a trot, then a run, finally a sprint, and just managed to hoist himself on to the buffer and then the ledge of the last of the moving trucks. Spreadeagled against the rear of the last container, holding on to a piece of chain here and a handle there, he disappeared with the rest of the train up the track. Clouds of grey smoke billowed around him as the forest closed in.

CHAPTER 31

'This your train?' Sharon pushed her head backwards, careful not to move her hands from the top of her head.

'My train, yes.'

The old man in his loose grey patched and moth-eaten uniform was clearly not at ease in English. She switched to German but tried to keep it informal.

'Would you like to show it to me?'

There was a long pause and she noticed that a hectic flush rose on his high cheek-bones and the gnarled old hand that held the small black Mauser shook a little. Clearly the prospect excited him. He gestured with the muzzle, indicating that she should turn, lead the way along the track. Surely, she thought, he should be wearing a monocle, have an iron cross round his neck. On her trips Stateside to stay with her Pa's family, he used to make a thing out of making sure she saw the sort of war films that are still popular in the United States and the UK but never get much of a showing in Germany.

'Could I put my hands down? I'm not armed. See?'

She turned, faced him, and very slowly undid the leather buttons of her sheepskin coat, letting it fall open over a scarlet polo-necked lambswool sweater and black woollen leggings. Both were tight fits. They bulged, but in the right places.

'OK? Now show me.'

There were fifteen trucks, cattle-trucks. They were cages mounted on standard truck chassis, built at least sixty years ago out of solid, well-seasoned timber. Rain, frost and sun had washed and burnt off every last residue of paint, creosote, whatever, leaving the substantial planks white like bones – or the sea-scoured timber one sometimes finds on beaches.

The dessicated skin, bones, hair and even scraps of clothing were much the same colour, though the skin often had a yellowish, parchmenty tinge. They had died on their feet because there had not been room for them to fall. They stood behind the slatted timbers like small trees, planted too close, that had been hit by a blight. But no forester had come to clear any of these dead copses, crammed into small oblong spaces with no nourishing earth at their roots, just the boards of the ancient trucks.

If beetles, termites, birds or animals had made any significant inroads into them Sharon saw no sign of it. The steel wheels and overbangs would have deterred rodents, the gaps between the timbers were too small for carrion-eating birds. Perhaps smaller birds nested there in the spring, using an upturned palm or the hollow between neck and shoulder, plucking thin hair from skull-like heads or shredding the hem off a jacket or a cuff.

Around the wheels and over the roofs of the trucks there were the spiky left-overs of summer: wild lupin and willowherb, lady's bedstraw and lady's mantle, vines, woodbine, perhaps, or wild hops over the roofs. It would be a very different place in the summer, almost hidden beneath its shroud of flowery green. Filled with airy, dappled sunlight it would have a sort of beauty, even happiness.

She was shocked at first, of course, but not revolted – no more than one is in a museum exhibiting an exposed burial, or at an embalmed saint in a glass case. She felt a sort of sadness, which might, if she allowed it, lead to tears. She guessed the old man in his ridiculous but horrid uniform might judge tears a weakness.

She turned to him and said brightly, 'And you are in charge?'

'Now, yes. There was a sergeant, an old man but he died of a heart attack when the Bolshevik planes machine-gunned us. They missed. But he died anyway. I took over.'

'And you have been here ever since?'

'Oh no.' Wheezy laugh. 'I went back to Berlin, to what became West Berlin. For fifty years, nearly fifty years, there was no way back. But when the frontiers opened I came back. I felt sure they were still here and waiting for me. They were. They are.'

She began to walk past the waggons, slowly, not looking too closely, listening to him. His booted feet crunched in the friable debris of summer or squelched where the melting snow had left muddy puddles.

'How often do you come?'

'Normally, only once a year. I came a week ago.'

'So why have you come back again today?'

'There is danger to my train. I have heard them discussing it. On the other side of the wall.'

She thought he meant the Wall, and that this was just another sign of his madness.

'You see, I was put in charge when the sergeant had his heart attack. It is my train now. No one must touch it.'

But suddenly she was no longer listening. They had come to the sixth waggon and there were differences. In this one the leathery skins of the corpses looked darker, all had black hair. Whereas in the first five almost all had been men, here there were as many women as men and a lot of children, even babies, too. Old people as well. And these people had died fighting, fighting to get out. Hands clawed at the timbers, were thrust up at the roof, reached down towards the earth as if searching for food. Faces were twisted in anger, fear, determination, despair, but never resignation. Most awful of all was a couple at the end of the waggon, a man and a woman clasping each other in a deep embrace. Each had his or her teeth in the other's shoulder – it was as if they had chosen to try to live by feeding off each other's blood.

This time Sharon did begin to weep. The old man approved. He grunted, coughed.

'They were brave, yes? Such pointless heroism is moving.'

From Deniz Enver's penthouse Herbert Doe looked out over the trees of the Tiergarten to the Siegessäule, the gilded winged Victory, and beyond it to the square stubby towers and pinnacles of the Reichstag. To its right he could make out the patinaed horses on top of the Brandenburg Gate, a good three miles away but clearly seen from this height through rain-washed air. The stacks of cloud had moved on east, their sides and tops now pure white in the midday sun, their lower slopes black and filling the air below them with curtains of purple rain. In front of the rain a small flock of gulls flashed white sickles in the bright sunlight.

'Should be a rainbow somewhere,' Herbert thought.

He turned, swished Glenlivet over the remains of ice at the bottom of the cut-glass tumbler the tall, athletic PA had poured for him. He liked a good scotch, did Herbert, hoped she'd freshen it for him, but having done the drinks she'd gone. The rest were all there. Hamdija, the consul with the daft eyes that looked two ways at once. Sayeed, the smooth Palestinian millionaire, operated as an arms-dealer, some said, out of Turkish Cyprus. Lot of dodgy people there. Then Sam Pratchard, trying to hide his small but round fat body in the biggest armchair, clutching his document case, had hardly touched his drink, and the Gaffer, Harry Sheen, chain-smoking, coughing, constantly brushing ash off his trouser leg even when there wasn't any.

Ruling the roost, in a leather executive chair behind her big desk, Deniz Enver. A woman carved from granite, Doe thought, except her eyes, which were jet or agate and constantly, watchfully, flickered over all of them, checking them all out even when she was talking.

The three Moslems talked with each other, perfunctorily, short bursts stabbed into the longer silences.

Then, at last, the telephone. Deniz Enver picked it up with her right hand and with her left detached a chunky gold and polished ruby ear-ring, Paloma Picasso, from her right ear. She answered whoever was on the other end with swift, short *evet*s and *ja*s so Doe could not be sure whether the guy at the other end was speaking German or Turkish. At last she put the phone down, slipped her ear-ring back on, laced her stubby fingers together and leant over them across the desk.

'There is,' she said, in English, 'good news and bad news. I'll give you the good news first. All of those Serb gangsters are dead, including Vojislav Milošević. We are very pleased with this. He was a brutal murderer, a rapist, who organised mass killings. The chances he would ever be brought to legal justice were infinitesimal. But justice has now been done. Thank you. You will be paid what we promised.'

She took a sip of mineral water and cleared her throat. Her voice was deep but not mannish, her accent marked. Gold on her fingers and wrists flashed and chimed when she moved her hands.

'Your eight men from Hamburg are all unharmed apart from one very minor wound and they are now on their way back. They have been paid by Walery Kalinka, who is handling the Polish side of this affair. He will require you to reimburse him through Piotra Grabowski, and we shall of course reimburse you . . . Mr Doe?'

He was white. His head was shaking, his fists were bunched.

'El,' he rasped, 'Eloise, she should have paid them. Why didn't she pay them?'

'Eloise Harman is dead. And so two are the brothers who led your men . . .'

Doe hurled himself on Sam Pratchard, smashed him about the head, punched him savagely in the nose, hauled him out of the chair and head-butted him. Pratchard went to the floor and Doe got in two hard kicks to his coccyx and the pit of his stomach before the blonde PA, summoned by a bell, was able to get an arm-lock on him.

All through this Doe bellowed. 'You evil, fat bastard, you should have gone, you should have taken the money, not El, not Eloise.'

Deniz Enver was angry too.

'Get him out before he bleeds on the floor any more.'

For a moment Herbert Doe stood in the middle of the room looking wildly around him as if trying to search out more people, more things to hit and break. Harry Sheen was hunched forward, elbows on his knees, face buried in his hands. His latest cigarette smouldered on the parquet flooring.

Doe got a grip, shrugged his old but still massive shoulders, rubbed the knuckles of one hand with the palm of the other and then the other way round. He went back to the window, listened to the pounding of his heart.

There was a rainbow now, over in the east, all its colours staining the horses on the Brandenburg Gate.

The train slowed and suddenly the forest opened out into the big oblong clearing where it and the other three trains had been parked. But this time it continued across the top of the sidings, rocking and swaying as it negotiated the points. Just as it came to a standstill, Kim caught a glimpse of groups of men standing in the open and two large helicopters. He dropped to the rail and went the other way, putting the train between him and them. The forest was very close on this side. He walked back ten yards until he could see the small marshalling-yard and the people in it, and took cover behind a tall larch with an almost black trunk. He saw Kalinka, Wisa and Piotra approaching the men.

Kalinka was in front, the two women hung back. He put himself in front of the largest of the visitors. This was a big fat man wearing a very expensive fur-collared overcoat beneath a black hat with a stiff, wide brim. He held a large cigar beween his black-gloved hands and when he drew on it the aromatic smoke billowed round him like the smoke from burnt offerings. It was clear that the people around him, who included uniformed soldiers of some rank, represented both a court and a Prætorian bodyguard.

Kalinka put himself near enough to make it possible for one more step to bring them close enough to shake hands – but Herr Drenkmann was having none of that.

His voice boomed. 'It went all right, then?'

'Not perfectly. But good enough.'

'These things never go perfectly. Good enough is fine. You got your money?'

'Yes.'

'Then let's get this over with.'

'Yes. But first we're going to walk the track – it's not far, three hundred metres beyond the bend – to check there's nothing on the track, fallen tree, anything of that sort. Perhaps you would like to see for yourself the cause of all this trouble?'

But Drenkmann shuddered, turned away, chucked his

cigar and began banging his gloved hands together, although it was no longer cold.

Kalinka, Wisa, Piotra and the four railwaymen set off down the track. Kim followed them, but remained in the forest edge. He moved silently. He had been trained not only to kill but not to be killed.

The single track wound sinuously through the forest – none of the bends was sharp, but all sufficient to keep all but fifty or so metres in front hidden. The last bend, and they could see the buffers twenty metres away on the end of the first cattle-truck. And, standing between them, Fritz and Sharon. He was holding her upper right arm with his left hand. He was not threatening her with the Mauser. But he certainly was threatening the Poles.

'You have come to destroy my train.'

His high old voice was more a snap than a bark. The Poles came to a halt. Piotra coughed, called back.

'Come on, Fritz, you know we wouldn't do that.' She shook her head, thinking desperately. 'We just want to have a look at it. It has . . . historical interest.'

'You're lying, Piotra. I have heard your conversations through the wall. Your conversations with the Englander.'

'You don't speak English.'

'I don't?' Fritz switched to that language. 'I have had a lot of spare time in the last fifty years. I can also speak Spanish. ¡Habla español? French too . . . Parlez-vous . . . but never mind. You are a traitor. I shall shoot you all, but I shall shoot you first.'

He raised the Mauser. Christ, thought Kim, he means it. He pulled from his belt the Smith & Wesson his grandfather had killed himself with.

Sharon aimed a scything kick at the old man's shin and his head went down. Kim's first bullet smashed into the timber above him. Fritz's crashed through the undergrowth to the side. The Poles, including Piotra, hit the track. Sharon got a grip on Fritz's right wrist. In her strong hands the bones felt like twigs.

'Don't shoot him,' she shouted.

But Kim did, carefully, through the chest, close to the heart, it was the shot that was least likely to hurt this strange black woman who seemed to have come from nowhere. It need not have killed him, but he was seventy-five years old and in poor health. Later Kim said if he'd known Sharon was a trained police officer he might have obeyed her. Might. But now he walked down the track by the side of the trucks. He, at any rate, wanted to see what it had all been about. When he came back he turned on Piotra.

'Fucking lucky for you I re-tightened the screw.'

She shrugged. Taking into account Sharon's intervention, she wasn't too sure he was right.

'Listen,' she said, 'those men who came to your room were not meant to hurt you. We only wanted to keep you out of this. They' – she nodded towards Kalinka and Wisa – 'told me to. We didn't know how you'd react.'

He shrugged, wanting to believe her.

They walked back, leaving Fritz where he had fallen, his head lolling against the tail-board, his neat black pistol still held loosely on the ballast between his knees.

Drenkmann wanted explanations of the shots. Kalinka told him to wait. The engineer and fireman got up a good head of steam, the explosives expert in Drenkmann's team organised the unloading of incendiary charges with some HE from one of the helicopters, and loaded them into the empty containers. He wired up timed detonators. Nobody showed any concern at all about what they were doing except the engineer, who grumbled beneath his thick moustache about the sacrilege of destroying one of the few steam locomotives, a Krupp Series 3, still in working order. Eventually all were satisfied that nothing could go wrong. The train trundled forward, clanking and wheezing. The fireman sounded the whistle, once, then he and the engineer let themselves off the footplates just as the train reached the speed of a brisk jog.

They waited. Rhythmically propelled puffs of smoke floated up above the trees. They heard the crash – not a big noise, just an extended scrunching, grating, splintering sound. Silence. Ten seconds. The explosives expert looked anxiously at a stopwatch. Then a long woooomph of a rolling bang, a fireball and seconds later a blast of hot air that made the trees bend, and plucked at their coats. Crows soared into the air, then a tower of smoke, some black, most white, and flaming ashes, also mostly white, fluttering down through the air like immolated butterflies. One landed at Kim's feet. He stooped, picked it up. It filled the palm of his hand and burnt it, yet he let it burn until the flames at the edges had moved into the centre, shrivelling the faded pink fabric. A pink triangle.

CHAPTER 32

'So. No coincidences.'

Back in the Brandenburgische Straße room. Smoking joints, drinking vodka.

'Chaos, yes. Coincidences, no.'

'Begin at the beginning.'

'Whose beginning?'

Yes, Kim reflected, that was a problem. So many beginnings. Back to the Dawn of Time.

'Let's start with you.'

'I don't see why, but then I don't see why not.' She took a toke, held it. 'I got myself here in 1980. A Solidarność chick, they let me in. Fund-raising, crap like that. I was on the game, sending funds back, making contacts, setting up blackmail scenarios. All sorts of shit. Lech gets elected and I'm suddenly nobody's baby. I'm also past it as a whore. I take to shoplifting. Work with a team, but we all rip each other off, and that gets to be a bad scene. I go solo and for some of the year starve and I'm too old now to be belting down the cycle lanes with a posse at my heels. Then cousin Walery gets in touch. There's a big scam he's putting together and he'll sub me what I need till we pull down the big one. Now this surprises me.'

'Why?'

'Let me tell you. He was a hard-line party member. As incorruptible as Robespierre. He was in charge of railway security right across Poland. Did a good job. Then, Lech gets in and of course he got the push, the old heave-ho. From a big job to a very small one, deputy controller of the Rzepin yards, with special responsibility for the bit that wasn't used any more.'

'And he found ... the train?'

'I suppose so. He certainly spotted Fritz on his annual walkabout and got me to follow him back here. And squat in this room so I could keep an eye on him.'

'Why?'

'I'm not sure. But he's a clever monkey, is Walery. Maybe he just thought it would be an asset, something he could use or fall back on. Make Fritz a fall-guy, whatever. That's how he works, all the time. He knew he had a commodity to sell, the train, he just set up ... possibilities, which he might use or not.'

'Seems strange.'

'No, it's not. It's the way people who make money or get power always work. They build up contacts, they have a network. They may only use a tenth of them, but there's always someone you can call in when you need to.'

'But this guy was a commie apparatchik?'

She looked at him with scorn.

'Same difference,' she said.

'So what happened next?'

'Shit, I don't know. But somehow he got wind of these Sheen people, and Jason and Ash, and then you wanting to come to Berlin, and he fixed it so you'd take this room at a price you couldn't refuse, and that way you'd meet me, and poor old Fritz—'

'Who would have killed you if I hadn't been there.'

'Who would have killed me if that black girl hadn't been there. Who was she?'

'I've no idea. But within days of getting here, I'm commissioned by Jace to find buyers of Russian ammunition and I tell you, and then the buyers turn up. Why? I don't follow all that.'

'Everything was in place. It was time to go to market.'

The whole affair got very controlled coverage. In Germany the media still, on the whole, do as they're told if the magic words 'national security' are whispered. Trains containing Russian ammunition which had somehow got into Polish marshalling-yards had become the cause of a battle between rival groups from the Balkans, both trying to take possession. The arms-dealers and their thugs had been rounded up by the Polish and German authorities working together. Four containers of ammunition had exploded during the brief conflict.

Drenkmann leant across his desk, with his big hands folded in front of him. This was not going to be easy. Fechter had not only demanded full explanations, but had already tendered her resignation.

'Kalinka,' he began, 'came to us with the news he had a train load of corpses. Actually, they must have been on their way up from Auschwitz, which was evacuated ahead of the Russians in January 1945. There was no way we were going to pay Kalinka. Too easy to trace the money back to federal reserves or whatever. So we agreed he could make whatever he could elsewhere, on the side. And it was out of that situation that the whole thing grew. The idea that there were trains out there, near Rzepin, filled with ammunition, that could be sold. For a time there was a sort of truth in it. For a time, a year ago, it really did seem forty-two trains had gone missing. It really was a clerical, a computer error, but even then, back then, Sheen Associates were sniffing. So we decided to make it just four trains. Kalinka, with a little help from us, got in touch with Sheen Associates.'

Drenkmann pulled out his pipe, stuffed it, lit it. Through the smoke he continued. 'We altered the records to make it seem four trains had disappeared—'

'Why four?' For the first time Renata Fechter felt bound to interrupt.

'Research showed it was the minimum to get interested buyers making bids, and the whole thing depended on Kalinka getting a sizeable cut. Oh, I know the whole thing was impossibly inelegant and clumsy, and as it developed we had to improvise—'

'We?'

'A committee.'

'Ah. A committee.'

That explained a lot.

Renata thought for a moment, sought inspiration through the smoke from *Cohesion 3*.

'Why a committee?' she asked.

Drenkmann sighed. 'It was too big for one person.'

'Why?'

'Oh, come. Think of it. The discovery of a train load of Jews on the way from an extermination camp to Bergen—Belsen? The repercussions. Israel demanding some sort of grand ceremony. Acts of repentance. Remorse. Oh, goodness me, it would have been intolerable. Opening endless old wounds, a shot in the arm for the anti-racists here, the anti-anti-Semites. And the Israeli right would have had a ball – just as we're all trying to let the Holocaust, well, find its niche in history along with all the other great atrocities. The Poles agreed with us, of course. After all, back in the forties they colluded, my goodness did they collude. They said to us, sweep it up, you can have a free hand. Just tell us how we can help, but keep us out of it. So there you have it.'

'And why was I brought in?'

'Well, my dear, that's surely obvious. Having put it about that four trains of ammunition had gone missing, it would have been highly reprehensible not to have had a cross-regional team looking for them.'

'But you did not expect us to get very far. Just to cover your arse.'

Drenkmann looked at the ceiling and filled it with smoke.

'Of course, you did very well,' he muttered.

'Better than you had expected. Considering you brought me in when my baby was only five weeks old. Furtwanger misled us the first time. Was that because we were getting close?'

'Furtwanger? Oh yes. The acting freight supervisor at Brandenburg. Poor man, he did his best, but he was an alcoholic and he never could quite remember who was meant to think there were thirty-eight trains, and who had to know there were forty-two.'

Renata left that on one side, got to the thing that really mattered, was closer to home.

'Did you arrange the kidnapping?'

He was suddenly angry, or simulated anger very well.

'Of course not. Certainly not.'

'But Carmen's arrest for not having her ID brought up to date?'

His shrug was a guilty plea.

Renata stood.

'Well,' she said, 'I'll give my future some thought. Meanwhile, there's one thing you should know.'

He looked up at her. Big, cunning, old and experienced though he was, he felt a sudden tremor of alarm. What was this woman coming up with now?

'There were no Jews on that train. Sharon King checked it out. There were four different groups. Gays. Gypsies. Clapped-out workers from the labour camps, socialists, Danes, Dutch and Frenchmen who had been worked into the ground to the point where it was no longer worth feeding them. The last waggon was filled with Down's syndrome people, spastics, club-foots, that sort of thing. People with the sort of genetic failings new age fascists are even now seeking to weed out at an earlier stage of their development. But no Jews.'

Drenkmann sighed and sighed again. Then he battered his pipe on the edge of his copper bowl so sparks and clinker flew. Clearly he was in a sort of dumb rage.

At last he said, 'No Jews? Then really we need not have bothered. We need not have bothered at all.'